BREATHLESS

Trent turned toward Noelle and tilted her chin up with his fingertip. The intensity of his expression caused Noelle to tremble beneath his gaze. She held her breath. When he looked into her face, all the promises that he'd made to himself vanished.

"I want to kiss you again, Noelle." His eyes swept searchingly over her face. "What do you say to that?"

For a moment she couldn't think, couldn't breathe, as his head slowly lowered. His muscular arms encircled her. His lips gently touched down on hers, once, then twice ending with his tongue awakening every nerve in her body.

Noelle grasped his forearms, mostly to keep her balance, but also to assure herself that this was no dream.

Trent eased away, planting one last kiss on Noelle's parted lips. "There's more," he groaned in a thick voice. "Believe that."

Donna Hill
Temptation

PINNACLE BOOKS
WINDSOR PUBLISHING CORP.

PINNACLE BOOKS are published by

Windsor Publishing Corp.
850 Third Avenue
New York, NY 10022

The P logo Reg U.S. Pat. & TM off. Pinnacle is a trademark
of Windsor Publishing Corp.

First Pinnacle Printing: October, 1994

Printed in the United States of America

Prologue

Fast.

The sleek bronze-toned Mercedes-Benz convertible sped down the black tarred San Francisco freeway. Jordan had purchased the car for her a year ago, to celebrate her twenty-seventh birthday and their fourth wedding anniversary. Just before. . . . Noelle shook her head and stepped on the gas. She wouldn't think about it.

Faster. The turbo charged engine hurtled forward. Her honey-colored hair, fashioned after actress Halle Berry, whipped around her coppertoned face. Maybe if she drove faster she could make the memories rush past like the scenery that graced the precisely manicured lawns. Rush past the incompleteness that was her life, now that Jordan was dead.

She'd allowed herself to be totally transformed by the charismatic Jordan Maxwell. He'd taken a scrawny, uneducated girl from the New Orleans bayou and turned her into one of the most powerful women on the West Coast. She'd come so far from where she'd been, her past was almost a blur. She was in limbo. She could never go back, and the powers that be, would keep her from going forward.

Without thinking, she adjusted the black sunglasses on her nose. The simple gesture had become habitual. The designer accessory had become her signature for nearly a year.

Noelle didn't wear the blacker than black glasses so much for sun, or to hide the tears that so frequently welled up in her eyes. She wore them more to camouflage the emptiness that had taken up residence in the dark brown orbs.

She couldn't let them see the void or the fear that kept her walking the floors at night. There were too many jealous onlookers—so-called friends that couldn't wait to see her fail. She knew that they snickered behind her back and that hurt her more than she'd ever let on. And no one was more outraged at her success than Trent Dixon.

Noelle rounded the hairpin turn with ease and recalled a conversation she'd stumbled upon at a party one night. *It was not only amusing that Jordan hadn't turned his company reins directly over to her, but expected,* she'd overheard. Noelle was an heiress to an empire with no throne. Trent had been with Jordan when he'd hit his first big deal in the Sudan. Trent knew everything there was to know about the import-export business. Noelle supposed that it was only fitting that Trent be handed the reins. As far as she was concerned, Trent Dixon could take the company and go straight to hell.

She'd never had any interest in the import-export business and Jordan was fully aware of that fact. Her views and his remained in opposition throughout their marriage. Nonetheless, she'd continue to receive her share of the profits whether she took over or not. What she really wanted to sink her teeth into was the villa, Liaisons. The villa that Jordan had willed to her. She had plans for that. Big plans. She'd make a name for herself on her own terms, not on Jordan Maxwell's coattails, and certainly not under the tutelage of Trent Dixon. He was the last person she wanted anything to do with.

Every time she thought about Trent Dixon she got a headache. Her body began to overheat and she couldn't think straight. There was no way that she was looking forward to their impending meeting, since their long-distance phone conversations over the past year had been anything but cordial. They had been treading the thin line between chilly politeness and outright sarcasm. Anytime he called to advise her that her signature was required on a document, even over the scratchy phone connection, Noelle could practically taste his indignation all the way from the Sudan. But he would never know how deeply she despised him. There was nothing that he could ever say or do that would make her believe that he didn't have something to do with Jordan's death. And for that she'd never forgive him.

He was scheduled to arrive in the states in two weeks. She'd never met him face to face. For some strange reason the thought of his arrival made her nervous. Because of that, it was more important than ever that Liaisons be perfect when he arrived. There was no one better than Tempest Dailey to pull off that miracle. And she'd done precisely that. The gala opening of Liaisons was scheduled for the following evening.

Tempest and her husband Braxton were two people who had risen above the others and proven themselves to be true friends. Noelle couldn't wait to see Tempest again.

Noelle stepped on the gas while smoothly cutting around a red Porsche. She checked the digital clock on the dash. Twenty minutes before Tempest's plane was to arrive. If she kept up the 85 mph speed, she'd beat the plane with time to spare.

One

The trill of soft music wafted across the warm San Francisco night. Hundreds of twinkling lights hung from the trees, the balustrades and windows, turning the enormous villa into a fairyland.

Noelle St. James-Maxwell, breathed a sigh of contentment. Everything was exquisite. The caterers had laid out a fare fit for royalty. Every imaginable delicacy was there for the taking. She smiled in satisfaction as she regally strolled across the grounds, nodding and waving, greeting the guests, the curious, the envious.

Noelle couldn't call any of them friends, she thought, ruefully, shaking hands with the president of NBC studios. She knew they'd all come to gawk, to pass their comments, stir more rumors and most of all, to see if the young widow of Jordan Maxwell had what it took to run his empire.

They wanted her to fail, she knew, smiling graciously at the arrival of Whitney and her superstar husband. The circle of elite associates that her late husband surrounded himself with were a tight-knit, cliquish group. They turned their noses up at any who were not one of them. Background, education and family trees were more important than personal substance. Noelle couldn't count a friend among them. The group had yet to adjust to the fact that Jordan Maxwell, owner of one of the largest import-export companies in the U.S., a man who could have any woman he chose, had plucked a no-count waitress from the bowels of the Louisiana swampland and dropped her in their midst. They were still reeling from that indignity five years later.

Jordan had groomed her for a world that she had never fully adjusted to and was never accepted in. Liaisons was her first real attempt at anything independent of Jordan. The thought of failure terrified her, and failure would solidify every negative comment ever said about her. For that reason, she'd never let them see the loneliness or the fear that lived in her soul, visible only through her eyes. For now, the darkness would hide her secret.

But tonight was her success, she thought, shaking off the disturbing thoughts. Liaisons was the culmination of her dreams, a tribute to Jordan, and no one was going to ruin it. Not even Trent Dixon.

"Noelle! Noelle!"

She turned in the direction of the familiar voice, the smile she displayed being genuine for the first time in hours.

"Tempest."

The two women embraced warmly, then quickly stepped back to assess the other.

"That dress is fabulous, girl," Tempest enthused, admiring the silk sheath of champagne gold that seductively stroked Noelle's notorious curves, reaching just above her slender ankles. The daring side split gave a teasing view of a perfect copper leg from ankle to hip.

Her soft creole accent floated through the air. "*Merci*. But of course you have outdone yourself, *chère amie*. Red was always your color."

Tempest smiled at the compliment. With a wicked grin she asked, "What do you wear under something like that?"

Noelle smiled slyly, "Absolutely nothing."

The two women laughed in unison, drawing the attention of one who stood apart from the growing crowd.

Quietly he watched the two beautiful women, but his attention was riveted on Noelle. He'd instantly recognized her. She was more magnificent than any newspaper clipping or photograph, he realized with a jolt that shot straight to his loins.

Her skin brought to mind the tangy taste of cinnamon. The silky head of chestnut hair, begged him to run his fingers through it. Her statuesque form screamed sensuality. Yet she had a presence that demanded respect. She was a woman who could make a man want to keep her in bed and never let her out. By just looking at her, the stirrings of arousal swept through him. He began to imagine what she would feel like moving beneath him.

Damn, man, what the hell are you doing? Fantasizing about making love to your best friend's widow?

He took a quick sip of champagne. In all of the

years that he'd worked with Jordan, he'd never met the woman who'd captured the icon's heart. His years of work in the Sudan had kept him out of the States. Now he could see exactly why Jordan had remained so faithful even when he was away from home for months at a time.

Being home again was going to take some getting used to. Especially since he knew he was not welcome here. But he had a job to do. He'd taken an unbreakable oath and he would fulfill Jordan Maxwell's wishes. His beautiful widow would just have to accept that.

As if reading his thoughts, Noelle slowly turned her gaze in his direction. The contact was electrifying. She felt hot and cold at once. His unwavering deep stare seemed to see right through her. The dark eyes were unreadable and she felt naked and vulnerable under their appraisal.

What he saw in her eyes shook him to the marrow of his bones. There in the depths of the nut brown eyes was a haunting loneliness, a well of vulnerability and a compelling pain that made him want to pull her into his arms and make her know that he would make everything right with her world.

Then, as quickly as the force had taken hold of them, the contact was broken when Noelle's attention was diverted by Tempest.

"Noelle? Are you all right? You look like you've been hit by lightning," Tempest said.

Noelle shook her head. "I'm . . . fine." She

passed off a weak smile at Tempest, whose eyes turned in the direction of Noelle's gaze.

"Who-is-that?" Tempest asked, admiring the man who defined tall, dark and handsome and made her wish her own gorgeous husband was there to wrap herself around.

"I'm not sure," Noelle answered slowly, noticing that her pulse was racing.

"Well with the vibes that the two of you are giving off, I suggest you find out. Don't you?"

"Maybe later," Noelle answered absently, not trusting the rush of emotions that swirled within her. She expelled a breath. "Where's Braxton?" she asked, needing to change the subject, while forcing calm into her voice.

"I was just thinking the same thing." Tempest checked her watch. Briefly she scanned the blooming crowd, while noticing that the handsome stranger had not taken his eyes off Noelle.

Braxton was not in sight. Tempest frowned. Over the past few months, Braxton's absences and late arrivals had become a bone of contention between them. "He should have been here by now. His flight was scheduled to arrive nearly an hour ago."

"You know how those flights from Morocco can be, *chère*. They're always delayed."

"Hmm. You're probably right. But in the meantime," she added, lowering her gaze to the ground as she spoke, "cutie pie is coming this way."

Noelle angled her head to see him coming toward them. For some inexplicable reason her heart thundered so forcefully she momentarily felt breathless. The closer he came the quicker her pulse galloped.

He didn't just walk, Noelle realized with growing alarm. His every move sizzled, tossing electric sparks in his wake.

Raw was the word that leaped into her brain. Raw, animal sexuality poured from him like sweat after hours of erotic loving. She felt dizzy.

"Good evening ladies." His mellow voice warmed Noelle like brandy in winter. Politely he inclined his head toward Tempest, who smiled knowingly.

"Listen, Noelle, I'm going inside to call the airport. Please excuse me," she said to both. Without another glance she walked up the small incline toward the main entrance.

"I hope it wasn't anything I said," he quipped, flashing a smile that made Noelle's insides quiver.

Smoothly she returned his smile. "I'm sure it wasn't. She's expecting her husband. It seems his plane has been delayed."

"In that case, I feel better." His smile stroked her. "At least about it not being my fault." He made a small show of looking over the grounds, if only to take his mind temporarily off of the face and body that was making him lose his sense of perspective.

In profile, Noelle stole the chance to observe him up close. He had to be over 6'3", she noted, as he stood head and shoulders above her 5'8" height plus heels. His hard muscular body told her that he took care of himself. He had a strong chis-

eled face of smooth sienna, a well-tended beard
that outlined his rugged chin. His eyes were wide
and dark, shadowed by thick black lashes and
thicker brows. His full, sensuous lips promised un-
measurable pleasure.

He had a real *GQ* look. Even in semicasual attire
he gave the impression of power and confidence.
He wore a suit of navy linen, that hung loosely on
his body, as was the fashion. He chose to wear a
V-neck T-shirt of white silk. The low collar en-
treated her to run her fingers across his chest. She
curled them into a fist to quell the urge.

He returned his attention back to her and her
flesh warmed under his gaze, shooting flashes of
liquid desire to her center. She felt the tips of her
breasts ripen under his open perusal, which made
her even more self-conscious.

She feels it, too, he realized, her ardor boldly
evident through the revealing dress, even as he
fought to control the turbulence of passion that
raged within him.

He forced his mind to clear. "This is a beautiful
place you have. You've done wonders with it."

Noelle's tapered eyebrows arched. "You're familiar with the villa, *monsieur*?"

"Actually," he replied in a confidential tone, "I
was with Jordan when he purchased it almost ten
years ago. He always had intentions of working on
it, but . . ." His sentence drifted off. "I'm glad to
see that his very beautiful wife decided to take it
over."

His dark eyes held hers a moment too long and Noelle felt lightheaded. *It must be the champagne.*

She cleared her throat. "It seems that you know a great deal about me, *monsieur* . . . ?"

"Noelle! Noelle!"

Noelle turned around to see Braxton and Tempest coming toward her. Her face lit up when she saw Braxton approach. It had been months since she'd last seen him. After the completion of the interior architecture and the landscaping, he'd had to fly off to Morocco.

Now that both of the honored guests were present the official opening of Liaisons could commence.

Braxton embraced her in a warm hug. "It's good to see you again, Noelle. I'm sorry to be so late, but my plane . . ." He gave her that smile that had imprisoned Tempest's heart for life.

Noelle looked at her relieved girlfriend. "I told you," Noelle admonished. She took Braxton's arm and turned back to make introductions.

He was gone. All that remained was his erotic scent that seemed to have seeped into Noelle's pores.

"Oh . . ." she muttered, a bit confused and somewhat embarrassed, looking over the heads of her guests.

"Is something wrong?" Braxton asked.

"No . . . I was just talking with . . ." She expelled a breath. "Never mind." She smiled brightly. "Now that you're here, I can make the announcement to open the house for the tour. That's what's important."

* * *

For the next hour, Noelle, Tempest and Braxton were bombarded with congratulations and enthusiastic approval of the three-story villa.

Noelle's jaws began to ache from the continual smile that she had carved on her mouth. But her thoughts were elsewhere. In every free moment, she subtly tried to locate the man whose image she couldn't get off of her mind. He seemed to have vanished, and she didn't even know his name.

"You're completely distracted," Tempest said, surprising Noelle with her nearness.

She laughed, embarrassed. "Is it that obvious?"

"Very." Tempest followed Noelle's gaze. "You're looking for him aren't you?"

Noelle's shoulders slumped. "I am transparent, aren't I?"

"Only to those that know you. So—who is he?"

Noelle turned her palms upward. "I still don't know."

"Excuse me? You mean that the two of you were practically undressing each other on the lawn and you don't know who he is? You're losing your touch."

An underlying sadness scored her voice. "I've had no reason to be interested in a man in a very long time."

"Yes, I know," Tempest said softly, placing a comforting hand on Noelle's bare shoulder, "but you're a healthy, vibrant, beautiful woman. You can't stay in hibernation forever. And you can't use Liaisons to shield yourself from the world."

Noelle's voice quivered. "He's only been gone a year. I . . . I just couldn't . . . He was my life, my world. He . . ."

"He was just a man, Noelle," Tempest said gently. "Just a man. Not the god that everyone, including you, made him out to be. I can't believe that Jordan would want you to remain alone for the rest of your life. He groomed you to be a part of the world, not just the world that he created."

Noelle lowered her eyes, struggling to fight back the tears that burned her eyes and seared her throat.

Her life had changed irrevocably. It was due to Jordan. Everything that she had, what she was, what she thought, was because of Jordan. He'd rescued her, brought new meaning to her life, gave her reason to want to get up everyday.

He'd turned her life around and now he was gone. He'd left her to deal with this evil, hungry world alone. To face his enemies that would just as soon help her as stab her in the back.

Five years ago, sweating in her aunt Chantal's tiny cafe, darting the grubby hands of the male customers she would have never imagined that her life could have ever been any different. Not until the moment that Jordan Maxwell walked into her life. Since that day nothing in her life had ever been the same.

Forever would she recall the way he looked at her when he walked through those doors. . . .

Two

"Noelle! Stop daydreaming," her aunt Chantal ordered. "We have customers."

Chantal wiped her hands on the once-white apron, and shook her head in annoyance.

"For a woman of eighteen, you sometimes act like an *enfant*," she sputtered, tossing up her hands. "Get your head out of the clouds. There's no knight waiting to rescue a poor orphan girl like you. This is your life, *chère*."

Chantal marched off toward the kitchen, demanding and instructing all who came in her path.

Noelle sighed deeply, knowing all too well that her aunt was right. This was her life. Here in the bayou of New Orleans, forever at the disposal of someone else.

She knew her aunt meant well, even when her words were harsh. Chantal had immediately taken in Noelle when her mother, Vivian, had died. And Chantal had given her a home. With her father's whereabouts unknown, Chantal became the only family Noelle had. Being Vivian's older sister, Chantal felt it her duty to take in her niece. But not without a price.

Noelle had to drop out of school in order to work in Chantal's cafe. Her aunt felt that an education was a waste of time. Once a person knew how to add, subtract and read the alphabet, school was useless. Common sense and a strong back would be how Noelle would make her way in the world.

Noelle had missed her school years. She missed her friends, she missed her youth. She felt doomed to a life of hard work and poverty.

Many nights she'd lie awake imagining beautiful clothes, a house that didn't always smell of gumbo, and a wonderful husband who adored her. *Dreams*. But her aunt was right. Who would want her? She had nothing and would never *be* anything more than a poor, orphaned waitress.

She pulled her shoulder-length hair behind her ears and walked out of the supply room into the small cafe.

As usual, the dinner crowd had packed the cafe. Although, Chantal's was on the outskirts of the city, patrons came from far and wide to sample the renowned cuisine.

Noelle put on her trained smile and began her routine of checking on customers and seating the incoming diners.

After seating one of her regular customers, she returned to her station at the door, and there stood Jordan Maxwell.

Immediately she knew that this man was different from all of the others. His clothing spoke of wealth, his posture indicated confidence and his smile was warm and inviting, not like the leers that she was used to.

"*Bon soir, monsieur.* May I help you?"

"I hope so," he answered in a voice that vibrated through her like currents on the shore.

She felt suddenly nervous, and childlike under his steady gaze. She lowered her eyes, focusing them on her notepad.

"Will you be dining alone?" Irrationally she hoped that he was.

"Fortunately."

Her head snapped up in question. Her face was hot with embarrassment, as if he'd read her mind. "*Pardon?*"

Jordan chuckled at her discomfiture while enjoying the lilt of her creole accent. "Fortunately, because I hope that you may be able to join me."

"Oh, no, *monsieur,*" she mumbled, both flattered and afraid. Nervously she looked around for her aunt. "That is not possible."

"Maybe not now. But you will. Perhaps next time," he said, fully confident that it would be a reality.

Jordan looked at the lovely young woman and smiled. He was used to having what he wanted and from the moment he set eyes on Noelle, and saw the spark of eager intelligence in her eyes and the pride with which she wore her stained uniform, he determined that she would be his.

"In the meantime, I'd like a table and a bottle of your best wine—to toast the occasion of our meeting."

Noelle felt her heart flutter. She didn't know which way to look. Instead she turned and quickly guided him to a vacant table near the piano.

For the balance of the evening, she consciously avoided going near Jordan's table. But it didn't stop him from following her with his eyes.

Throughout the night, each time that Noelle dared to look in his direction, he raised his glass in a toast. Then, in an instant, without warning, he was gone.

Several months passed and Noelle didn't see Jordan again. But she couldn't seem to forget him or the way he'd made her young heart feel. *Special*. No one had ever done that before. Each time that she strolled through the teeming New Orleans streets, she thought she spotted him in the crowd. At night she dreamed of his face. The strong caramel features, wide dark eyes and hair that reminded her of the first sprinklings of snow.

Then, when she was beginning to believe that seeing him again was an impossibility, he reappeared one steamy night in August.

Noelle saw him standing in the doorway. A flood of heat swept through her and for several moments she stood immobile, unwilling to believe that he had returned. She willed her legs to move.

"You're just as beautiful as I remember," he said, his deep timbre thrilling her.

No one like him had ever called her beautiful. She smiled in response.

Her heart raced. "What brings you back after so long, *monsieur?*"

He took her hand in his. "I thought you'd be ready to have dinner with me now."

Noelle felt her body tremble. She quickly looked around the cafe. She spotted her aunt scowling at her from the rear.

She looked up at him, her eyes begging him to understand. "Please, *monsieur*, my aunt . . ." She looked over her shoulder.

Jordan looked beyond Noelle and spotted Chantal.

"Let's tell your aunt that you'll be leaving." Gently, he pulled Noelle behind him and walked up to Chantal.

That was the last day that Noelle worked in the cafe. Jordan had smoothly convinced Chantal that her niece had the potential to achieve wonderful things, and he was going to be sure that she did. In exchange for Noelle's services, Jordan dutifully sent a very large check to Chantal each month, which seemed to appease her. However, it was difficult for Chantal to believe that a man like Jordan Maxwell could see any value in her meek, little niece. But if he was willing to pay for Noelle's absence; who was she to argue? Perhaps Jordan saw something in Noelle that she, herself, had missed all of these years. She could only hope that Noelle would be happy in her new life.

For a man who had conquered every obstacle in his life, Noelle was a new challenge for Jordan. Somewhere, deep in the recesses of his soul, Jordan saw in her a part of him that was missing. Her naïveté intrigued him. She didn't have a greedy, or pretentious bone in her body. She was unlike any woman he'd ever known. But he knew that in order to fit into his world she would have to be molded as a sculptor models clay into a work of art.

Noelle was instantly caught up in Jordan's vision of what he wanted for her. His dream became hers. She was overwhelmed by his expectations, thrilled at the possibilities yet frightened of the doors that he intended to open for her.

"You have talents that you have yet to discover," he'd said to her. "I intend to bring them to the forefront for all of the world to see."

The first step in her transformation was her education. Jordan hired private tutors to help refine her speech and catch up on her studies. Studies that were conducted in the cozy apartment that he'd selected for Noelle. With that completed, he sent her to the University of Virginia, where she'd met Tempest and Braxton. Her graduate work took place in Europe, Africa, the Orient. She purchased her leather from Italy, her jewels from Africa, her silks from Hong Kong. She visited the finest *haute couture* houses in Paris.

Noelle didn't have time to think about what was happening to her. She felt as though she were in some magical dream world where Jordan was the magician who could make anything happen. But Jordan was a hard taskmaster. "Can't" was not in his vocabulary. He demanded perfection from everyone around him, and accepted no excuses for anything less. He readily used ridicule as a weapon to propel you. Ultimately you produced, if for no other reason than to prove him wrong. In the end, you achieved what you thought was impossible, and secretly you thanked Jordan. He, in turn, received your loyalty.

With no close friends nearby, and her only family hundreds of miles away, Noelle was enveloped in the cocoon that was Jordan Maxwell. She relied on him for everything.

Noelle always felt as if she were in a never-ending dream. She agreed with every suggestion, critical comment or word of effusive praise that Jordan uttered, afraid that if she ever challenged Jordan's wishes, for her, she'd wake up from her dream and find herself back in Chantal's cafe.

Her transformation took five years to complete, and in the fifth year, Jordan married his creation.

Jordan Maxwell had literally swept Noelle off of her feet and into a world that she had only imagined. Only now it was more magnificent than she'd ever dreamed. She was only beginning to see the power that Jordan wielded. With a simple phone call he could have planes, boats, cars at his disposal. With a dash of his signature he could transfer millions of dollars. By simple request, he could secure the company of politicians, diplomats, movie stars. "Everyone has a weakness, Noelle," Jordan often told her. "Find it and you have conquered them."

Her sheltered years in New Orleans had left her naive about the ways of the world. Even her travels across the globe were chaperoned. She never imagined how much subterfuge, envy, and viciousness that existed in Jordan's everyday life and did not believe the rumors of darker dealings.

What she did understand, however, was that she did not truly fit into his world. All of the fine clothes, the culture, the money, the power would not change the fact that she was only a cook from a backwater cafe. And to Jordan's friends and associates, she always would be.

Jordan protected her as much as possible from the gossip. She, in turn, worshipped the ground that he walked on. But deep in her heart, she wondered if Jordan truly loved her. She knew he loved what he could do for her and he loved the person that he'd created. But did he truly love her? She didn't think so.

"I didn't mean to upset you, Noelle," Tempest said softly. She gently stroked her arm, pulling Noelle back from the depths of her memories.

Noelle blinked back the images. She gave Tempest a faltering smile. "I know," she whispered. "These are my ghosts. I'll find a way to banish them. One day." She forced a smile. "In the meantime, I have a half dozen guests that have reservations for the opening weekend. So, shall we get them settled?"

Three

Trent moved like a caged panther around his suite, tossing his belongings around as if they were to be discarded.

Noelle St. James-Maxwell had unnerved him. That's all there was to it. He'd never met a woman capable of doing that to him, especially without even trying.

He blew out an exasperated breath and jammed his hands in his pockets. How in the world was he supposed to accomplish what he'd come to do, if he couldn't be in the same room with her without losing his cool? To compound the problem, once she realized who he was, he was sure she wouldn't come within ten feet of him.

He ran his hand across his bearded chin. Perhaps he could get around that little inconvenience, he thought. At least until he won her confidence.

He stopped pacing. The wheels began to spin. He was sure that he could pull it off. All he needed was a few weeks, two months at best, and his work would be finished.

He strode across the room to the phone and picked up the elaborate Liaisons brochure that had

only been distributed to the selected few. He dialed
the private number.

The illuminated numbers on the bedside clock,
were reflected in Noelle's weary eyes. In little more
than an hour the sun would rise across the bay.
She hadn't slept more than a few minutes all night.

Instead of succumbing to the fatigue that enveloped her, she tossed and turned, reliving the moment she'd heard of Jordan's death. She never
confided her true feelings to anyone about that
moment.

She'd always been too ashamed.

No one really knew or understood her relationship with Jordan. On the surface, they appeared
to be the fairy tale couple come to life. In a way,
they were. They looked great together. Their goals
were one. They were perfectly complementary. Yet
her life was anything but a fairy tale, it was simply
all that she knew.

While she respected and adored Jordan, he left
her empty. She was a shell, a product of his creation. She missed something she had no name for
and every so often pangs of loneliness would hit
her. How many times had she questioned her reasons for remaining with Jordan? How many nights
had she spent alone, unfulfilled, but too loyal to
her husband to commit the unspeakable? Jordan
sensed it too and inexplicably he provoked her, intentionally trying to drive her into another man's
arms.

Yet through all of her hurt and loneliness, she understood Jordan like no one else. She saw through the ruthlessness, the drive, to the vulnerable man beneath the facade. And she knew that as long as they remained husband and wife she would stay committed to her wedding vows. Vows that she believed in with all of her heart. "What God has joined together . . ." For that reason, she knew, deep inside, Jordan was grateful for her tenderness and compassion. In turn, he showered her with gifts, cars, jewelry. They traveled, they danced, they met dignitaries, they dined in all of the exotic places across the globe. But they never truly loved. Not in the same sense that a husband and wife loved. More like two dear friends who were truly indebted to each other for their very existence. An existence that was cruelly snatched away from her and she had only one man to blame.

It was nearly noon when Noelle emerged from her room. She'd finally fallen into a deep sleep shortly before sunrise, with dreams filled with vivid images of the man she'd met at the opening. The titillating dreams left her more on edge than before, which only added to her anxiety for having overslept.

She went directly to the lower salon to check the guests who had stayed over. Spotting Liaisons's manager, Gina Nkiru, she quickly crossed the polished marble floor to Gina's desk. As she approached she wondered, once again, why Gina had

chosen the hotel industry as a career. With her
exquisite streamlined looks and penchant for top
of the line clothing, she could have easily been a
success in the world of high fashion. Nonetheless,
her credentials were above reproach.

Gina's auburn head snapped up from her paperwork when she sensed a presence above her.

"Oh. Good morning, Mrs. Maxwell," Gina
beamed. She quickly rose and smoothed her mauve
skirt. Gina felt honored to be asked to hold the
highest position at Liaisons. Gina's years of work
in the hotel industry, working as her father's aide
at the embassy of Ghana and her multilingual
skills had served her well in vying for this job. But
all of her experience could not have prepared her
for the mystique of Liaisons. It was something out
of the most vivid imagination. She'd lost count of
the celebrities and public figures that had graced
the building the previous night. To think that
many of them would become regular patrons was
almost too much for Gina to comprehend.

Gina wished that she could tell her friends and
family about everyone that she'd seen. But all employees were bound by legal contract never to di-
vulge that information. That along with her
uncompromising professionalism would never allow her to breach a trust.

Anonymity was the big draw of Liaisons. Each
and every guest was secure in the knowledge that
their identities and their dalliances would remain
secret. Hence the name Liaisons. That and the

$2,500.00 per night fee and the exclusion of any media, effectively deterred the foolhardy.

Even with that knowledge she was still stunned to be holding a cashier's check for $75,000.00 for the new arrival, Cole Richards.

"How is everything Gina?" Noelle inquired, briefly scanning the guests as they milled about.

"So far, so good, Mrs. Maxwell." She took a peek at the occupancy list that indicated, only, which suites were in use. "We have a total of ten guests. There are two vacant suites on level two, a vacancy on level one and one suite available on the penthouse floor."

Noelle nodded. Satisfied. She allowed herself a brief moment of relief. "Let me take a look at the private register."

Gina retrieved the leather-bound journal from the safe and handed it to Noelle.

Noelle scanned the names, nodding at each familiar one, until she reached the name Cole Richards. She frowned. "Who is this?" She pointed to the last entry.

Gina peered across the desk to the line that Noelle indicated with a French manicured finger.

"I'm sure I saw him last night, Mrs. Maxwell," she assured with confidence. "He checked in about an hour ago. He's on level three. He gave me this." She showed Noelle the check.

Noelle's brown eyes briefly widened in surprise. "$75,000.00?" She did a quick mental calculation. "He intends to stay for an entire month?"

"That's what he said."

"Did he provide the required references?"

"Yes. I filed them away. Would you like to see them?"

"Please."

Gina exited through the door directly behind her desk into the back office. Momentarily she returned with a sealed folder. She handed it to Noelle.

"I'll just take this to my office. I'll be sure to return it before the end of the day."

"Of course." Gina started to feel uneasy. A tiny spot just beneath her left eye began to twitch—a sure sign. Her father always said that she was psychic, and her feelings were generally on target. She only hoped that this time her intuition was off.

Noelle turned to leave.

"Mrs. Maxwell?"

Noelle came around looking at Gina quizzically.

"Didn't everyone who was here last night receive a personal invitation?"

"Yes. Unless they were the guest of someone who did. Why do you ask?"

"Then Mr. Richards must be a friend or the guest of someone that you know."

"That remains to be seen." She smiled briefly and headed in the direction of her office.

Gina swallowed back her trepidations. As she marked Noelle's departure, she had the unsettling sensation that trouble was on the horizon. But she had her own secret to concern herself with, and it would take all of her diplomatic skills to keep it under wraps. If Noelle were ever to find out, she would surely lose this fabulous job.

Noelle took the short ride on the glass elevator to the lower level where her office was housed.

Within moments she'd broken open the plastic seal and had methodically run over the details that it contained.

There was a personal letter from her friend Senator Richard Thomas of California. He described Cole Richards in glowing terms, saying that they had been associates for several years and he was very familiar with Mr. Richards' entrepreneurial skills in the aeronautical industry.

Planes. The thought evoked painful memories. She shoved them to the back of her mind. She set the letter aside and looked over the brief personal profile.

He was 35 years old, preferred privacy, home state New York. He would be staying for one month in suite number 9. He listed his occupation as an Aeronautical Consultant. No guests were expected.

Pensively she looked across the room and focused on the Picasso abstract, absently replacing the pages and closing the folder.

Suite number 9. That was on the east wing, set off by itself, she recalled. Braxton had designed it specifically for those that wanted the utmost privacy.

For some reason, Cole Richards had sparked her curiosity. She leaned back in her leather seat and Jordan's words of wisdom echoed in her mind.

*Never leave anything to chance. You always stay ahead
of your opponent by already knowing what they're trying
to find out.*

Slowly she pushed herself away from her desk.
Perhaps she'd pay a personal visit to her special
guest. Just to satisfy her curiosity, of course.

Hesitantly, Noelle stood in front of suite number
9. Maybe this wasn't such a good idea. After all,
the profile did indicate that Mr. Richards wanted
his privacy. Then again, she reasoned, as owner of
Liaisons it was her responsibility to be assured that
her guests' anonymity was not compromised by any
unscrupulous individual, which this Cole Richards
very well could be. She felt mildly justified.

Inhaling deeply she knocked on the door, then
waited for what seemed like an eternity. She was
beginning to truly feel ridiculous. She turned to
leave just as the door was snatched open.

"Yes?"

The familiar voice vibrated down her spine and
momentarily held her in place. As she turned
around to face him, her eyes locked on the bare,
wet chest then drifted down to the white towel that
scarcely covered his middle. Her mouth went dry
and her face felt flushed, and for the life of her
she couldn't think of anything logical to explain
her appearance. Standing before him she, once
again, felt like the young inexperienced waitress instead of the twenty-eight-year-old businesswoman.

He merely stared at her, seeming totally nonplussed by his half-naked appearance. His cavalier attitude snapped her to her senses.

She cleared her throat. "I'm sorry, Monsieur Richards. It seems that I've come at a bad time."

He gave her a crooked smile. "Now why would you say that, Mrs. Maxwell?"

She quickly realized from his tone that he was teasing her, apparently taking great pleasure from their encounter.

"Would you like to come in while I—uh—put something on? I was expecting room service."

Noelle straightened her shoulders and forced her gaze up from below his waist to focus on his eyes. She quickly discovered that wasn't much better.

"I want to make a practice of visiting all of my guests," she replied. "Especially those that intend to stay with us for a while."

The smooth cadence of her voice reminded him of hot nights on sandy beaches with a full moon glowing above. *Sensual.*

"But I think I should come at another time. I'm sorry to have disturbed you." She made a move to leave.

He reached out and touched her shoulder and she swore that must be what an electric shock felt like.

His voice was low, throbbing. "I hope it's not a problem that I'll be staying for a while." His fingers began to burn with the contact. Reluctantly he removed his hand. "I need the rest." His smile held an invitation.

"I didn't mean to give the impression that your

stay was a problem." She touched her hand to her chest. "I apologize."

"None needed." His eyes held hers.

Noelle was the first to look away.

"I, I must be going. If there's anything you need . . ."

"I'll be sure to let you know."

Noelle gave him one last fleeting look, turned on her heel and walked quickly down the carpeted corridor.

Trent leaned casually against the door frame watching her hasty departure. The cool mint green linen dress just barely skimmed her knees. Last night he thought he'd had the perfect view of those luscious legs. Now he knew what had been left to the imagination.

He surprised himself with the control he exerted while she stood in front of him. It had taken every ounce of self-restraint to still the urges that pulsed through his loins, while she stood there looking so flustered, assured and delectable all at once.

Now that she knew he was there, the next phase of his plan had to be executed.

He shut the door. In a little more than ninety days, the notes would be called in. Everything that Jordan worked for would come tumbling down. The only person who could salvage his empire was Noelle. And the one she needed to learn the ropes from was him. The last man on earth she'd have anything to do with. He had to get her to trust him. Or at least trust Cole Richards.

Four

En route to her office, Noelle made good on her statement to Cole Richards. She took a short stroll through the gardens, the three dining rooms, the pool and the exercise room. She made a point to speak to each guest personally. Everyone that she met confirmed that the service and accommodations surpassed all expectations.

She should be elated, but instead she felt more under the microscope than ever. All eyes would be on Liaisons and her for the next few months. Everything had to be better than perfect.

The fact that Cole Richards was to be a long-term guest, mildly complicated matters. He made her feel things, think things, want things. She couldn't allow herself to be distracted by him or anyone. Not now.

Arriving in her office, Noelle sorted through the mail and reviewed the bills that required her signature for payment. She casually flicked through the stack until she came across a plain white en-

velope addressed to her from Jordan's attorney in
Los Angeles.

Curious, she tore it open. As she read the un-
believable contents the words began to blur and
her hands trembled.

Screaming denial rang in her brain. This must
be some macabre joke. But as she continued to
read the familiar scrawl she knew that it was true.

The light knocking on the door, nearly caused
her to cry out. She cleared her throat and swallowed back the tears. The knock came again. She
pushed control into her voice.

"Yes? Come in."

The door swung open. "Well. Good afternoon."
Tempest whisked in closing the door behind her.
She took a seat on the low sleek, leather couch.
"Whew. I'm exhausted. What a night."

"I know. It was better than I expected," Noelle
answered absently.

Tempest frowned. "You don't sound like you're
too pleased."

Noelle briefly shook her head. "Of course I'm
pleased. Why shouldn't I be? Liaisons's opening
surpassed everything that I ever dreamed," she
concluded, pointedly avoiding Tempest's steady
gaze.

Tempest pursed her full red lips and crossed
her legs.

"How long have we been friends, Noelle?"

The question caught Noelle off guard. She
forced a laugh. "For more than eight years. Why?"

"We've always been honest with each other, right?"

"Of course. What are you getting at?"

"Something's bothering you. And I want to know what it is. Maybe I can help."

Slowly Noelle rose from her seat and turned away to face the window that covered the expanse of the wall. Her view took in the outdoor pool and rested on Cole Richards as he emerged from the water. His muscles rippled with every move. Her pulse picked up its pace while she watched him stride across the pavement into the villa.

She turned away from the window and forced a smile as she faced her friend. "I only wish there were something you could do."

Tempest rose. "Is there a problem with Liaisons? Are you ill? Talk to me," she pleaded softly.

Noelle's lids fluttered as she tried to hold back her tears. She crossed her arms, embracing herself as if the act could contain the torrent of emotions that threatened to overflow.

Alarmed, Tempest hurried to her side, bracing Noelle's shoulders. "Noelle, what is it?" She guided Noelle to the couch. "Whatever it is, it can be worked out," Tempest assured, her soothing voice washing over Noelle.

Noelle solemnly shook her head and wiped the tears away from her cheeks.

"It's just so bizarre."

Tempest heard the strain in her voice. "What is?" she coaxed.

Noelle angled her chin toward the desk. "Over there. On the desk there's a letter. From Jordan."

Trent returned to his suite. His body felt rejuvenated after the vigorous swim. His mind was clearer. Physical exercise always had a positive impact on him. Whenever he felt stressed or worried he found a way to expel it in some form of activity.

Swimming was just one outlet, but flying was his passion. He'd been flying since he was eighteen. He'd gotten his pilot's license at twenty and was a certified instructor by twenty-two.

His skills as a pilot became public knowledge after a stint with the airforce. His unit, led by him, had successfully pulled off a rescue mission of an American diplomat held in the Middle East.

From there he wrote his own ticket. He became a pilot for hire, flying anywhere, anytime. Which was how he met Jordan Maxwell and became his personal pilot and business partner.

Without warning, images of Noelle pushed thoughts of Jordan out of his mind. He clenched his teeth. He had to stay focused.

He stepped out of his wet trunks and strode naked across the room. It was now or never, he thought as he dialed the villa operator.

"Yes, Mr. Richards?"

"I need to rent a car within the hour.

"That's no problem. Just follow the instructions

on the voice-activated system when I switch you to
the rental department."

"Thank you."

Exactly as he'd dictated, a midnight blue Lexus
LS was waiting for him when he exited the facility.
He slipped behind the wheel and headed toward
Los Angeles.

Tempest read the letter with a mixture of disbelief and alarm. It was obvious, after the first few
lines, that Jordan had written this letter well before
the accident. She could easily understand and sympathize with Noelle's shock. What was curious,
however, was her nagging sensation that Jordan
seemed to have known well in advance that he
wouldn't be returning home. She wondered if
Noelle had the same feeling.

Gently she placed the letter on the desk and returned to Noelle's side.

"Are you all right?"

Noelle nodded.

"Noelle, was there something going on in Jordan's life that could have prompted him to write
this letter?"

She shook her head slowly. "No. Nothing that I
know of."

Tempest took a thoughtful breath before speaking. "It's just that . . . well, it sounds as if he knew
something. Or had planned something."

Noelle sprung up from the couch. Her brown eyes blazed. "Are you trying to imply that Jordan planned his own death?" Her voice rose to a tremulous pitch. "Are you?" she demanded.

"Noelle. Calm down. The letter just doesn't sound right. He says that you would know what to do. That your life together was what made him go on for as long as he did. That he'd trust you to be able to run his business and everything would fall into place. Noelle, whether you want to accept it or not, this is a farewell letter."

All of the restraint that Noelle had maintained crumpled at those telling words. She seemed to deflate like a pierced balloon. The tears that she'd held at bay ran freely down her chiseled cheeks. But her voice was surprisingly strong when she spoke.

"I didn't want to believe it," she said slowly, "I didn't want to think that he would intentionally abandon me. Then to ask me to trust Trent Dixon is more than I can bear."

Tempest stretched her arm across Noelle's shoulders. "I know that you hold this Dixon guy responsible for the plane crash. I know that it's hard for you to accept that he survived and Jordan didn't. But if Jordan trusted him, why can't you?"

Noelle tossed her head in dismissal. Her eyes pierced Tempest's. "Yes, Jordan trusted him. He trusted him with his life and Trent Dixon destroyed that trust!"

"It was an accident Noelle. The inquiry cleared Dixon of any wrongdoing. It was a malfunction."

"But Trent was responsible for the maintenance of the plane," she countered. "He was responsible."

Tempest began to feel that she was fighting a losing battle. She tried one last time.

"You don't even know Trent Dixon. Did it ever occur to you that he's going through his own hell? Jordan left the reins of his enterprise in Dixon's hands. Whether you like it or not, you're going to have to deal with him. At least until the terms of the will are fulfilled. As this letter says, after the year is up, Dixon is to turn the company over to you."

Noelle's lids briefly lowered in reluctant acceptance. "I've never been interested in running Jordan's business. He knew that. He *knew* that. We were always completely at odds over his business practices and his vision for the company. For all I care, Trent Dixon can have it."

But with those words an eerie thought rushed to the surface.

She turned to Tempest, her eyes wide with awakening. "Suppose this letter is just a ploy by Dixon to lure me into a sense of security so that he could take the company from me without a fight?"

Tempest wrestled with the idea for a moment. "But how would he have gotten Jordan to write this letter? This is Jordan's handwriting isn't it?"

Noelle stood up and began to pace, biting on her thumbnail as she thought.

"It looks like Jordan's writing. But Trent was the

closest person to him. He could easily have studied his handwriting over the years."

Tempest slowly shook her head and sighed. "Where did the letter come from?"

"It was hand delivered this morning from our attorney's office in L.A."

"Have you called your attorney?"

"That would be pointless. Joseph Malone was more Jordan's attorney than mine. He's one of those types that sticks to the letter of confidentiality. I'm sure he's under some strict instructions."

"Then who else may know something?"

Noelle turned back toward the window. Snatches of her conversation the night before rang in her head.

"The man I met last night," she said slowly. "He said he was with Jordan when he bought the villa." She turned toward Tempest. "He's here. Now. Cole Richards knew Jordan."

Five

Trent spent the better part of the day in his other hotel suite in Los Angeles. He had an arm's length of calls to make to the Maxwell headquarters in Sudan and Hong Kong. He couldn't risk them being billed to him at Liaisons.

According to the reports that he'd received, everything was in order. Or at least as well as could be expected with the revolution in full swing. Import and export of anything other than food and medicine was out of the question. The United Nations was taking steps to intervene, but there was no telling how long that would take.

Finally, wrapping up his business late in the day he headed back to Liaisons.

As he sped across the winding highways in the rented Lexus, he questioned his tactics. Maybe he should have been honest with Noelle and absorbed her eminent outrage. But it was too late now. He had no other choice than to follow through. Noelle Maxwell believed that he was Cole Richards and it would remain so until the time was right to tell her the truth.

He made the last curve into the long drive of Liaisons and turned into the underground garage.

Tonight, he thought.

Noelle took special care to prepare herself for the evening ahead. After the shocking ordeal of the morning she needed the time to relax before mingling with the guests.

Her attempts to subtly locate Cole Richards had proven to be fruitless. He'd apparently left the villa earlier in the day and had yet to return.

She sighed as she sat before her mirror applying her makeup to the flawless copper skin. She felt certain that Cole Richards held the key to some information about Jordan and the fatal plane crash. What it was she couldn't be certain, but she would have to find a way to gain his help.

Satisfied with her polished look, she crossed the room and selected a fitted gown of black lycra. The off-the-shoulder neckline was dotted with tiny rhinestones. She slipped the gown over her nude body. The simple act wrought steamy visions of how Cole Richards looked at her the previous night and how sensual he'd made her feel.

Unconsciously, standing before the full-length mirror, her hands involuntarily stroked her heated body. Briefly she shut her eyes as powerful flashes of long unfulfilled desire ripped through her.

What would his hands feel like, his mouth, his . . . Her eyes flew open. Her breath came in short, choppy waves. She stared unbelievably at herself in the mirror, her hands still cupping her full breasts.

She flung her hands to her sides. With a shuddering breath she spun away from the telltale image.

Forcing herself to concentrate, she stepped into her strapless black heels, picked up her rhinestone purse and walked purposefully from her room.

The glass enclosed dining room, situated on the rooftop of the villa, had already begun to fill with eager diners. Part of the policy of Liaisons was to cater to the guests' every dietary whim. Upon arrival, every guest filled out a complete guide to their special requirements and the Liaisons' chef met their requests with verve. The immense kitchen was stocked with everything from Nathan's hot dogs to exotic Far East cuisine.

Momentarily, Noelle stood at the threshold of the dining room quietly observing the guests, and hoping to catch a glimpse of Tempest and Braxton, to no avail. However, she was totally satisfied that her fantasy hideaway had become her reality. Maybe now the gossipmongers would begin to take her seriously. There was no way that anyone could doubt that Liaisons was a huge success. And she'd only just begun.

"Checking on your guests again?"

The decidedly intimate voice came from behind her.

Noelle stole a glance over her shoulder to see

Cole Richards standing a mere breath away. Her pulse shuddered as her brief glance told her that he was even more handsome than when she'd last seen him. If that were possible.

He stepped around to stand at her side.

"It's my responsibility to make sure that everyone at Liaisons is well taken care of, *Monsieur* Richards."

His slow smile taunted her. "I'm sure that everyone appreciates your conscientiousness." He paused, noting the seriousness of her expression. "Please call me Cole. I'm sure we'll be seeing enough of each other to be able to drop formalities."

Her expression slowly relaxed. "I suppose you're right. You must excuse me if I seem . . ."

"Anxious?" he said completing her sentence.

Her smile was tremulous as she nodded.

"It's just that I've worked so hard for so long to," she spread her hand in explanation, "make this all happen. I just want everything to be perfect."

He saw the shadow of doubt flicker in those beautiful brown eyes and he had to reassure her.

"Believe me, I can't imagine anyone thinking otherwise." He lowered his gaze and then looked directly at her and added gently, "I'm sure Jordan would be very proud of what you've accomplished."

"You knew my husband well?" she asked, smoothly sidestepping the compliment.

"Yes. Very well."

Noelle recognized her opportunity. She straightened her shoulders and tilted her head.

"Would you care to join me for dinner—Cole?"

He took her elbow and grinned. "I thought you'd never ask. I'm starved."

Dinner conversation was easy, unstrained and at times filled with laughter. They talked about old movies, the economy, hobbies, places that they had been and found that they had a lot in common. The unspoken realization was tantalizing.

"Your chef is magnificent," Trent complimented, pushing slightly away from the table. "I can't remember ever having poached salmon that could compare to this."

Noelle smiled appreciatively.

"Jordan and I met Paul, the chef, when we were in Paris," Noelle explained. "I decided then and there that if I were to ever have this dream of mine come true, I would make sure that Paul was my chef."

Trent brushed his lips with the linen napkin then tucked it beneath his empty plate. "So you thought about Liaisons for a while?"

Noelle nodded. "All of the years that I worked at my aunt's cafe in New Orleans, I envisioned a place of my own. Something unlike any other," she added wistfully,

"You've outdone yourself." He looked around the elegant dining hall, then back at Noelle. When his dark eyes settled on her, she felt her insides flutter. "I can't imagine all the time and work it took to put this all together."

She sighed. "I had a good teacher."

For several moments they sat in companionable silence, sipping the last of their wine, each caught in momentary memories of Jordan Maxwell.

"Would you like to take a walk with me around the grounds?" Trent asked. "I haven't had a chance to see very much."

Noelle smiled. "I'd like that very much."

They talked softly as they strolled across the grass covered slopes, with Noelle pointing out her favorite spots and explaining where some of her ideas had arisen.

"I wanted to try to recreate some of the wonderful things that I'd seen in my travels and bring them all together in one place.

"Like the fountains over there." She pointed in the direction of the enormous marble fountains. "I'd seen those in Greece. The ideas for the pillars came from seeing the ruins in Rome. The hieroglyphics on the stone wall in the steam rooms came from my visits to the tombs in Egypt."

Trent was visibly impressed, Noelle noticed with a touch of pride.

"You've obviously traveled a great deal. Not many people are that lucky."

"Jordan tried to make sure that the whole world would be an education for me."

Noelle slowed down and stopped walking. Trent halted his step and turned toward her. His expression registered concern.

"Is something wrong?"

She stood still for several moments framing the questions in her mind. "How well did you know Jordan? When did you see him last?"

He knew the questions were inevitable, and had dreaded this very moment from the time he mentioned that he'd been with Jordan at the purchase of Liaisons. Careless. He hated having to lie to her. She was so beautiful, so sincere, nothing like the person that he'd envisioned. But he felt he had no other choice.

He stepped cautiously closer. She looked so fragile and vulnerable. Her luminous brown eyes were wide with expectation.

"We worked—together," he began, "on several projects."

Noelle's brow creased. "I don't remember Jordan ever mentioning you."

He thought quickly. "I was more of a consultant. He called me in from time to time."

She lowered her gaze to the ground. Her voice was barely above a whisper. Trent strained to catch each word.

"I hadn't seen Jordan for three months before the—accident. He'd spent his time traveling and then when the revolt started, he told me he couldn't get away, there were too many things to take care of."

Slowly she looked up, her eyes glistening with memories. "I'm sorry," she said, swallowing back a sob. "I didn't mean to drag you into my problems." She sniffed and smiled weakly.

His gut twisted with guilt. "It's all right," he assured her softly. He pulled a monogrammed handkerchief from the breast pocket of his midnight blue dinner jacket and handed it to her. Instantly he realized his error.

The initials TMD hypnotized him. He held his breath while Noelle dabbed at her eyes.

"Thank you Cole." She handed him the handkerchief. His relief was almost palpable. Noelle read it as discomfort. "I didn't mean to embarrass you. I don't usually do this kind of thing. Especially around strangers."

His eyes roved over her face. "I was hoping that we were more than strangers." He grinned mischievously. "Especially after this morning, Mrs. Maxwell," he teased, his look bringing back swift memories of their earlier encounter at his suite. His crooked smile made Noelle laugh in spite of herself.

"I guess you're right." She eyed him coyly surprising herself with her directness. "So what does that make us—exactly?"

He stepped closer, until he was near enough to feel the heat from her body, and was sure that she could hear his racing heart.

She felt the intimate caress of his eyes when he looked at her and held her breath as he spoke.

"I'd say that makes us two people who are on their way to something very," he touched her chin with the tip of his finger, "very special."

When she looked up into his eyes, he saw a mixture of longing and doubt. "What do you say to that?" he asked softly.

She hesitated, reluctant to say what she was truly feeling. Things were moving too fast.

"I'd say it's time that we changed the subject."

Trent smoothly recovered without missing a step, much to Noelle's relief. The feelings she had about Cole Richards were coming too hot, too fast. She had to put on the brakes.

He grinned and shoved his hands in his pants pockets, reminding her of a little boy caught with his fingers in the cookie jar.

"And to what would you like to change the subject?"

Noelle breathed deeply. "What exactly did you do for Maxwell Enterprises?" She looked directly into his eyes.

Trent casually averted his gaze. "I was responsible for recommending particular aircrafts to suit the need." He spread his hand in explanation as he continued. "I compared capabilities, costs, shopped around, kept up on the latest models, made necessary negotiations." He shrugged, offhandedly. "Things like that."

Slowly Noelle nodded while she absorbed the information. Then her head snapped up.

"Would that cover personal aircrafts as well?" Her pulse raced and so did Trent's. He thought he knew where this was headed and he didn't like the direction. But he couldn't divert the inevitable collision.

"In some cases," he replied with caution.

"Cole." She stretched out her hand and clasped his arm. "I want you to find out what happened to my husband's plane."

"What?" That request he didn't expect. "I—I, didn't the FAA rule it as an accident?"

"I don't care what the FAA said!" Her slender hands clenched into fists. "I have a feeling that something happened. Something that the FAA and my own investigator were unable to find. Jordan was too careful, too conscientious about everything. He never would have flown in a plane that had even the remotest problem."

Her dark brown eyes locked with his. "And neither would Trent Dixon. Unless he knew . . ." Her voice trailed off with her thoughts.

"Knew what?"

She shook her head in uncertainty. "I'm not sure," she said finally. "All I know is that I'll never be able to go on with my life until I do know—for sure. And I believe that you're the one who can help me."

He read the silent plea in her eyes and he almost weakened.

"But you even said that you'd hired an investigator and he couldn't come up with anything. The FAA couldn't come up with anything. Why are you so sure that I can?"

Her features softened when she spoke. "You don't have to answer me now. Just promise me that you'll think about it."

Trent briefly shut his eyes, realizing that at that moment, with her looking at him as if he was the only man on earth; if Noelle Maxwell had asked him to jump off of the Golden Gate bridge in his birthday suit he would have agreed. He nodded.

"Thank you," she whispered.

With that aside Noelle took up their stroll again, heading back in the direction of the main house. She spoke softly as they walked.

"Sometimes," she began, "I feel as though I'm trapped in some sort of limbo. Unable to go forward, unable to go back. My unresolved feelings have me locked into a fortress without windows or doors."

"But you are moving on with your life. You've opened Liaisons. It's obviously a success."

She laughed a self-deprecating laugh. "This is all part of the fortress."

His dark eyes squinted in confusion. "I don't understand."

She touched his arm lightly and instantly felt the heat spread through her fingers. "It's a longer story than I care to tell." She turned away.

For several moments he stood behind her, entranced by her solitary beauty. The iridescent glow from the half moon seemed to cast a halo around her black clad body, every detail of her form defined under the moonlight. He was spellbound by the sensuous voice, moved to undeniable arousal by her very existence in his life and pained by the fear and loneliness that was her life. Damn it Jordan! What have you done to her—to me?

He eased closer and turned her around into the circle of his arms.

"Maybe one day you'll tell me," he said gently. His eyes trailed languidly over her face and he felt her heart slam against his chest.

She stared at him, transfixed by an overwhelming anticipation that was almost unbearable. She struggled to control the spiraling emotions and failed as his head lowered. His mouth met her parted lips.

The contact was as fiery as an arson's blaze. She felt her entire body ignite, yet she shivered in his arms. He pulled her closer, molding her body to his.

His own mind and body convulsed in a barrage of explosive emotion. His thoughts ran in circles as he tried to control the instantaneous passion that welled within him.

He felt as if he'd known her forever and then not at all. He wanted to taste every inch of her, make her his own. His eager tongue explored her mouth and when she willing responded he knew that he was lost.

Noelle searched his mouth. Her slender arms clung to him, her only means of knowing that she was still on earth finding herself within the warm cavern.

How long had she waited to feel this way? A day? A week—forever? Somehow she believed her search was over. Cole would show her what it was like to be a real woman.

Then reality stung her with vehemence. She couldn't. Not with this man. Not with someone who knew Jordan. Then their long-kept secret would be discovered. She couldn't do that to Jordan's memory.

Without warning, she tore herself from Trent's embrace. She shook her head warning off his spontaneous approach.

"No. Please. I shouldn't have done that." She turned away and started up the small incline toward the entrance.

Trent took off after her, reaching her just before she came to the door. He grabbed her arm. "I wanted to," he said in a raspy voice.

Noelle remained with her back to him afraid to see the truth that she sensed would be in his eyes.

"I've wanted to from the moment I saw you, Noelle. So don't blame yourself."

Slowly she turned to face him. He saw the doubt in her eyes. He reached out and cupped her cheek in his hand.

"What are you so afraid of?" he asked gently.

She tilted up her chin, exhibiting a confident air. "You've got it all wrong. I just don't want you to think that I was trying to . . ." She searched for the word.

"Romance me into helping you," he said finishing her sentence once again. The beginnings of a smile tilted his full lips. "Like I said, Mrs. Maxwell, I wanted that kiss."

The light in his eyes ignited. "And I think you wanted it, too."

He moved his hand down to stroke her arm.

She stared at him for a brief moment. "Good night, Mr. Richards." Her tone was suddenly formal. "Please let me know if you'll accept my request."

Without another word she turned away, hurrying into the safety of the villa.

For several moments Trent leaned against the ornate pillar, silently fuming. He could have kicked himself. He'd obviously misread her. He shook his head at his own macho stupidity. Just because he let his hormones lead the way didn't mean that she was on the same wave length.

He slammed his fist against the pillar. Damn it! This was going to be even more difficult than he thought. Not only did he have to hide his identity, and keep his feelings for Noelle in check, he also had to get her to realize that he wasn't some oversexed, oversized teenager on the make.

Noelle lay in her bed staring sightlessly up at the sheer netting that draped her bed. For years she'd kept a lid on her desires. She'd willingly substituted gratitude and loyalty for physical pleasure. And now, in one fell swoop, Cole Richards walks into her life and opens up the trap door to her heart.

She squeezed her eyes shut. She couldn't let herself be swept away by a torrid desire for a man she hardly knew. And even if she did, which was highly unlikely, she'd had no experience with casual affairs and wouldn't know how to conduct one. For all the years of her marriage she'd stuck to the letter of her vows. *Forsaking all others.* She'd never allowed temptation, unhappiness, or physical incompleteness to lead her into infidelity. Although she wasn't particularly religious as an adult, her childhood years of churchgoing had left its indelible mark.

In any event, Cole Richards appeared to be the type of man who would never settle down and she knew she could never tolerate that.

Could she even trust a man, any man with her feelings, with them knowing who she was and the millions that she represented? Why would Cole Richards be any different from the others who had been attracted by the wealth and power? This time couldn't be any different. Could it?

She turned on her left side, trying to still the racing beat of her heart. Even as she did visions of Cole, the scent of him, the feel and taste of him filled her.

She flipped onto her right side, pushing her face into the pillow. She'd just have to find some way of dealing with the irresponsible way he made her feel. She'd disguised her true feelings for years. This time wouldn't be any different. Because Cole Richards was going to help her prove that Trent Dixon caused Jordan's death whether he wanted to or not.

Nothing could interfere with that.

Six

Tempest spotted Noelle across the courtyard and waved to her.

Even before Tempest reached where she stood, Noelle saw the lines of strain beneath the striking hazel eyes.

"Are you all right, *chère?*" Noelle asked when Tempest approached.

"Just a little tired," Tempest answered lamely.

Noelle looked hard at her friend. "Now how long have we been friends?" Noelle taunted, tossing Tempest's own question back at her.

Tempest sighed heavily and sat down on the bench beneath a huge transplanted palm tree. Noelle sat beside her and waited.

"Braxton left last night," she blurted out.

Noelle frowned. "Just like that?" She snapped her fingers for emphasis.

"Yes. Just like that." Tempest repeated the gesture.

"I don't understand."

"He claims he has another job in Brazil that needs his immediate attention."

"But isn't your daughter, Kai, coming in today?"

Tempest nodded. "I'm on my way to the airport now to meet her and Mrs. Harding."

"I thought Braxton was going to use this time to spend with you and Kai?"

"That's what I thought," Tempest complained. "We spent the entire night arguing about it. He still insisted that he had to go."

That would explain why she didn't see them at dinner last night, Noelle guessed. She searched for something comforting to say. "Perhaps it is important. I can't imagine that he would leave without seeing his daughter if it wasn't urgent."

Tempest stood up, smoothing the aqua-colored suit jacket. She looked off toward the horizon.

"Things have been very strained between Braxton and me for a while," she admitted softly. She turned toward Noelle. "Our schedules are so hectic we hardly see each other. Then when we do—" her voice trembled, "it's almost like we're two strangers. It was never like that between us, even after being separated for those six years after I left Virginia and went to New York. When we found each other again it was like those lost years had never happened."

Noelle was shocked. She'd always imagined that Tempest and Braxton were the perfect couple. If you had wanted to write a book about a happy marriage, they would be the ones to write about. They had been through so much to be together. It was hard for her to believe that their marriage could be in trouble. But then Noelle examined her own marriage. Everyone believed that it was *My Fair Lady* come true. But at what cost?

Noelle stood up and put her arm around Tempest's shoulder. "I didn't know," she said gently. "I only wish that I had the answers to make things better. All I can say is that as long as you and Braxton continue to love each other, everything will work out. You'll see."

"I hope you're right. And I do know that I love him, more than anything in the world." She forced a smile, still unable to put into words what was truly troubling her. She pushed aside her troubles. "How about you? Are you feeling better today?"

Noelle wanted to tell her about her evening with Cole, about the way she felt when she was with him. She decided that it wasn't the best time to discuss her budding feelings for Cole in light of Tempest's problems.

"Actually, yes. As a matter of fact, I thought about what you said about the attorney. Maybe I will call him."

"I think that's the right decision. The worst that could happen is that he won't tell you anything."

Tempest checked her watch. "I've got to go. The flight is arriving in L.A. Mrs. Harding got my instructions wrong and booked the flight into LAX airport."

An idea came to Noelle. "Would you mind some company?"

"Of course not. It's not the shortest drive in the world."

"Maybe I'll just pay my attorney Monsieur Malone a surprise visit."

Tempest brightened. "Perfect. I love surprises. If you catch him off guard he won't have time to prepare a story."

"Exactly!" Noelle grinned. She linked her arm through Tempest's. "Let's go."

Trent meticulously reviewed the data that had been faxed to him on Liaisons. He'd set up a small office in his hotel suite in L.A. It was fully equipped with a computer, printer, a copy and a fax machine. He'd already had his computer linked via modem to the main headquarters in Sudan and in Hong Kong.

The financial stability of Liaisons was excellent. He'd verified the credibility of the accountants, attorneys and had conducted a background check on all of Liaisons's staff.

As he leaned back in his chair he breathed a sigh of relief. Noelle Maxwell was unquestionably an astonishing businesswoman, not merely a woman in business. There were no outstanding debts. All of the structures exceeded building codes and revenue was pouring in.

If he had any doubts about her capabilities they had certainly been laid to rest.

He closed the thick manila folder and stood up, shoving his hands in his jeans pockets as he did. To look at her one would easily assume that she was merely a pampered heiress with delusions of grandeur, he mused. To the contrary, Noelle was a woman of substance, with talents yet untapped. But did she have what it took to manage an empire as complex as Jordan's? More importantly would she be able to handle the truth once it was revealed to her and possibly give up her one dream to save Jordan's? Of that he was still unsure.

His own personal feelings about her seemed to be clouding his judgment. He wanted her. He wanted her like he hadn't wanted any other woman. And the intensity of his emotions made him feel vulnerable. A feeling that was totally foreign to him.

He'd already revealed too much to her last night. It had probably cost him his credibility in her eyes. He couldn't let that happen again. He owed it to Jordan to see that the instructions of his will were carried out. Emotional entanglement with his widow was not part of the package.

"I'll see you later this evening," Noelle called out as Tempest waved and drove away.

For several moments Noelle stood in front of the building that housed Joseph Malone's suite of offices. He was obnoxious as far as she was concerned and she knew that he didn't hold her in very high regard. Whatever civility he showed her was purely due to the very large retainer that Jordan had paid him.

She pushed through the glass door and boarded the elevator to the third floor, wondering all the while what made her think that he would tell her anything.

The reception area was paneled with dark maplewood. Any semblance of sound was easily absorbed into the thick grey carpet. It reminded her of a scene from some old black-and-white "B" mystery movie. *Yuk.*

She walked directly to the secretary's desk, with her three-inch, sling-back heels sinking into the carpet with each step. She had the hilarious notion of being swallowed by grey quicksand.

Alice Bernstein, the middle-aged secretary, looked up at her over her wire-rimmed glasses.

Her face flushed when she recognized Noelle. "Mrs. Maxwell, what brings you here?"

Force of habit compelled her to quickly check the appointment calendar on her desk. "I don't see your name in *the book.*" She said the last word with an almost holy deference. "Was someone expecting you?" She removed her glasses and looked every bit like the affronted secretary.

"No Alice, I don't have an appointment. But I would like to see Monsieur Malone. Is he free?"

Alice Bernstein's silver curls seemed to spring to life.

"Oh—Mrs. Maxwell, you know that it is quite impossible to see Mr. Malone without an appointment." She reshuffled the small, neat stack of files on her desk. Alice took pride in the one fact that her life was dictated by order. Any interference threw her completely off balance and the sudden appearance of Noelle Maxwell had done just that.

She didn't like it one bit. She reached for her always handy cup of water and took a sip. She immediately felt more composed and in control. She squared her chin.

"If you'd like to give me a date and time when you're free, I'd be happy to . . ."

"I'm free right now, Alice. And I'd like it very much if you'd tell Monsieur Malone that I'm here," she stated firmly.

Noelle stood her ground tossing back the icy stare with one of her own. Generally, Alice Bernstein had the ability to unnerve Noelle. Even as she stood before her, she had the inclination to make a bee line for the elevator. But she wouldn't let the old general intimidate her today. She wasn't leaving until she had accomplished what she'd come for.

Alice was completely astonished. She wasn't used to anyone not following her instructions. Especially Noelle Maxwell. All one usually had to do was raise an eyebrow and she'd back down. When did she finally get some backbone? Alice had to admit, although never to Noelle, that she admired her nerve.

Alice loudly cleared her throat.

"If you'll just have a seat over there." With her pen she indicated a row of grey chairs. "I'll see if Mr. Malone can spare you a few moments." She picked up the phone.

Noelle released the long-held breath. "Thank you."

Moments later, Joseph Malone flung open his

door. "Noelle," he boomed in a deep basso voice. "Please come in."

It always amazed her that this reed of a man could have such a powerful voice. She supposed that's what made him such a master in the courtroom. He was just as rangy and taut as ever, she noted. He'd always reminded her of a predator ready to swoop down on an unsuspecting victim.

As Noelle approached, he placed his bony arm protectively around her shoulder, ushering her into his office. Noelle cringed.

"Now, what can I do for you?"

Noelle took a seat opposite the maplewood desk and crossed her legs. She reached into her pocketbook and produced the letter from Jordan.

"I'd like you to explain this to me."

Briefly he scanned the letter and returned it to her.

"I really can't see how I can explain the contents, Noelle. I wasn't privy to the . . ."

"Please don't patronize me, Joseph. You know perfectly well what I mean. Where was this letter? And why am I just receiving it from your office?"

Joseph pursed his thin, pale lips, placing his index finger thoughtfully across them.

"I had instructions," he said simply. "I was to have this envelope delivered to you, one day after the official opening of Liaisons."

"What? Jordan didn't even know that I would go through with it."

"Perhaps. But, if and when you did, you were to receive this letter."

Noelle exhaled heavily. "Is there anything else I should know, Joseph?"

The pain in her voice almost touched him, but he pushed it away. He was no longer obligated to her. The last retainer check had been cashed upon delivery of the letter. But why did she have to look at him with those eyes so full of anguish? Something inside of his chest twisted.

He cleared his throat. "There is a codicil to your late husband's will."

"What are you talking about? I was there when it was read."

Joseph nodded indulgently. "Yes and according to my instructions, the codicil was only to be read by Trent Dixon."

Her head began to pound.

"I see." She stood up. "And I suppose I'm not to be privy to that either?"

"I'm afraid not. My instructions were quite clear."

"Thank you for your time, Joseph," she tossed at him, more annoyed at herself for having thought that their encounter could have been any different.

He rounded the desk, reaching the door a step before her.

"I wish there was something else I could tell you, Noelle," he said with as much sincerity as he could summon.

Noelle only nodded as she crossed the threshold.

Joseph had a rare attack of conscience as he watched her leave.

"Maybe Mr. Dixon would be willing to tell you. I understand he's here in Los Angeles."

Noelle halted her step and turned around. "How do you know?" Her heart thundered.

"I called the headquarters in Sudan yesterday. I was told he'd come to California two days ago."

Trent finished the last of his paperwork. Languidly he stretched his tight muscles. He had to get out of this room. Hours on the phone and behind the computer had left him numb. A long flight around the countryside would be ideal about now. But what he really wanted to do was return to Liaisons and see Noelle. He hadn't been able to stop thinking about her. She seemed to creep into his thoughts at the most inopportune times. Like now.

The throbbing between his thighs was almost unbearable. Maybe what he really needed was a cold shower.

He switched off the humming machines, grabbed his denim jacket and headed out of the door.

Noelle exited the building and proceeded to walk, oblivious to the rows of boutiques and the flow of human traffic.

Trent Dixon was somewhere in Los Angeles. He was the only one who had the answers to her questions. The thought of his proximity unnerved her.

Why was he here? Had he come to spy on her? He could be anywhere, walking right beside her and she wouldn't know it. That fact raised her blood pressure. She didn't have the faintest notion of what he looked like. He'd never accompanied Jordan on his trips to the U.S., since he was responsible for operations in Jordan's absence. Trent Dixon could run her over with a Mack truck, right this minute, and she wouldn't know it was him. Her temper rose as her thoughts ran in circles.

The head-on collision knocked her purse from her hand.

"Noelle?" Trent instinctively grabbed her shoulders to steady her, then reached down to retrieve her purse. "Are you okay?"

"Y-es," she stammered, surprised and embarrassed to see Cole Richards in the middle of Los Angeles. "I'm fine. Sorry. I guess I wasn't watching where I was going."

"You must be deep in thought."

She gave him a weak smile. "Something like that." She took a quick look around, observing her surroundings for the first time. The large marquee of the hotel loomed above her head and her thoughts scurried off in a dangerous direction.

He was probably there to meet someone, she thought. Did he spend the night here after he'd left her weak from his kisses?

An unfamiliar wave of jealousy swept through her. Her body tensed.

"Did you think about my request?" she asked in a tight voice.

Confusion registered on Trent's face with the swift change in Noelle's mood.

"Is something bothering you, Noelle?"

"What else could be bothering me?" she almost snapped. She looked away unable to meet the questioning gaze.

Trent avoided answering the question, by posing one of his own. "I was going to get something to eat. I'd like it very much if you'd join me. Then we can talk. Would you?"

When she dared to look back at him, she was, once again, consumed by those onyx eyes that had haunted her nights, by the lips that she longed to taste again and by the captivating scent that heated her blood.

He'd begun to think that she hadn't heard him or had chosen not to respond—when she finally answered.

"Do you know your way around?" she asked in that sexy faint accent that drove him crazy.

"Maybe you can give me the tour again," he replied, his tone intentionally intimate.

Noelle cleared her throat. "There's a great outdoor cafe about a block down. I'm sure you'd like it."

"With you, I'm sure I would."

For a brief moment they both stared at each other, the busy world around them going totally unnoticed.

"We're going to cause a scene in a minute," Trent said, his smile teasing. "People are beginning to stare."

Self-consciously Noelle looked around, feeling that everyone could see what was going on inside of her.

Her voice was slightly tremulous. "Then I guess we should be going."

Trent slipped her arm through the curve of his. "Lead the way."

Lunch was brief, almost strained. Both of them were harboring their own thoughts and skirting the real issues that bubbled like molten lava beneath their composed surfaces.

"You were right about this place," Trent offered, breaking the rather long train of silence. "The food here is great." He smiled. "But they can't touch Liaisons's with a stick."

"I hope that everyone who comes will feel the same way." She fiddled with her napkin to avoid looking at him.

Trent reached across the table to still her fingers. He covered her hand with his. The immediate warmth spread through her.

"I thought about your request to . . . find out what happened."

She looked directly at him and his stomach lurched with longing.

"And?"

"And I've decided to help you."

The brilliant smile that he received was worth all the deceit.

"Thank you. I'll make it worth your while. Whatever the price."

His brows creased both in disbelief and guilt. "I couldn't possibly take any money from you." His voice rose in agitation. "I'm not doing this for the money."

"I didn't mean to offend you, but I think it would only be fair. In fact, I insist."

Trent's jaw clenched. He looked away. How could he possibly accept money from her knowing that the person she was looking for was sitting right in front of her and that he would have to do whatever was necessary to keep that information from her until the time was right.

His gaze returned to her. "I won't accept anything from you until after the job is done. That's the only way," he added firmly.

Noelle considered for a moment. "If that's the only way you'll agree, then I guess I don't have a choice."

"Then it's settled."

She nodded.

Trent leaned back in his seat and exhaled deeply. What in the hell had he gotten himself into?

"Do you have plans for the rest of the day?" he asked.

"No, I don't, actually. I was supposed to call the villa and send for a car and driver, but after my visit with Joseph Malone . . ."

The mention of Malone's name caused Trent's pulse to gallop. He'd completely forgotten about the carnivorous attorney. He was the one person who could identify him on sight.

". . . so your job may not be so difficult after all."

Trent slowly returned to the conversation. "What? I'm sorry."

"I said, Joseph Malone told me that Trent Dixon was here in Los Angeles."

Just great. "That will make things easier," he said lamely.

A thought occurred to Noelle. "You spent time in Sudan with Jordan," she stated more than asked. "Did you ever meet Trent Dixon? What does he look like?"

Oh, God. Trent cleared his throat. "I never had the chance to meet him. I guess our paths just didn't cross. Why don't we get out of here?" Trent suggested, before Noelle had a chance to respond. He swiftly wiped his mouth and pushed away from the table.

Before Noelle knew what was happening he was standing behind her chair to help her up.

Her eyebrows arched. "Why are you in such a rush all of a sudden? Is something wrong?" she asked in bewilderment.

"Of course not. But there's no point in sitting here when we can be exploring. You did promise to show me around." He forced a smile as they walked toward the door.

Noelle shrugged to camouflage her confusion. "I guess we could drive out to the movie studios, or into Beverly Hills." She looked at him skeptically. "What do you want to do?"

He wanted to say, get as much distance between me and Malone as possible, but instead, "How about a drive out to the beach? Next to flying, the waves always help me to think. The sun will be setting in a few hours. It's been a long time since I saw the sun set over the water."

His full lips curved into that sensuous smile that made her feel weak.

"It sounds wonderful."

Her voice felt like the brush of silk against his ears. "My car is in the hotel garage."

The mention of the hotel caused Noelle's initial misgivings and jealousies to resurface. It was ridiculous to feel this way, she knew, but for whatever reason, she couldn't seem to help it.

Trent watched the warm brown eyes turn suddenly cold and distant.

"Noelle, for the last time, what is it?"

"If we're going to the beach, we should get started," she answered in a cool tone.

Trent fell in step next to Noelle. He kept his confusion to himself in the hope that she would eventually reveal what was bothering her.

She couldn't keep doing this, she thought. It was unfair to Cole to suspect him of anything. And what if he was in the hotel with another woman. There were no strings tying them together. But still, she didn't like how the thoughts made her feel. If nothing else, they had to work together to find Trent and the truth.

If there was any possibility that what she was beginning to feel for Cole could ever be reciprocated, she needed to know what else or who else was in his life. She needed to put her concerns to rest.

As casually as she could, she asked the question that had been burning her tongue.

"So . . . what brought you into L.A.? I thought Liaisons had everything that a person could want. Please don't say that we're lacking something." She kept her eyes straight ahead as they continued toward the hotel.

Trent struggled to keep from smiling. So that was it! She saw me coming out of the hotel and thought I was with someone. *A woman.*

"Well, I came in town earlier this morning. I had a business appointment with a potential client." She could feel his eyes looking down at her with that smile that made her believe he could read her mind.

Noelle felt her whole body heat with embarrassment. Now she felt totally ridiculous again. Cole Richards had an uncanny knack for having that effect on her.

She swallowed the lump in her throat. "Oh," was all she could say.

They turned into the garage entrance. Trent handed the attendant his ticket stub and they waited for his car to be brought out.

Trent turned toward Noelle and tilted her chin up with his fingertip. The intensity of his expression caused Noelle to tremble beneath his gaze.

She held her breath and when he looked into that face, all the promises that he'd made to himself vanished.

His voice was low, penetrating. "I want to kiss you again, Noelle." His eyes swept searchingly over her face. "What do you say to that?"

For a moment she couldn't think, couldn't breathe, as his head slowly lowered. His muscular arms encircled her.

His lips gently touched down on hers, once, then twice ending with his tongue awakening every nerve in her body.

Involuntarily, she grasped his forearms, mostly to keep her balance, but also to assure herself that this was no dream.

But the intimate moment was cut short when the roar of the Lexus engine filled the torrid air.

Reluctantly, Trent eased away, planting one last kiss on Noelle's parted lips. "There's more," he groaned in a thick voice. "Believe that."

Seven

"But why did Daddy have to leave so soon? Why didn't he wait for me?" Kai demanded, her wide dark eyes piercing her mother's.

Tempest absorbed the pain of her daughter's disappointment so potently, it felt like a steel weight that had leveled her heart. *Damn you Braxton! How could you do this?*

Tempest sat down on the couch and pulled Kai down next to her. She put her arm around her daughter's slumped shoulders and eased her closer.

"Listen to me baby," Tempest said softly. "It was very, very important work that your daddy had to do. You know how much he loves you." She kissed the top of Kai's head. "He would never miss a chance to spend time with you if it weren't very important." *How many more lies will I have to tell my child?*

Kai forcibly tugged herself away and sprung up from the couch.

"It's always something," Kai said, her ten-year-old voice rising in anger. "He's never around anymore." She spun around to face her mother.

Those large black eyes, identical to her father's, were glistening with unspent tears.

"I'm tired of traveling all over the world. I want to live like the rest of my friends. I want to have a regular life and a regular family."

Tempest rose and took Kai into her embrace, fighting desperately to hide her own tears.

"It'll be all right, baby. I promise," she cooed. "We're going to be a regular family. I promise you."

Tempest peered over Kai's head at Mrs. Harding. Clara Harding had been a part of Tempest's life since she was six years old. Clara was more of a second mother than a housekeeper and she treated Tempest and Kai like they were her very own children.

"Clara would you run a bath for Kai, please? Then afterwards I'll take both of you on a tour of Liaisons. We're going to make the most of this visit."

She forced herself to smile when she looked down at Kai's upturned face.

"And I think my beautiful daughter hasn't seen anything until she's seen Liaisons."

She turned Kai toward Mrs. Harding. "So get moving. There's plenty to do. And I know your godmother is waiting to see you."

Kai smiled slightly at the mention of her godmother, Noelle. Reluctantly she did as she was told and followed Mrs. Harding out of the room.

Tempest smothered a sob with her hand. "I'm not going to let you keep doing this Braxton.

You're not going to keep hurting us like this. No more!"

She stormed off into her bedroom and placed an overseas call to Brazil.

"I'm glad I keep a blanket in my trunk." Trent stretched his long muscular limbs. "Old habit." He turned his head to see Noelle perched gingerly on the edge of the blanket.

"Relax, Noelle," he urged, raising up on one elbow.

She laughed nervously. "This outfit isn't exactly beachwear."

He took a quick glance at the lemon yellow, sleeveless linen dress and matching strapless shoes. He wanted to tell her that he could fix all that by simply helping her out of it. But he knew that wouldn't go over too well.

"What was it like living in New Orleans?" he asked instead. "It's one place I've always wanted to visit."

Noelle visibly relaxed. She sighed with a wistful smile. "It was all I knew for most of my life. Mardi Gras, hundreds of tiny cafes, seafood, crowds. I thought every place in the world had all-night jazz clubs, and hordes of people roaming the street in bizarre costumes on holidays." She laughed at the recollection, then sobered. "We were poor, and I thought I was happy." She peeked at him over her shoulder. "I guess that's how it is when you have nothing to compare it to."

"And now?"

"Hmmm. Well, I suppose most people would think I have the perfect life. Clothes. Money. The ability to travel whenever and wherever I want. I've seen my life displayed in so many magazines and newspapers I almost started to believe the stories myself . . ." Her voice trailed off. "But I think deep inside I'm still that simple girl, working in my aunt's cafe. I still have dreams and hopes."

Trent traced circles in the sand with his finger as he listened. Hesitantly, without looking up he said, "I would think that with Jordan all of your dreams would have come true." He instantly saw her withdraw at the mention of Jordan and regretted uttering his name.

"Things aren't always as they seem," she said.

He inched closer, needing to know. "This may be none of my business," he ventured, "but—were you really happy in your marriage?"

Noelle lowered her head and hugged her knees to her chest. Trent strained to hear her.

"At times. I think Jordan truly believed that showering a person with gifts and buying them anything that they could ever dream of would make them happy. But that kind of happiness is only temporary." She looked off toward the horizon. "That's not to say that we never shared joyful times together, because we did. Then at others I felt like I was trapped in some sort of nightmare." She shook her head as visions of ugly fights sprung before her eyes.

"If you were a real woman you'd find a way to

satisfy me." Jordan had yelled. "Go on, find your-self another man! I'll even pay for it. Like I've paid for everything else in your life." With those painful words he'd stormed out and locked him-self in the guest room leaving her alone in their enormous bedroom. Yet she'd stayed because she saw beneath the outward rage. It was never her that he was truly angry with. She was simply his available target.

She'd always felt that if she could somehow de-stroy the barrier that Jordan had constructed around himself, he would release all his insecurity.

She shook off the vision with a toss of her head. "What about you?" she asked, needing to change the subject.

Trent chuckled softly. "I definitely didn't have the fantasy storybook life. I was adopted when I was about two. I never knew my natural parents. But I was always happy. I had two of the greatest people as parents anyone could want. They made sure I had the best they could afford, which in-cluded four years at Columbia University.

This revelation deeply touched Noelle. She could sense by his tone the depth of his feelings for his parents. And she envied him. Then some-thing he said struck her. "You said you had two of the greatest parents." She hesitated a moment. "Did something happen?"

Trent inhaled deeply remembering all too viv-idly the day of James Dixon's heart attack.

"My father died when I was in my sophomore year of college. Heart attack."

Instinctively Noelle touched his arm in a comforting gesture. "I'm sorry," she said softly, knowing all too well the feelings of loss.

Trent nodded. After several moments he went on to tell her about his two adopted sisters who he obviously adored, and his twin niece and nephew who both swore that they were going to be great pilots just like their uncle.

"They all live in Philadelphia," he concluded. "We don't see each other much," he chuckled in that deep baritone, "but we do have a helluva phone bill!"

Noelle laughed with him as she realized how their lives were parallel in some respects. She felt that invisible bond, that had been present since their first meeting, intensify. Her one regret was that she didn't have the loving family that she so much wanted.

"Do you plan on having a family someday?" she asked tentatively.

"Most definitely! I want a house full of kids, so I can give them all the things that I had. And more." His eyes roamed slowly over her face. "Most of all—I want a wonderful woman to share my life with."

She felt breathless and hot as he stared at her as if she were the only person in the world. "That . . . sounds . . . wonderful." Her eyes held his as he leaned, slowly closer.

The warmth of his lips brushed her shoulder like the whisper of a breeze. A tremor rushed through her and her eyes slid closed.

Trent slipped his arms around her, sliding his hands down her thighs. He eased closer, pressing his chest against her back.

Her hands grasped his roving fingers, locking them above her knees.

"Cole," she whispered in a strangled voice.

"Sssh. No . . . time for . . . talking."

The setting sun cast a brilliant orange glow across the horizon, bathing them in its iridescent light. Giving this intimate moment an almost surreal aura.

He planted a row of kisses along her neck, her shoulders. "You're beautiful," he whispered in her ear.

Instinctively she arched her back when his hands trailed teasingly up her waistline. She'd fantasized about this moment from the very first night that they'd met. She imagined his strong hands roving freely across her body, tasted his lips against her own, inhaled his scent until it became a part of the very air she breathed. Now it was real. She'd never felt such a powerful attraction towards anyone. Not even when she first met Jordan. This was different. And for her this wasn't something totally physical. She trusted Cole. She trusted him with her heart.

Trent smoothly leaned Noelle back into the cradle of his arm until his face was only inches above her own. He felt his heart hammer mercilessly and he was sure that Noelle must think he was some oversexed gigolo on the prowl. But he couldn't stop himself as he moaned against her neck. He couldn't stop the waves of excitement that shook his body.

Yet, even as he kissed and caressed her, seeping between the vapors of his longing were faint strains of doubt. Noelle had been married to and loved by one of the most powerful black men in the world. A man who had made one of the greatest impacts on his life. His friend. His mentor. A surrogate father in his young adult years. Yes, he'd had his share of romances, crisscrossing all the barriers. But Noelle. Noelle, she was different. Whatever happened between them, he knew, would change them both forever.

He wanted everything to be perfect. He wanted to be sure that with every move he made, her moments with Jordan would dissolve from her mind like sugar in hot water.

As he held her like she was the most precious and delicate of jewels, she felt herself come alive for the first time in her life. She wanted him. Desperately. She wanted to know and feel, fully, what it was like to be totally loved—like a woman. She wanted what she had been denied for all the years that she'd been with Jordan.

She felt herself being swept away by the hunger of desire that seemed more powerful than the force of the crashing waves.

But she couldn't do it. She couldn't allow this man, her husband's friend, to discover what had been kept secret for the duration of her marriage.

She couldn't dismantle Jordan's image in Cole's eyes.

Trent lowered his head to, once again, kiss her the way he'd dreamed.

Noelle suddenly turned away, and with surprising strength, pushed him off of her, forcing him onto the sand.

"What, the . . ."

"No . . . Cole . . . I'm sorry . . . I can't." Her heart thundered. Her skin was aflame. She couldn't face the accusing look, the disbelief and hurt that she knew hung in his eyes.

With as much grace as she could summon, she rose from the blanket, purposely keeping her back to him, wrapping her arms protectively around her body.

Trent pulled himself onto his hands and knees until he was in a crouched position. He dropped his head onto his knees. He felt like a first-class fool.

He was so sure that this was what Noelle wanted too. This time. The atmosphere, the fire between them. All perfect. He'd gone against his better judgment. He knew he shouldn't get involved with her. It was too complicated. But he couldn't seem to help himself. He was falling for her. Hard. And that fact made what he was doing to her that much more despicable.

"I'm sorry." His voice barely reached her.

"No. I'm the one that's sorry," she said solemnly. "It's not your fault."

She turned around to face him and he looked

up. Her brown eyes glistened with tears and it pierced his heart. Trent believed them to be tears of sadness, but they were tears of longing. She wanted him so desperately it was an almost physical pain and to see the look of anguish on his face only added to her own misery. She trusted him. But could she trust him enough to tell him the truth?

Slowly she knelt down in front of him. "Cole," she began softly but then couldn't go on.

He looked at her with an intensity that set her soul on fire. She gently stroked his bearded jaw and he clasped her hand against his lips, kissing her palm.

"Whatever it is, Noelle, you can tell me. I'll understand. If you're not ready, if I'm not what you want, you can tell me." He kissed her palm again. "You can," he whispered urgently.

Sadly she shook her head. "It's all so complicated." She tugged on her bottom lip with her teeth. "And sordid, and I . . . don't want to talk about it. Not now. I can't." She looked away.

"Noelle," he turned her face toward him. He kept his hand on her cheek and she cradled it against her shoulder. "Whatever you want, I want for you. Whenever you're ready, I'm here."

She smiled weakly. "Thank you, Cole."

Each time that she said the name Cole, his gut twisted with guilt. How much longer could he keep deceiving her? How much longer before she discovered the truth on her own? Then what?

"I'll tell you what," he offered, forcing cheer

into his voice, "why don't we head on back and have one of Paul's fabulous meals and relax?"

Noelle nodded with relief. But the mention of Liaisons brought back her conversation with Joseph Malone.

Frowning she looked at Trent. "If Trent is in L.A. why hasn't he contacted me? He wasn't scheduled for another two weeks. What do you think he's up to?"

Trent looked away toward the darkened horizon, forcing his thoughts to catch up with the change in topics. He stood up and brushed off his jeans, but kept his eyes focused on his shoes as he continued to brush off his clothes.

"Maybe your attorney got his information wrong."

Noelle shook her head emphatically. "Joseph Malone never has the wrong information."

Don't I know it. He began to move restlessly, eager to change the topic.

"Then maybe Dixon decided to visit friends," he shrugged dismissively, "or relax for a while before he came to see you." *Please change the subject.*

"Maybe," she sighed, not totally convinced.

"Just wait until he turns up," he advised, finally daring to look at her. "There's no point in stirring things up. And I'll find out what I can until then. I've already sent for the FAA report."

She slipped the dark glasses in her purse. "I guess you're right," she admitted half-heartedly. Trent relaxed a little. "I just wish I knew why he was here two weeks early."

He put his arm around her waist, and snatched up the blanket with his other hand. Noelle tucked her purse under her arm.

"I'm sure we'll find out soon enough. In the meantime, let's get back. Your guests await!"

Noelle grinned up at him. "Thank you," she said softly, but her eyes said so much more, and Trent wondered again what secret bound her heart.

After Trent dropped Noelle off at Liaisons, she headed straight to Gina's office to get a rundown on the day's activities.

"I know there's nothing we can do right now," Gina said softly into the phone. "But we have to be patient. You know that. Everyone will just have to understand. When the time is right."

The sharp knock on Gina's office door made her jump.

"I have to go. Someone's here. Yes. As soon as I can. Bye." She quickly hung up the phone.

"Yes. Come in," she said in her cheeriest voice.

Noelle stepped into the small, neat office and closed the door behind her.

"Sorry to disturb you, Gina."

"No. No problem, Mrs. Maxwell." Gina cleared her throat as she stood up. "Please sit down. I guess you want the report."

Noelle looked at her quizzically. "Is something wrong? You seem . . . edgy."

"Oh. It's nothing. Just a slight headache. Nothing that two aspirin won't cure." Noelle noticed that Gina's smile didn't quite reach her eyes.

"Well be sure to take care of yourself. I know how hard you push yourself. Tomorrow is your day off isn't it?"

Noelle tucked away every bit of information about her staff in her head. It was a gift that constantly amazed Gina. And she was sure it was one of the reasons why Noelle had such a good rapport with her employees. That's why it made her so damned angry when she'd hear some of those wealthy bitches talk about Noelle as if she were some incompetent child who'd gotten lucky. Noelle had more class and intelligence than all of them rolled up together.

"Yes it is," Gina answered. "I think I'll just stay home and relax."

"You be sure you do that," she admonished, pointing a flawlessly manicured finger at Gina.

"I promise," Gina grinned. "Here's the report." She picked up the two-page report from her desk and handed it to Noelle.

"Thanks." Noelle rose from her seat. "Don't forget what I said," she warned.

"I won't Mrs. Maxwell."

"See you when you get back. And how is your father by the way?"

"Oh," she smiled, "he's doing very well. As a matter of fact he may be going over to the Sudan on behalf of the United Nations, depending on what happens over there in the next few weeks."

"If anyone can have an impact on the rebel

forces, Kenyatta Nkiru can," Noelle offered, remembering quite clearly the dynamic impression that he'd left on her when he'd come to see this "magical place" that his headstrong daughter had opted for instead of a career in politics. He was certainly a man to be reckoned with.

Noelle was updated periodically on the impact that the revolution was having on Jordan's business, but had steered clear of interfering. She had some very definite opinions on what should be done. However, she'd never give Trent Dixon the satisfaction of shooting them down. Let him handle it. She intended to stay as far away from Maxwell Enterprises as possible.

"Anyway, enjoy your day off and give my regards to your father."

"I will."

Noelle left the office with the vague sensation that Gina had something else on her mind beside a headache. But, then again, everyone was entitled to their secrets. She had enough of her own to attest to that.

Tossing aside thoughts of Gina, they scurried off in the direction of Cole. She'd had a wonderful afternoon with him. He was everything that she could hope for in a man.

She frowned. And yet she still wasn't sure about giving herself to him completely. She knew he wanted her as much as she wanted him. But would he wait around long enough for her to come to grips with the ghosts of the past? As she headed for her office a cynical inner voice penetrated her

conscious thoughts. It was curious that both he and
Dixon were pilots and both of them had worked
for Jordan. But the similarity ended there, she decided. There was no way that . . .

"Auntie!"

The all-too-familiar childlike voice snapped
Noelle out of her reverie. Her face lit up when
she saw her goddaughter run toward her, the unsettling comparison immediately forgotten.

"Kai!" She swept her up in her arms and
squeezed her hard before putting her down. "How
are you sweetheart? You've grown up so much since
I last saw you."

Kai beamed. "I'm in the fifth grade now," she
said proudly.

"And I'm sure you're the smartest and the pret-
tiest girl in your class."

Kai's cheery expression changed.

Noelle kneeled down. "What's wrong, *chère?*"

Kai pouted. "I never stay in one school long
enough to find out," she spat out with a vehemence that shook Noelle.

She looked over Kai's head to see Tempest
standing behind her daughter. The expression on
her face said that there was much more to be told.

"But you're such a lucky girl, Kai. There are so
many children who would love to travel around the
world," she said gently.

"Not me!"

Noelle looked up at Tempest who only shook
her head sadly.

"Well, since you're here, why don't we make a deal?"

Kai looked up with a bit of interest.

"What kind of deal?"

"I'm going to make sure that you have the best time possible. And you're going to put all those . . . thoughts out of your head and enjoy yourself. How's that?"

"Can I have room service?"

Noelle grinned and kissed her cheek. "Of course."

"Okay. It's a deal."

Noelle stood up and took Kai's hand. Her smile was full of compassion when she looked at Tempest. "So," she breathed, "what have you both been up to?"

"Just trying to get Kai and Mrs. Harding settled in," Tempest offered. She placed her arm around her daughter.

Noelle looked down at Kai. "I bet your mother hasn't shown you the stables. I know how much you like to ride. Would you like to ride before dinner?"

Kai jumped up and down. "Yeah!"

"Great. Wait right here and I'll have someone take you over. I'll be right back," she said to Tempest.

Moments later she returned with Gina.

"This is Gina Nkiru, Kai. She runs things around here and she loves horses, too."

"Hi," Kai said shyly.

"Hello, Kai. Mrs. Maxwell told me how much

you love to ride, and I know just the horse for you," she smiled. "Are you ready?"

Kai nodded happily.

"Then let's go. I'll have her back to her room before the dinner hour," Gina assured both women.

"Thank you," Tempest said.

When Kai and Gina were out of earshot, Noelle turned to Tempest. "Let's take a stroll over to the atrium. You look like you need to talk."

Tempest nodded, thankful, once again, for Noelle's perceptiveness.

They settled comfortably on the cushioned bench. The airy space offered a sense of peace and tranquility. Enclosed in glass with a beveled skylight, the large space was amass with tropical plants and trees from around the world. It was like bringing the very essence of nature right to your feet.

Tempest slowly began to relax, allowing the serenity to replace the hurt and turmoil that raged within her.

"Talk to me," Noelle coaxed.

Tempest shook her head. "I wish I knew where to begin."

"Start anywhere."

Tempest took a long deep breath, then blurted out the words that had tormented her. "I think Braxton is having an affair." She covered her mouth with her hand as if the very act could take back the damnation.

"No. Not Braxton," Noelle sputtered in disbelief. "Why, why would you think something like that?"

"What else could it be, Noelle? He's changed. He's always busy, always away. Hushed conversations, special meetings." She turned toward Noelle, her hazel eyes flashing. "What does that say to you?"

For a moment Noelle couldn't find the words to dispel Tempest's accusation. No one knew Braxton better than Tempest. If she believed that Braxton was having an affair, she had good reason. The thought that he could hurt Tempest in such a way enraged Noelle. But in the midst of Tempest's hurt it would do no good to display her true feelings. That's not what she needed now.

She spoke calmly. "Have you spoken to Braxton?"

"No. I called the construction site in Brazil and was told that he was unavailable. Humph. *Very* unlikely. Braxton can always be reached."

"Before he left, did he say when he would be back in the States?"

"He said he wasn't sure. If he couldn't get back before we leave in two weeks, he'd meet us in New York."

Noelle took both of Tempest's hands in her own. "Listen to me. There's no point in building a case against him until you've talked. You and Braxton have a second chance at a life together. Not many people do. Don't throw that away with unfounded suspicions.

"Be patient. I know it's hard. But if your marriage is as important to you as I know it is, just be patient.''

Noelle's smile was gentle. "When you talk with him, be honest about how you feel. Take the chance. Tell him your fears, and what you want. It's the only way he'll know."

Tempest succumbed to a weak smile and sniffed. "When did you get so wise?" she asked softly.

Noelle's eyes drifted around her garden of Eden, then back to Tempest.

"Right this minute," she answered in a voice filled with revelation. Maybe what she longed for was right at her fingertips, she thought. And maybe she should take the chance.

"And what brought it about?" Tempest wanted to know.

"Cole Richards," she answered simply.

Eight

Trent immediately returned to his room. He had work to do in order to pull this whole bizarre plan off. Under the pulsing surge of the steamy shower, he tried to keep his mind focused on his objectives. But no matter how hard he tried to concentrate on contracts, bank loans and Maxwell Enterprises, his thoughts shifted to Noelle.

With each passing day, he mused, lathering his hard body with Aramis soap, he became more drawn to her. She was everything he could ever wish for in a woman. Having gotten to know her, she had unconsciously changed his whole perception of her. Not only was she beautiful, but she was sensitive and had more business sense than many seasoned veterans.

The streaming water rushed over his face. He braced his hands against the black tiled walls, letting the water pound against him in the futile hope that it could somehow wash away the unending desire that coursed through him.

He stood to lose it all. The woman. The job. Everything. All because of a promise to a dead man.

He shut off the water and wrapped a towel around his waist. He had no choice. He'd never go back on his word. Maybe by some miracle, when this was all over, she'd find a way to forgive him.

He checked the clock. He had about two hours to return to L.A. in time to meet his friend Nick Hunter. Nick was due in town to check into some potential real estate for his new club. It had been a while since they'd seen each other, but they made a habit of keeping in touch. He'd contacted Nick before he left Sudan to let him know where he'd be staying. He was glad that he did. It would do him good to talk with someone he trusted. When Trent had offered to put him up during his stay, Nick was more than happy with the idea of utilizing Trent's hotel room.

He grinned sardonically as he towel-dried, imagining what his caustic buddy would say about his latest liaison.

Noelle sat in front of her dressing room mirror, absently brushing her hair while she recalled her confession to Tempest. She had to admit that she felt better having finally gotten her feelings for Cole off her chest. Tempest had been elated for her and urged her to pursue the budding relationship. She had every intention of taking her advice.

She smiled. Even in the middle of everything that was going on in Tempest's life, Tempest still was happy for her and supportive of her. That was a true friend.

Dressed for dinner, in an emerald green, crepe cocktail dress, Noelle entered the rooftop dining hall, hoping to see Cole. Not spotting him, she wandered over to the bar where two women were engaged in animated conversation. She heard her name mentioned and stopped in her tracks.

". . . the place looks good," one woman said to the other, whom Noelle recognized as Suzanne Donaldson, editor for one of Los Angeles's leading women's magazine. "But," she continued, "we all know that beauty has nothing to do with brains. She'll probably run the place into the ground in a matter of months. She may have the Maxwell name, but she'll always be just another waitress!"

The two women nodded in agreement, with Noelle still going unnoticed.

"I still cannot imagine how Jordan Maxwell, of all people, would have reduced himself to marrying such backwater trash."

"You know what they say: you can take the girl out of the swamp," Suzanne continued, "but you can't take the swamp out of the girl!" They both fell into affected laughter.

"What always amazed me," Noelle said in a silky voice, taking pleasure in the horror registered on their faces when they saw her, "was that backwater trash isn't strictly reserved for New Orleans. Have a lovely evening, *ladies*. And I use the term *ladies* very loosely."

They both tried to sputter explanations and apologies which fell on deaf ears.

Noelle's flesh burned, her ears rang, her pulse raced. She wouldn't scream. She wouldn't go running to her room like a wounded puppy. Not anymore. She'd do like she'd always done, store the humiliating comments in that secret compartment that no one could reach.

She should be used to it by now, she thought, swallowing back the lump of anger that welled in her throat. But how did you get used to the pain?

She put on her best smile and stopped at each table to ask a question here, make a comment there or offer a dinner suggestion. Then she was gone.

She desperately wanted to escape to the sanctity of her room, she thought, taking the outdoor elevator to the lower salon. But that would be the equivalent of running away. She wouldn't give them the satisfaction.

She emerged on the first level and ran into Tempest and Kai who were on their way to dinner.

"Have you eaten already?" Tempest asked, surprised at Noelle's unusually early departure.

"No. I'm not really hungry." She looked down at Kai, purposely avoiding Tempest's searching gaze. "And how was your ride, sweetheart?"

"It was great, auntie. I'm going to ride Blaize again tomorrow."

"Wonderful. I knew there'd be something here that you'd enjoy." She turned toward Tempest. "You two have a good evening. I'm going to check on a few things, then go over to my office. I have some paperwork to clear up." Her smile was empty as she absently patted Kai on the head.

Tempest wasn't convinced, but decided against pursuing the issue until a later date.

"If you're sure."

Noelle nodded. "They're running a Denzel Washington marathon in the theater downstairs, if you want to go."

Tempest looked down at Kai, who grinned broadly. "Maybe we will. I'll talk with you later." Their eyes held for a moment and they parted.

Noelle strolled to the garden in the hopes of finding Cole, to no avail. She thought about going to his suite, but changed her mind. Just thinking about being alone with him again, in close quarters, made her anxious.

Tomorrow was another day. She headed for her office, before turning in for the night.

"How in the hell did you get yourself into this mess?" Nick asked, shaking his dark head in amazement. He lifted his glass and took a sip of cognac, eyeing Trent over the rim. "And Jordan's widow on top of that." He took a long swallow and closed his eyes as the fiery liquid slid down his throat. "Man you have truly gone over the edge."

"Listen man," Trent interrupted, knowing that at any moment, Nick would be on a monologue roll. "I've said the same things and asked the same questions myself." He dropped down on the sofa, stretching his long legs out in front of him. He

leaned back, bracing his head with laced fingers.
"I'm in it and I can't get out of it. And quite
frankly," he gave Nick a pointed look, "I don't
want to."

"She really means that much to you? So
quickly?" Nick asked in a combination of amazement and acceptance. He and Trent had been
friends since the air force. He'd roamed the country with Trent. They traded clothes, secrets and
sometimes women. He'd seen women come into
and go out of Trent's life and never had he seen
Trent care one way or the other. Until now.

"Yeah," Trent nodded solemnly. "She does." He
leaned forward resting his arms on his thighs. "But
once she finds out who I am, and why I'm here,
it'll be all over. I don't want to lose her."

"So what are you gonna do?"

"I've been asking myself that very same question."

Joseph Malone rolled over and snuggled closer
to the warm body next to him. When he first met
her, nearly two years prior, she had made an immediate impact on him.

Her vibrancy, candor, razor-sharp intelligence,
not to mention natural beauty, had been just the
medicine he needed after a very ugly divorce. She
made him feel human again.

It was his inside connections that had placed her
in the front running for her very lucrative position.
He had fallen in love and at times he believed that

he was actually mellowing. The positive effect that she had in his life had slowly begun to radiate outward. He was beginning to feel compassion for other people. The incredulity of that notion still amazed him.

Gina sighed softly as her eyes slowly opened to see Joseph smiling down at her.

"You look like you're thinking pleasant thoughts," she whispered, while her warm brown eyes went sweeping over him.

A broader smile tugged at his mouth, softening the often hard look that was his trademark.

She stroked his chiseled chin as if seeing him for the first time. When she'd truly come to know Joseph, she saw in him what many others couldn't.

His tough-guy exterior was all a facade. He'd grown so accustomed to dealing with irascible clients, cutthroat attorneys, huge fortunes, and corporate treachery, that he'd surreptitiously assumed the mantle in order to survive. Beneath it all was a lonely man who needed someone to look after his needs for a change. And that's what Gina intended to do.

Although there was nearly fifteen years difference in their ages, they were compatible on every level—Cut from the same cloth, as her father would say.

"I was thinking about you," he responded in that basso voice that made many quiver in their footsteps. "I'm tired of hiding us from the world, Gina. I want to marry you, and having a secret wife will be a bit difficult."

Gina came fully awake and shifted in the bed. They'd had this conversation a half dozen times over the past year and her answer had always been the same: "We have to wait." But just how long would he wait for her to tell her boss that she was marrying a man who had always been less than decent to Noelle—tell her father, who would be outraged at a mixed union? What would Noelle think of her and her choice? Would she assume that Gina was there to spy on her and take information back to Joseph? And ultimately to Trent Dixon? Gina admired Noelle for her courage, her strength and her achievements. What Noelle and her father thought of her mattered a great deal. But was it more important than salvaging the best relationship she'd ever had? These were the questions that rattled her, and Gina knew she'd have to make a decision soon.

She sat up and tossed the dark paisley sheet off her nude body, simultaneously swinging her long legs over the side of the bed to stand up.

"We decided to wait, Joe," she said without much conviction, keeping her back to him and giving him an ample view of her shapely bottom.

"*You* decided we should wait," he countered, running his fingers through his tousled salt-and-pepper hair. He got out of bed and crossed the room to stand behind her, his suntanned body in sharp contrast to her ebony tones.

His voice dropped to a lower octave. "I don't want to wait any longer," he said, brushing his lips across her shoulders. He slipped his arms around her narrow waist. "And I want you to make a decision one way or the other."

Gina spun around inches from his face. Her eyes narrowed. "Is that an ultimatum, Joseph?"

His jaw clenched. "Yes."

"You should know me well enough to know that I don't take ultimatums very kindly. Even from you, Joseph."

She tugged away, snatched up her discarded clothing from the floor and stormed off into the bathroom, slamming the door behind her.

Trent returned to Liaisons shortly after midnight. He'd explained his plan to Nick, who after several hours of debate had reluctantly accepted defeat. In days gone by Nick wouldn't have batted an eye at such an outrageous plot. But since he'd settled down with his wife, Parris, and opened his own nightclub in New York, Nick Hunter was a changed man. Trent shook his head in amazement. What love could do to a person . . .

He opened the door to his suite and switched on the recessed lights. Was he doing the right thing? he wondered for the umpteenth time, discarding his jacket on a nearby chair. Or was he only complicating matters further?

He couldn't be sure. But the one thing that he was certain of was that he had fallen in love with Noelle and he'd do whatever it took to share that love with her. If only for the moment.

First thing in the morning he would reserve a plane.

Bright and early the following morning, Noelle sat at her desk reviewing the total revenue against the accounts payables. She couldn't believe her eyes.

Liaisons had been open for less than a month and already they were three million dollars in the black. Her check from Maxwell Enterprises had arrived in the mail, adding to the growing revenue. But she had made plans for that money, just as she had done for the past four years. She tucked it away, and smiled, knowing exactly how she would put it to use.

She scanned the guest list. Reservations were booked through the entire year, with a waiting list for the following. To say that this venture was a success was a complete understatement. Potential patrons were so eager to secure a suite that deposits were still pouring in months in advance.

"I wonder what those two wenches would have to say to that?" she asked out loud, the astonishing success temporarily offsetting the hurting comments.

Satisfied, she closed the large green ledger and pushed away from her desk, thankful, once again, that Jordan had insisted that she take business management and accounting courses.

Jordan. She still felt slight pangs of melancholy when she thought of him. Although their marriage had been far from ideal, they had found a way to be good for each other. Somehow they filled a need in each other's lives. He was the strong older man who had never been present in her life, and she was his greatest accomplishment.

She turned toward her panoramic window which looked out across the entire lower level of the west wing and the indoor, Olympic-sized pool. From the other side, the imported, tinted glass looked like a mirror—it allowed her to look out while maintaining her privacy.

Watching the early morning swimmers brought back vivid images of Cole when he'd emerged from the pool. Instantly her body became infused with a pulsing heat. She wanted him. There was no longer any doubt in her mind. And at the very next opportunity she would show him just how much.

A knock on her office door intruded on her steamy thoughts. She took a settling breath and smoothed the raw silk shirtdress of red and gold. Jordan had had it specially made for her on one of his numerous trips to Hong Kong.

"Come in."

The door came slowly open and Trent stepped in.

At once she was taken aback by this blatantly gorgeous man. His white cotton shirt was open down the front, almost to his navel and the black baggy pants brushed teasingly against the muscular thighs when he moved. He carried a black leather jacket over his arm and an inviting smile was on the bearded face.

She stood completely still behind her desk certain that her knees, which had suddenly turned to Jell-O, wouldn't carry her one step.

Her smile matched his.

"Good morning." He stepped fully into the room. "I'm sorry about not seeing you last night." His mouth tipped in a half smile. "I guess I was more exhausted than I thought."

"No problem. I had plenty to keep me busy."

Their eyes held and neither spoke, as though afraid that any movement, any spoken word might disturb the hypnotic pull that transfixed them at that moment.

Trent slowly walked forward, stopping on the opposite side of Noelle's desk. He leaned across, bracing one hand on the desk, the other cupped Noelle's face. He drew her closer until their lips met.

"It was a problem for me," he whispered against her mouth. "I dreamed of you all night." He pulled slightly back so that he could look into her eyes. "I don't want to just dream about you at night, Noelle. I want you to be there with me. Especially when I wake up in the morning."

Her pulse pounded so loudly in her ears, she couldn't be sure that she'd heard him.

He straightened. His dark eyes were holding her in place. "I want you to come away with me for the weekend. I want us to have the time to get to know each other. Better. I know," he continued, suddenly feeling that he was treading on shaky ground, "that I may be presuming too much. I've made some mistakes where you and I are concerned. But I just feel that we have something special going on here, Noelle. And I think you feel it, too.

"The hell with waiting for the right time. Time doesn't wait for anyone. Come away with me. Let me show you just . . ."

"Yes," she whispered, feeling the flooding of uncontrollable joy whip through her. "Yes," she repeated, "I'll go away with you."

Without another word, Trent rounded the desk and pulled her hungrily into his arms, molding her against him. His mouth swept down over hers, his tongue urgent and demanding.

And she responded. The velvet warmth of his kiss was sending spirals of passion racing through her. She allowed herself to succumb totally to the full domination of his lips, and knew that this was only the beginning.

Nine

Trent eased back. "You won't regret this. I promise you," he said against her mouth. "I can arrange it for us to leave tonight. If you're ready."

Noelle's heart sank. "I can't. Not tonight. Gina is off today. She won't be back until tomorrow." She sighed. "That's the earliest I can get away."

Trent straightened, looking at her with warm eyes. "I can wait." He checked his watch. "I have some errands to run. I'll see you at dinner?"

"Sounds wonderful," she responded in that voice that thrilled him.

He gave her a long breathless kiss that left her longing for more.

"See you later." He made a move to leave.

"Oh, Cole, before you go—have you gotten any information yet?"

He fought to keep from averting his gaze as the lies formed on his tongue.

"As a matter of fact, I'm going to pick up the report this afternoon. I have someone who'll be working on it while we're away."

"Really. Who?"

"You'll meet him soon enough. I've got to go," he added hurriedly.

Before she had a chance to respond, he was out of the door.

Briefly she wondered who this *someone* was, but decided that she'd put her faith in Cole so she would just let him handle it. She felt confident that whoever he had selected to help uncover the truth about the crash, he was someone competent.

In the meantime, she thought, with her excitement building, she had plans to make, and a million details to attend to before she left.

Momentarily, she closed her eyes, and tried to imagine what an entire, uninterrupted weekend with Cole Richards would be like.

Just as Noelle had promised Kai, room service had delivered breakfast to their suite. She ate the full-course breakfast with relish, completely amazing her mother and Mrs. Harding with her enormous appetite.

Tempest shook her head and smiled as she watched her daughter consume everything on her plate.

"Where do you put it all, Kai?" Tempest teased.

"Hmmm, all over" she answered with a mouth full of syrup-drenched pancakes. "I have to keep my strength up," she added. "I have a big day today."

Tempest's hazel eyes widened in curiosity. "Is

that right? And would you mind sharing what this big day is?"

Kai downed her glass of milk and wiped her mouth with a linen napkin. "Well, the man that works in the stable said he would have Blaize ready for me this morning. And I met a girl yesterday on the track. She's here with her parents. We're going to the dance class in the gym. Then we're going to play with her dolls." Kai's eyes lit up. "She has dolls from all over the world! And she said I could play with them. Then we're going to get our hair done at the hair salon downstairs."

"Get your hair done?" Tempest asked incredulously.

Kai's head bobbed up and down. "Yeah, I talked to the lady in the salon yesterday. I told her that my mother designed this w-h-o-l-e place and that Noelle was my godmother." Kai grinned. "She said we could have the full treatment," she concluded triumphantly.

Tempest was momentarily speechless. Was this the same girl who only yesterday was on the border of misery?

"Well I see you have your day all mapped out. I would like to meet this new friend of yours and her parents."

"Okay."

The phone rang in the background and was quickly picked up by Mrs. Harding.

"Tempest," Clara called from the next room, "the phone is for you."

Tempest pushed away from the table and entered the small sitting room. "Who is it?" she asked as Clara stood with the phone in her hand.

"It's your husband." She handed Tempest the phone, looking at her with eyes full of compassion. Gently she patted her shoulder as she left.

Tempest had been the daughter she'd never had. She'd helped Tempest's grandmother, Ella, raise her. When Tempest had returned home from college, pregnant and afraid, Clara had rallied to her side. Everyone, except her, thought that Tempest's marriage to David Lang was the answer to their prayers. That turned out to be disastrous. Not only because David proved himself to be nothing more than a greed-driven politician, but because Tempest had never stopped loving Braxton, the father of her child.

Clara would move hell and earth to see to it that Tempest and Kai were happy and protected. She knew how much Tempest adored her husband and she knew all that they had been through to be together.

She could only pray that whatever the trouble was between them that they would work it out. She had never seen two people who loved each other more. It would just about kill her to see them apart.

Clara returned to the small dining room to check on her often-mischievous charge.

For several moments, Tempest held the phone against her chest searching her mind for the right words. Slowly she put the phone to her ear.

"Hello, Braxton."

"How are you? How's Kai?"

"We're both fine." She paused. "You really disappointed her, Braxton. You know that don't you?" She felt her adrenaline begin to pump. She fought to control the rising anger that was becoming evident in her voice.

"It couldn't be helped. I thought I explained that to you."

"You explained it. But that's not good enough and you know it." She took a calming breath. "You're going to have to decide what it is you want, Braxton."

On the other end of the world, Braxton felt the weight of Tempest's hurt and confusion. If only he could tell her. But the time wasn't right. Not just yet. He could only hope that what he was doing could make up for all of the disappointments that he had caused.

"Listen to me, baby, everything is going to be fine. I'll be back by next week. There are just a few things I have to take care of first and then I'll be on the first plane out of here."

Tempest was not satisfied and couldn't resist twisting the knife of guilt just a bit deeper. "Then when's the next plane? Will it be on Kai's birthday this time or the day before our anniversary? Christmas? New Year's? When?"

"This isn't getting us anywhere, Tempest," he tossed back. His voice rose. "I didn't call to get into an overseas argument with you." Braxton struggled to control his own erupting temper, knowing that the reason why they were arguing at all was because of him. He tried to believe that the way he was handling things would be best for everyone. But at what cost?

"Listen, T, I'm sorry. I know you're upset. I know Kai was disappointed. I didn't set out to hurt you or her."

Tempest struggled with her swirling emotions. Listening to him, in that voice that she loved, she could almost believe anything he said. Times like this reminded her of how they used to be. How they could be if he'd just let them.

"Can I speak to Kai?" he asked, the hesitation apparent even over the distance.

She cleared the knot in her throat. "I'll get her."

"Wait. Before you go, I just want to say that we do have some things to talk about. Our future." She felt her stomach twist. "It's just that now isn't the time. I promise, I'll be there as soon as I can. We'll straighten everything out then. And in the meantime, just remember that no matter what—I love you."

Without responding, she placed the receiver on the table and went to find Kai. *No matter what.*

Trent arrived at his suite in L.A. to find Nick comfortably playing his saxophone.

"Hey man," Nick greeted, looking up as Trent breezed through the door. "I didn't expect you until later."

Trent pulled off his leather jacket as he crossed the room and tossed it in a vacant chair. "Yeah, I know, but I talked to Noelle this morning."

"And?"

"And she agreed to go away with me for the weekend." He flopped down on the couch.

"Great! Then why do you look so gloomy?" Nick gently placed the sax on the floor.

Trent blew out a frustrated breath, and shook his head. "I know I should be thrilled. It's what I wanted since the first time I met her. But . . ."

"But what?"

"It's all gotten so complicated. Maybe if I'd told her the truth in the beginning, we still could have worked things out." But even as he said the words, he knew that was an impossibility.

"But you didn't."

"I know that!" He jumped up from his seat and jammed his hands in his pockets, pacing. "And I'm going to complicate things further by sleeping with her. Then what?"

"Then you'll just have to deal with it." Nick leaned back and looked at Trent hard. "Or you could tell her the truth, now, before this scheme of yours really blows up in your face and everybody else's."

Trent ceased his pacing and turned on Nick. "And what about the company? What about the thousands of people who will be out of jobs? What about my promise to Jordan? Not to mention the loans from the bank that are gonna come barreling down any minute." He tossed his hands up in the air and looked toward the ceiling as if searching for the answers. His voice lowered. "She hates Trent Dixon, Nick. She blames him for causing Jordan's death. Even though the reports say something different. Do you honestly think that she's going to shower me with love and affection when she finds out the truth? When she finds out that she's slept with the man she thinks killed her husband? There's not enough explaining in the world to pull that one off."

He turned away, disgusted with himself and what he'd done.

"You can fix all of that by telling her now. You know it and I know it. Let the decision be hers."

Trent was audibly silent.

"You can't. Can you?"

Trent's jaw clenched. "No. I can't. I want her too much. If I can only have this one time with her, then so be it. Because I know, as sure as hell, that once she finds out she'll never come near me again. All I have, Nick," he continued, hoping that his friend would understand, "is now."

Noelle completed a series of phone calls to tie up some loose ends with the villa. Then she stopped by Tempest's suite and shared her good news, and was enthusiastically ordered to have a great time. Then she went to check on Carol, the young trainee who filled in for Gina.

Upon arriving at the reception lounge, she was surprised to find Gina in her usual spot behind the long counter.

"Gina. What on earth are you doing here? You're supposed to be off today."

Gina tried to smile. "I know. I had a change in plans and decided to come to work instead."

"A change in getting some rest?" Noelle asked, perplexed, quickly reflecting on the conversation of the previous day.

"I guess I didn't need as much rest as I thought," she responded, trying to keep the edge out of her voice.

Noelle hid her surprise at Gina's obviously annoyed reply. "Well, you know what you need," she said, trying to sound pleasant and take the tension out of the air. "How's that headache?"

"Much better thanks." Gina kept her eyes focused on the ledger. "Is there something I can do for you?"

"Actually, I just came up to check on Carol. I thought I would have to wait until tomorrow to go out of town, but since you're here, I can leave sooner than I anticipated. That is, of course, if you feel up to managing things yourself. You will have to spend the weekend here." Foresight had prompted Noelle to include several small suites for staff members who might have to stay over for an unexpected reason. In a state plagued by earthquakes, floods, fires and mudslides, one just never knew.

She angled her head to the side and peered at Gina quizzically.

Gina finally raised her eyes up from the book in front of her. "I don't see a problem." She forced a smile. "If there's anything special I should be alerted to, just let me know. I'm sure everything will be fine."

"Wonderful. You have all the schedules and the reservations are in place. So . . ." she grinned, raising then lowering her shoulders, "I guess Liaisons will function fine without me for a few days."

"Don't worry about a thing, Mrs. Maxwell. Your villa is in good hands."

Noelle stretched her hand across the counter that divided them, and she placed her hand over Gina's. "I know you'll do a wonderful job, Gina. I have all the trust in the world in you and your capabilities." She smiled again. "I'll stop by before I go."

"I'll be here."

Noelle turned to leave, confident that with Gina at the helm she had nothing to concern herself with. Nothing at all.

Ten

A misty rain had begun to fall as Trent pulled the Lexus into the underground garage of Liaisons. He hurried across the manicured grounds. He swore under his breath. The last thing he now needed was to catch a cold. His decision to have a secluded suite precluded him from using the elevator that only went to the main wings. This was one time he really could have used that convenience.

By the time he reached the entrance, the rain was falling in buckets. Maybe it was best that he and Noelle weren't able to get away tonight.

Ever since the crash, he had steered away from flying in anything but clear weather. Flashes of that last flight with Jordan still plagued him. Many nights, he'd wake up in cold sweats, screaming and trembling like a frightened child, his body racked with pain from the many breaks that his body had suffered when they plunged into the sea. Especially nights like this.

He pushed through the glass doors and entered the main lobby, just as a flash of lightning illuminated the heavens. Shaking off the dripping water and ominous thoughts, he crossed the marble floors and headed for the elevator, anxious to get out of his drenched clothing.

He hadn't been in his room for more than a few minutes, having only taken off his shirt when there was a hesitant knock at his door.

"Who is it?" He ripped out the words impatiently, while running a towel across his wet hair. A blast of thunder muffled the response.

He snatched the door open and his whole demeanor quickly changed.

"Monsieur Richards, I seem to always catch you at a bad time," she grinned mischievously.

He reached across the threshold and grabbed her arms, pulling her into his. "There is no bad time when it comes to you," he whispered against her mouth. His tongue traced the soft fullness of her lips, sending tremors shimmying through her body.

Reluctantly he eased away without completely letting her go. His eyes swept hungrily over her. "To what do I owe this very pleasant surprise?"

"I have news."

"Come into my parlor," he teased, bowing low as she passed him.

". . . so we can leave tonight," she concluded, quite pleased with the way things had turned out and anxious to leave before she had any pangs of doubt.

Trent was decidedly quiet.

"Is something wrong? I thought you would be happy."

"No. It's not that, of course I'm happy. It's just

that . . ." he could never tell her the real reason, the root of his fears.

"Just what? You've changed your mind, is that it?" She was beginning to feel utterly foolish for having rushed over to him ready to throw herself in his arms like some, some . . .

"Tonight would be fine, Noelle. I'll just have to make a few calls to confirm the changes. That's all." He kissed her lightly. "What time will you be ready?"

"How's six?" she answered, relieved.

"No problem."

"There is one thing, though, Cole."

"What's that?"

"I'd rather meet you somewhere." she looked at the floor. "I mean, I don't . . ."

He cupped her chin, forcing her to look at him. "Believe me, you don't have to explain. I understand perfectly. Meet me at Cochran Airways, it's about . . ."

"I know . . . exactly . . . where it is." She swallowed. "Jordan used to fly from there quite often when he flew in his . . . private plane."

How could he have been so stupid? Of course Jordan used that private airstrip. Hadn't he made enough reservations on Jordan's behalf?

His smile was both apologetic and teasing at the same time. "I hope you won't hold it against me," the words rekindling for her the night that they'd first met.

"There's no way you could have known," she said softly. She breathed deeply. "And just where are you taking me, Cole Richards, that we need a plane?"

"Now if I told you that, you'd know as much as I did. And there'd be no point in all this being a surprise. So get going and I'll meet you at six."

Noelle pretended to pout as she was escorted to the door.

Trent kissed her tenderly. "Until later."

"Bye," she whispered.

He closed the door behind her and shut his eyes. Please don't let the nightmares come. Not tonight. Please, he silently prayed.

Noelle tossed her overnight bag in the trunk of her Mercedes, and hurried around to the driver's seat. Normally, it would take about forty-five minutes to arrive at the airstrip, but in this weather she had allowed herself an extra half hour. The last thing she wanted was to get stuck.

The windshield wipers worked wildly to keep the driving rain off of the windows. It was a losing battle. She slowed the car to fifteen miles per hour as visibility was almost impossible.

How in the world would they be able to fly anywhere in this weather? she worried. It was a night very much like this one that . . .

This was different, she assured herself. She wasn't flying on the open seas. She wasn't traveling in a faulty aircraft. She wasn't flying with someone who didn't check every detail. Cole Richards wasn't Trent Dixon. Cole was someone who could be trusted.

The lights from the airstrip loomed ahead. Another ten minutes and she'd be there. Her heart picked up its pace as she contemplated the trip.

This was a big step she was taking. This was the first man she'd been with since Jordan's death. The first man period. The thought began to frighten her.

What if she couldn't measure up to Cole's expectations? What if he were turned off by the fact that she was . . . No, he wouldn't do that. He would be gentle. He would be loving. He would fulfill her as she'd been longing to be fulfilled. He would teach her and she would be a willing student.

Still, she was afraid. Afraid of what Cole's discovery would do to his image of Jordan. The persona that Jordan presented to the world was infinitely important to him. He reveled in his power and masculinity. But before the next few days were over, that image would come crumbling down. Was she ready to do that to him? Even after all of this time?

She pulled onto the dirt road that led to the hanger. She saw the Lexus parked up ahead. For several paralyzing moments she sat in her car, unable to get out.

It isn't too late to turn around, an inner voice warned. She took a deep breath and opened the door, retrieved her bag from the trunk and entered the hanger.

Her legs felt weak as she walked the few yards

to where Trent was animatedly engaged in conversation with the owner's son. Trent turned when he heard footsteps approach. The panicked look on Noelle's face stopped him in midsentence.

"Noelle, what's wrong? Is everything alright at Liaisons?" He crossed the floor in quick strides to where she stood.

"Y-yes," she muttered. "It was just a bumpy ride. The weather is terrible. Are we going to be able to fly?"

Trent put his arm around her waist. "Mr. Cochran assures me that our flight path is relatively clear. The storm is moving away. We'll just have a tail wind to contend with."

"You don't have a thing to worry about," Bill Cochran assured. If you'll both follow me, I'll take you to the plane." As the three crossed the large open space, Bill Cochran wondered why this man had insisted that he not mention his real name. He'd dealt with Trent over the phone on numerous occasions and always had Jordan's plane in tip-top shape. Trent Dixon's credentials as a pilot were above reproach. Now Trent was with Maxwell's widow, pretending to be someone else. Why? Then again it was none of his business, the huge fee that he'd been paid was enough to dismiss any questions.

"Please excuse my manners, Bill," Noelle apologized as they neared the plane. "How is your father?"

"Arthritis has him pretty bad. Days like this keep him indoors. But other than that, he's as grumpy as ever," he chuckled.

Noelle easily recalled the burly older man whose every word sounded like an order. It must be a result of his years in the army she'd always concluded.

Bill Cochran briefly ran a perfunctory check of the instruments, made mention of where everything was located, and handed Trent the flight plan.

He patted Trent on the back as Trent took his seat in the cockpit.

"Y'all have a safe flight, now," Bill Cochran ordered. He tipped his hat toward Noelle. "You take care Mrs. Maxwell. It was good seeing you again."

"Thank you, Bill. You, too. And please give my regards to your father." Noelle eased down into the passenger seat, directly behind Trent. She strapped herself in, as Bill exited the plane.

"All set?" Trent said over his shoulder.

"As ready as I'll ever be."

The engine rumbled beneath them and within minutes they were in the air.

Gina tried to be patient as she explained yet again to Suzanne Donaldson that she could not issue refunds in the form of cash.

"I'll be more than happy to write you a check. But that's the best I can offer on such short notice."

"Well if that's all you can do, I suppose I have no choice," she scoffed. "I'll stop down to pick it up on my way out. Do have it ready." She turned away in a huff and sauntered off toward the elevators.

"I'm more than happy to be rid of you," Gina said under her breath. Suzanne Donaldson was a royal pain. She carried herself around as if the whole world owed her something. Good riddance. She could easily have given her a refund from the vault, she smiled wickedly, but why make life easy for her? She didn't like her from the moment she set foot in the door. She'd overheard several of the nasty comments she'd made about Noelle to the other guests and that just added spice to her distaste.

The phone rang. "Liaisons. Gina Nkiru speaking. May I help you?"

"Yes, Ms. Nkiru," answered the masculine voice. "I certainly hope you can help me. This is Senator Thomas speaking."

Why was that name familiar?

"Yes, Senator Thomas. How may I help you?"

"I'll be in town for a few days, and I was hoping that there was a possibility that you may have a vacancy."

Now she remembered. He was the reference for Cole Richards.

"As a matter of fact, Senator, we do have a vacancy. We had an early checkout."

"Wonderful."

"When would you be arriving?"

"I'll be arriving by mid-week. I'll be staying for three days."

"I'll be sure to have your suite ready."

"By the way, is Mrs. Maxwell around?"

"No. I'm sorry she's out of town for the weekend. She'll be back on Sunday."

"Very good. I'm looking forward to seeing her again."

"I'm sure she'll be happy to see you, too. And Mr. Richards also."

"Excuse me?"

"Cole Richards, the gentleman that you referred."

Senator Thomas paused. "You must be mistaken. I don't know anyone by that name. And I certainly didn't recommend anyone."

A hot flush swept through her. "I probably am mistaken," she said, hoping that the panic wasn't evident in her voice. "There've been so many reservations lately, I must have gotten the name confused."

"Well, in any case, if you should hear from Mrs. Maxwell, do tell her about my arrival."

"I will."

Gina replaced the receiver with a shaky hand. Oh, God. Not only had she done the unspeakable by mentioning another guest by name, that guest's references were false. And if his references were false what else about him didn't ring true?

She hurried into her office and retrieved Cole's file. There it was, a glowing reference letter from Senator Thomas. Her heart thudded. It was her responsibility to verify all references. But Cole Richards just seemed so above board, and he'd left such a large deposit, she just didn't think . . .

She shoved the folder back in the file. She couldn't tell Noelle. She'd lose her job for sure.

What had she done? And who was Cole Richards?

Eleven

By the time Trent and Noelle landed in the Napa Valley, the rain had all but stopped, replaced by a growing chill in the air. A car was waiting to pick them up and twenty minutes later, they pulled up to a quaint little bed and breakfast inn, named Meagan's Place.

"I hope you like it," Trent said nervously, as he guided Noelle across the cobblestone path. He chuckled. "It doesn't compare to Liaisons, but I thought you might enjoy a slower pace for a few days."

Before they reached the door, Noelle tugged on Trent's hand, causing him to turn around.

Worry was reflected in his eyes.

"I'm sure I'll love it," she said softly, allaying his fears with a heavenly smile. "And I'll love it even more because you took the time to think about me."

"That I did," he responded. "This whole weekend is for you, Noelle. I want everything to be perfect for you."

"It already is."

Gently, he took her in his arms and kissed her tenderly, then eased away. "Come on," he said in a low, intimate voice, "I want to show you our room."

* * *

Noelle welcomed the fire that was already roaring in the fireplace, taking out the chill that had seeped through her bones.

Her eyes ran over their inviting quarters. The partially drawn drapes gave them a splendid view of the mountains with the sun hanging low over the peaks. The entire room was done in warm prints, the wallpaper matching the throw pillows and bedding.

But the focal point of the room was the enormous four-poster, mahogany bed that sat at an inviting angle near the bay window. Draperies in the same pattern, hung over the posters. Overstuffed pillows and thick down quilts begged the observer to sink onto them. Small, rectangular tables of the same mahogany were adorned with bowls of fresh flowers, giving the entire room an outdoor scent.

Everything about the room said, Welcome.

She spun around, her face beaming when she looked at Trent. "It's beautiful. I could stay here forever!"

He walked toward her, pulling her against him. "That's the whole idea," he growled into her neck. "But first," he moved away and took her hand, "I say we get something to eat before we barricade ourselves in here." His smile was teasing.

"I thought you'd never ask."

There were only two other couples present in the homey dining room. The menu was simple but appetizing.

Noelle ordered clam chowder for starters, a tossed salad, and fried catfish strips with yellow rice.

"This reminds me of New Orleans," she said biting into a tempting morsel of fish. "I haven't had catfish this good since my aunt made it."

Trent grinned. "I'm glad you like it." He cut into his two-inch porterhouse steak. "When was the last time you saw your aunt?"

Noelle leaned slightly back in her chair. "It's been quite some time," she admitted. "She hasn't been well over the years. She wasn't able to come to Jordan's funeral. We, Jordan and I, usually visited her once a year." She smiled at the memory. "She never changed over the years. Right up until the last time I saw her she was still giving orders and demanding sweat and blood from her staff."

"Seems like a very interesting lady. Maybe that's where you get your tenacity from."

Noelle's eyebrows arched in an unspoken question.

"You're a determined woman, Noelle," he said, by way of explanation. "There's no doubt about that. I believe that if you put your mind to it, you could do anything you set out to do." *Even run Maxwell Enterprises.*

She sighed heavily. "Perhaps. I really don't see myself as the extraordinary businesswoman that some have made me out to be. I'm just doing what I like. I've always enjoyed seeing people happy and well fed," she added with a grin. "I just feel fortunate to have the financial ability to do what I want. Not many people have that opportunity."

"You're a very lucky woman in many regards, Noelle."

"I feel especially lucky now," she said, looking into his eyes. "More so than in a very long time."

"I hope I'm the reason."

"Maybe," she teased. She focused on her plate. "This place is really lovely. You were right, I did need a change."

"I thought we could take a flight out to the wineries tomorrow."

Noelle nodded in agreement. "It's funny, but as long as I've lived in California, I've never been to a winery. It was something I always intended to do, but never got around to it."

"Then it'll be a new experience for both of us. Something I can go back and tell the folks at home about."

Noelle took a sip of spring water. "What do you plan to do when you . . . leave California?" she blurted out.

The question had been gnawing at her ever since she'd accepted his offer to go away for the weekend. *This was the nineties,* she tried to remind herself, but at heart, she was still old-fashioned. She wanted to at least pretend that there was some future for them on the horizon. Even if it was only for a little while.

The suddenness of the question caught Trent off guard. What could he possibly tell her that remotely resembled the truth?

"I hadn't really thought about it," he answered smoothly. Then shrugged, "I don't have any new contracts at the moment. So maybe I'll just hang out here for a while." His look held her. "How would you feel about that?"

"I think I'd like that very much," she answered without hesitation.

He reached across the table and took her hand in his.

"I'm not going to fill your head with promises, Noelle. I'm not going to tell you that there's a rosy future for us, although I'd like it to be. But the reality is, my job takes me all over the world. I haven't been in one spot for more than a couple of months at a time in years. Maybe one day . . ." He looked deep into her eyes. "With the right ingredients, I could plant some roots."

Noelle was the first to look away. "I understand. I don't want you to think that I was trying to . . ."

"Tie me down?"

She nodded.

"I couldn't possibly think that. Not about you. Actually," his tone turned teasing, "getting tied down doesn't sound like such a bad idea." His lips curled up into a grin.

It took several minutes for the comment to sink in. When it did, Noelle felt her face flush with heat. She couldn't meet his taunting eyes, but started to laugh in spite of herself.

"Monsieur Richards," she gasped, affecting offense, "I'm not that kind of girl."

His voice settled down to a low throb. "Then I can't wait to see what kind of *woman* you are."

She glanced away, hoping that he didn't see the inexperience written all over her face.

"In the meantime," he said quickly, wanting to alleviate her obvious discomfort, "why don't we take a stroll around the grounds?" He pushed away from the table and came around to help her out of her seat.

The sun was slowly setting over the hilltops. For miles the lush green valleys resembled giant waves, permanently etched onto canvas.

A cool, after-shower breeze blew caressingly around them. Noelle snuggled closer to Trent as they walked, welcoming his warmth.

"I didn't know what I'd been missing all of these years," she said softly. "It takes your breath away."

He stopped and turned her to face him. "It's almost as beautiful as you Noelle." When he stood there looking down at her, he wished that it could always be this way with them. Open. Carefree. Full of wonder and expectation. But he knew that this brief moment in time was only temporary. He had no right to hope for anything more. But whatever he could take from their time together he knew it would have to last him a lifetime. A lifetime without Noelle.

He leaned down and kissed her with such tenderness that her heart felt like it would split in two. At that moment she felt that she would do anything to be with this man. To make a life with him. To forge a future with him. Did she dare to hope? To dream? If only for the moment.

In silent understanding they turned back toward the inn.

The only light in the room emanated from the fireplace, sending light and shadow dancing across the walls. She was grateful for the semidarkness, hoping that it would camouflage the anxiety that hung in her eyes. Her fingers trembled as she made a task out of unpacking her bag, for some inexplicable reason wanting to delay the inevitable.

She did want this, didn't she? she questioned, gingerly laying her chiffon gown across the bed, that had been turned down in their absence. She'd come this far. There was no turning back. Her heart thundered.

Trent stepped up behind her, kissing the back of her neck and she nearly leaped out of her skin.

"I didn't mean to startle you," he apologized, reaching around and handing her a glass of champagne. "Here, take a sip."

Obediently, she did as she was instructed. She didn't taste a thing.

Trent pinched the glass from her fingers and placed it on the bedside table. He turned her around to face him.

"I won't do anything you don't want me to do, Noelle. I realize this is a big step for you. You're not the kind of woman who would take . . . something like this lightly. Believe this, if you believe nothing else. This time with you is special to me. More than I could ever explain. I've wanted you from the moment I saw you, maybe even before. In my dreams." He gently stroked her face and she felt as if all of the air had been absorbed from the room.

His hands trailed down her arms and he took her hands in his, leading her out of the bedroom.

Trent pushed open the connecting door which led to a spacious bath. Without a word, he turned on the shower and within moments the room was filled with steam.

"I won't do anything," he repeated, untying the knot on her wraparound dress, "that you don't want me to." He kissed her neck, separating the folds of the dress as he did.

Noelle bit her lip to stifle a cry, when his mouth slid down to caress the exposed skin of her breasts.

The fine mist from the steam enveloped them, dampening her skin. The air seemed to sizzle as her dress slid off her to fall like a whisper around her feet. His hands lovingly explored the delicious curves of her body. His eyes, heavy with desire seared across her flesh. She trembled as the stroking of his fingers sent jolts rushing through her.

"You're beautiful," he groaned, slipping one strap off her shoulder and then the other. He cupped her full breasts in his hand, grazing her erect nipples with tantalizing flicks of his tongue.

Noelle felt lightheaded as wave upon wave of unsatisfied hunger engulfed her. She clasped his head with her hand as he took one succulent tip into his mouth and then the other.

From somewhere far off she heard ragged moans, almost a plea, and realized that it had come from deep within her. She tried to speak to tell him how wonderful he made her feel but she couldn't find her voice, as his hands trailed downward, pushing her black lace panties over her hips.

Hesitantly, he took a step back. His eyes refused to believe the magnificence of the person who stood in front of him. She was a pure work of art, a sculptor's dream. Her tall, voluptuous frame belied her outward slenderness. Full, erect breasts cried out to be touched. Her delicately narrow waist, flared out to rounded hips. Hips made for loving, was his one rational thought, as his eyes trailed downward to the long, shapely legs that he couldn't wait to be imprisoned by.

Standing before him, Noelle felt truly beautiful for the first time in her life. The look of pure adoration, that emanated from his eyes, not simply wanton lust, warmed her to her soul.

Tentatively she reached out a shaky hand and slowly unbuttoned his shirt. With more calm than she thought she was capable of managing, she pushed his shirt over his broad shoulders.

She wanted to discover him, to understand and commit to memory every inch of that glorious body. Boldly, she first unbuckled his pants then loosened the zipper.

Instinctively, his hand grabbed hers pressing it solidly against his throbbing member. She shud-

dered as the thudding pulse of his desire welled
within her grasp.

His intoxicating groan urged her on as she
stroked him, learning the curves, the sleekness, the
power of him.

He struggled for control, but knew that he could
no longer withstand the seduction of her caress.

His mouth covered hers hungrily, drinking in
the sweetness, exploring and discovering new
depths, new heights. He pulled her to him, pressing her soft flesh against the hard lines of his.

Unable to be denied a moment longer, he
guided her into the shower.

The surging water cascaded over their bodies,
drenching them, cooling them, heating them,
binding them.

He drew her nearer, sliding the jasmine-scented
soap over her form. The sensuous feel ignited unimaginable longing.

Her eyes slid shut as the foamy lather liquified
and dripped languidly down the crevices of her
body. She braced herself against the tile wall as
Trent neared.

He pressed himself against her. The frothy suds
were joining them erotically together.

Noelle stroked the hard contours of his broad
back, sending shivers of incendiary delight down
his spine.

"I want you, Noelle," he moaned against her
neck. His lips ran a path across her shoulders. "I
want to make love to you. Now."

Twelve

Lovingly and with tender care he placed her on the bed. The flames from the fireplace kept dancing off of her still damp body, giving her an almost surreal aura.

For several moments he stood above her, hesitant to touch her. Afraid that just the slightest contact would send him over the edge.

And then, as if in a dream, she reached out for him, beckoning him with her eyes. She whispered his name.

"Cole."

Slowly, hypnotically he lowered himself onto her waiting body. Only a breath separated them.

He touched her cheek then covered it with a kiss. His mouth closed over hers swallowing her quiet moan.

Expertly, his hard thighs separated her pliant ones. His wide hands caressed her thighs, her hips, raising them to meet him.

His mouth drifted down to take a taut nipple fully into his mouth. She cried out his name as he pushed against her and met resistance. Startled, he searched her face with his eyes. The unasked question hanging in the air between them.

She clung to him, arching her body to join with his. Urging him on. No longer caring what he discovered, only knowing that at this moment she must have him within her. His mouth came down on hers, his tongue dancing against the walls, stifling her cries. Her eyes squeezed shut as he pushed past the thin barrier that separated them.

The briefest moment of piercing pain was immediately replaced with an overwhelming sensation of sublime joy.

Slowly, tenderly he moved within her, bracing her hips to meet his rhythm, sending sensation after sensation of pleasure whipping through her.

She never imagined it could be like this. All of her unfulfilled days, and countless lonely nights had not prepared her for this ecstasy.

She wanted to please him and instinctively her innate sexual nature took over. She stroked him, called out his name, slowed the tempo, moved her hips solidly against his thrusts.

Trent groaned out loud, clawing at the sheets as her undulations steered him toward the brink of total submission.

Faster they traveled, discovering in each other a world that neither knew existed. Until now. In each other's arms, bound by a calling older than time.

Tears of exquisite joy ran down her cheeks as the pulsing, throbbing beat of release wound its way through her body.

She wanted to scream, to laugh, to cry. She

wanted this moment to last forever, but intuitively she knew that the climactic end was rapidly approaching.

Trent's heart raced. Every fiber of his being threatened to explode. This couldn't be real, he thought hazily, as Noelle's long legs tightened around his waist.

He sunk deeper within her, pulling her hips savagely against his final shuddering thrusts.

Through the cloud of dizzying fulfillment, he heard her cry out his name over and again as her spasmodic response drained the last of the fiery liquid.

Quietly they lay nestled in each other's arms. Trent cradled Noelle protectively against him, listening to her heart beat rhythmically against his chest. What had taken place between them still had him awestruck. How could it be possible that she was . . . ? His mind was still too cloudy to sift through the possibilities. He'd find a way to get her to talk about it. But all he wanted to do right now was hold her.

It was more than she could ever have hoped to expect. Cole was all that she'd imagined him to be and so much more, she thought. He'd awakened in her that strong passion that was always just beneath the surface. She felt complete, different somehow—as if some magical force had altered her life. That magic was Cole. She had no regrets.

Trent turned fully on his side. "Noelle," he said

gently, "do you want to tell me what went on with you and Jordan?"

She tried to turn her face away, but he wouldn't allow it.

"Does it change anything?"

"Like what, Noelle?"

"Like what you think about Jordan?"

"Jordan? Is that what's been bothering you all along? You were worried that if we made love I'd find out that you were still a virgin?"

She barely nodded. "I was worried about how your opinion of Jordan would change."

"Whatever went on between the two of you could never change the kind of man Jordan was, Noelle."

"It's just that Jordan always prided himself on his masculinity. Maybe even more so because of his . . . problem. I'm sure that's the reason why he was so driven." She bit her lip. "I was in a four-year marriage that was never consummated. It's almost too bizarre to be real. But it is. I lived it."

"Did you . . . know before you married him?"

She shook her head. "I had no idea. I always believed that he was being an old-fashioned gentleman and wanted to wait." She expelled a shuddering breath. "On our wedding night," she began hesitantly, "he made me . . . do things, then he taunted me, insulted me, told me that I was the reason that he couldn't make love to me."

She held back a sob. "I tried. Night after night. I did everything he told me, but nothing ever happened. I felt so inadequate as a woman, as a wife.

"Then one night, after another of our terrible

arguments about my incompetence, he finally just broke down. He told me how much he loved me, how he believed that he had finally found the one woman that could change him. But he said he realized that nothing could change the fact that he was no longer a "real man." And probably never would be again.

"He told me if I wanted to leave him he would understand. He even offered to let me have a lover on the side." She looked up into Trent's eyes. "But I couldn't do that. I wouldn't do that. My wedding vows still meant something to me. In sickness and in health," she said deliberately. "Jordan had been everything to me, mentor, friend, protector, provider. He opened up the world to me. I would never leave him because I'd come to realize that Jordan needed me, although he'd never openly admit such vulnerability. And I think he knew that I'd never leave. He appreciated me, and I guess he loved me in his own way. I guess Jordan hoped I would be the one to make a man out of him. And when I couldn't . . ." Her voice drifted away.

Trent was stunned by this intimate confession. He knew that it took a lot for her to reveal the most private details of her life with Jordan. But now, the pieces of the puzzle were beginning to slowly come together. He'd never understood why Jordan had requested such an enormous favor from him. It was becoming clearer. Now it all made sense, Trent realized. That would explain why he was never seen running around with various women and why he married an innocent like

Noelle. Jordan's illness had rendered him impotent. A man like Jordan wouldn't risk that crushing secret getting out because of some casual fling. He had to get married to maintain his image.

"But what about you Noelle? What were you to have? Jordan spent the majority of the time out of the country."

"I kept myself busy with my studies, traveling, trying unsuccessfully, to fit into Jordan's world. But he more than compensated for his shortcomings in our love life." She laughed mirthlessly. "Jordan showered me with gifts, cars, jewelry. All of my clothes are handmade, my shoes are imported."

"But what about you, Noelle?" he asked again.

It was several moments before she spoke. "He made me feel special, for the first time in my life," she said plaintively. "Jordan took me from a life of poverty and little hope, and gave me salvation. I owed Jordan. I admired him, looked up to him, depended on him. I know that he was cruel at times with his words, but his anger was not at me." She looked away thoughtfully. "He was angry at himself," for not really being the man that he presented to the world." She paused, her next words seeping out through the crevices of her loss. "In one careless moment all that I knew was taken away from me. And I have no one to blame except Trent Dixon. I hate him for what he's done, to me and to Jordan."

She swallowed. "But to answer your question, my life, at least the one I'd come to know, was empty as far as real love was concerned. Even with all of the trinkets to fill it up." Her voice softened and she looked at him with the discovery of love in her eyes. "Until I met you."

The blade of guilt twisted deeper into his gut. Noelle had worshipped Jordan. There was no question about that. She worshipped him as a child worships a parent, he realized with sudden clarity. He was the father that she had missed. Just as Jordan had become for him. He could never make that up to her. But damn it, it wasn't his fault. Or was it? He could have said no. He should have just refused. But he knew how important it was to Jordan. After all that Jordan had meant to him, he couldn't deny him that final wish. If Jordan couldn't get him to do it, eventually he would have found someone else. Perhaps someone not as competent as himself and that could have proven to be even more disastrous. More importantly, Jordan was determined that Noelle be spared . . .

"Cole?" The gentle, cadence of her voice pulled him back. "I didn't mean to put you on the spot. I just want you to understand. Until now, I've never discussed the intimate details of my marriage with anyone before. It's always been too . . ."

He put a finger to her lips and focused on her, seeing her from yet another perspective. "Yes, I do understand, Noelle. I understand more than I ever thought I could. I'm just glad that you thought enough of me to confide in me. You're a remarkable woman and you deserve nothing but happiness."

He leaned down and kissed her tenderly, then

slowly, patiently, he rekindled the flames that danced just below the surface, with the insistent circular motions of his hands.

This time, Noelle led the way, guiding him to all of the spots that she'd discovered aroused her. She felt a sense of wild abandon in his arms. Her own driving need shocked her. She wanted to learn everything, know everything at once. And she wanted Cole to teach her.

She was more than a dream come true, Trent gasped, as Noelle's velvet tongue trailed steadily down his chest. He visibly trembled when she took him in her hand, hesitating but a moment. Then all he felt was a searing white heat shooting through his body as she enveloped him.

Thirteen

A light tapping on the window permeated Trent's dreams. It was raining. He was in the air, trying to fly above the storm. His palms were wet from perspiration.

"This is crazy, Jordan," he yelled over the roar of the Cessna's engine. "We should turn back. You don't have to do this. There has to be another way."

"We made a deal, Trent. There is no other way," Jordan answered back as another sharp pain ripped through his insides. He doubled over. "You . . . can't back out now."

Trent's heart raced. What was he doing? The slightest error and they would both be dead.

A bolt of lightning blazed through the heavens.

"Did you make the adjustments?" Jordan asked, sweat beading on his forehead.

"Yes," Trent answered succinctly.

"I want you to make sure that every detail of my will is carried out to the letter." He spoke through clenched teeth. "She can do it. I know she can. And she deserves the chance. She thinks she just wants to run some hotel, but I know better.

She's better than that, because I made her what she is. Noelle has been groomed all of these years for just this moment. She just hasn't realized it yet. She'll see. You'll make her see, what power, real power, can do. She'll never have to feel inferior to anyone again."

The plane suddenly lurched to one side, being tossed around by the raging winds like sheets on a line. Jordan was seized with another attack of excruciating pain. An animal-like cry was torn from his throat.

Trent cringed at the sound. Jordan had gone on like this for months, Trent thought, as he fought to keep the plane in the air. He'd refused to see a doctor and wouldn't return home. "I can't let her see me like this," he'd said on more than one occasion. "And you'd better not breathe a word to her!"

They were several miles off shore, having flown out of Thailand on their way to Hong Kong. He and Jordan had been finalizing the reorganization operations with Mr. Takaka who was to take over the headquarters in Hong Kong. It was obvious to Trent and to Takaka that Maxwell Enterprises needed to rethink how it did business and find alternatives to expand. But Jordan had been adamant about not changing a thing about his corporation. He was positive that after the *minor* revolt in Sudan was settled, the exporting of goods would be resumed.

For all of Jordan's business sense he refused to see that his enterprise was in serious trouble. The fact that he had negotiated for close to fifty million dollars to refinance his shipping and airlines only compounded the problem. With trade being cut off at the knees because of the rebel forces, Maxwell Enterprises was losing thousands of dollars per day. They needed to diversify.

"How far are we from the shore?" Jordan asked, breaking into Trent's troubling thoughts.

"About fifteen miles."

"It's time."

Trent briefly looked over his shoulder and saw the look of absolute peace and resolution on Jordan's face.

They'd gone over the plan a hundred times over the past month. *It must be made to look like an accident,* Jordan had insisted. He didn't want Trent implicated in anyway. *If* Trent got out of the plane alive.

Trent adjusted the dials, set the controls on automatic. He reached for the headphone and called in the distress signal. When Hong Kong responded to the desperate call for help, he ignored it. Just as he had been instructed. He slipped on his life jacket and unfastened his seat belt.

His throat constricted when he rose from his seat. His eyes clouded with burning tears of regret, fear, and the imminent loss of someone who meant so much to him.

"No good-byes," Jordan said.

Trent dropped down on his knees and embraced him.

"Just go," Jordan croaked in a tight voice.

Then suddenly the plane shook like it had been

hit with enemy fire, tossing Trent across the small
seating space. Sparks shot up from the control
panel. The small twin-engine Cessna began a
stomach-pitching descent to the dark waters below.

Oh, my God, Trent thought desperately. It wasn't
supposed to happen like this. It was too soon. They
were going down. He wasn't going to make it.

The roar of Jordan's voice snapped him to his
senses. "Get out, Trent! Now, before it's too late.
Now!"

"Cole. Cole. Wake up!" Noelle gently, then with
more urgency shook his shoulder. He was drenched
in perspiration.

Trent's eyes flew open and he looked wildly
around as if he didn't know where he was. His
body was racked with unforgotten physical pain.

Noelle became frightened seeing the look of
pure terror carved on his face. "Cole, please," she
begged. "It's all right. You were having a dream."
Cautiously, she reached out and touched his cheek.
The contact seemed to draw him back.

Slowly his eyes began to focus. He breathed in
short panting breaths. He struggled to sit up, and
seeing the look of agonized concern on Noelle's
face, he knew it had happened again.

"Are you all right?" she asked gently, as her fear
for him was slowly ebbing.

He nodded. His voice was unsteady. "That must
have been some dream."

Noelle eased off of the bed and got a towel from the dressing table.

"Do you want to talk about it?" she asked, carefully drawing the towel across his damp body. "They say it helps."

He rubbed his eyes with the tips of his fingers. "You know, I can't remember what it was about."

"You can't remember?" she asked in disbelief. "You practically leap out of your skin, groan like you're being tortured and wake up bathed in sweat, and you can't remember what it was about!"

Trent took a deep breath, and hung his head in resignation. He flung himself back down against the pillows, and stared up at the ceiling. "All right, all right I do remember. At least some of it," he admitted. "I was dreaming about . . . a flight that I was on."

"And?"

"And, it was pretty scary."

"What was so scary about it? Was it when you were in the air force?"

"Yes," he answered, almost too quickly, thankful for a way out.

"We were on a rescue mission, in the middle of a storm. One of the planes was lost and mine almost went down." At least that was true, he consoled himself.

"Oh, Cole," she reached out and stroked his cheek. "I'm so sorry."

"I'm sorry that you had to witness that. I haven't had an attack in a long time."

"Well, it's over now," she soothed, easing down

next to him and cradling him against her breasts. "Try and get some sleep." She kissed the top of his head and held him, listening to his breathing return to normal.

Instinctively, she understood that when he crawled on top of her and entered her without so much as a word, it was solely an act to assure himself of his connection to life. He simply needed her at that moment, without question, without recriminations. She willingly gave herself to the driving thrusts that quenched her thirsty body, and she became one with the ragged moans of his release.

As Noelle finally drifted off to sleep, a nagging thought hovered just on the fringes of her consciousness. She could have sworn that Cole had called out Jordan's name in his sleep.

"How are you feeling this morning?" Noelle asked as she stood in front of the mirror brushing her hair.

"Pretty damned good," Trent grinned, sliding up behind her and nibbling her neck.

Joy bubbled in her laughter. "We'll never get out of here if you keep that up."

"Hmm," he slipped his arms around her bare waist, "that sounds like an excellent idea."

She swiveled around and leaned lightly into him, tilting her face upward to his. "Now, Monsieur Richards, I didn't come here with you to be ravished!" She giggled as she fought to maintain a sense of seriousness. "I came here to see the vineyards."

"Well, madame," he responded, pulling her solidly against him, "I think you've come to the wrong place." His mouth covered hers in a hungry kiss that left her weak with wanting.

"Last night was beautiful, Noelle," he whispered against her lips. His nimble fingers trailed up and down her back. "You were beautiful." His eyes washed over her. "I've never been with anyone who's made me feel the way you do."

"You made me happy Cole. More than you'll ever know. What happened between us was special." She looked away. "I know you've been with other women . . ."

"Don't."

"No. Please let me finish. And I could only hope that I made you happy. Because no matter what happens between us, I'll always remember this time together. Always." She looked up at him and everything that she felt was mirrored in her eyes.

Trent felt a surge of guilt sweep through him like a tidal wave. He'd taken away her most precious gift with lies, and deceit. Romanced her out of her virginity on the pretext of being someone she thought she could trust, could put her faith in.

What had he become? Had his own needs and desires superseded the feelings of others? Had he been under Jordan's tutelage for so long that he was becoming like him?

Then he was no better than Jordan Maxwell who

made the stakes so high the other players could never stay in the game.

He cupped her face in his hands. His eyes grew serious. "This—this is no casual thing with me, Noelle. You're too important to me for that. Don't you ever forget that. Ever." He seared her lips with a kiss.

"Maybe you're right," he grinned, leaning back and catching his breath, "I think we should get out of here." And he would have to find a way out of this web that he'd woven.

Nick studied the fax that had come over the machine moments earlier. Several of the Maxwell sites had been completely shut down. One of the jets was confiscated and its contents looted. There was complete anarchy in the streets.

He placed the long sheet of paper on the table. How would this affect the loans that Trent spoke about? Nick worried. If no money was coming in from shipping and air transport, how were they going to pay off the bank and all the other expenses? The letter didn't state how much loss had been sustained, but he could only imagine that it was in the millions.

This is what Jordan had left for Noelle to walk into? It was incomprehensible that Jordan couldn't have foreseen what was happening. He was too astute a businessman not to plan ahead. He breathed deeply. Trent did mention that there were other circumstances that compelled Jordan to handle things the way that he did. Must have been some mighty powerful circumstances, he thought, picking up his jacket.

Things would be so much simpler, he thought, if Trent would tell her the real reasons behind what had taken place that night. But he knew Trent as a man who stood by his word. He would never tell her, no matter what the cost to himself.

Nick walked toward the door. He'd make the call to Liaisons when he returned.

"If you'll follow me," the sunshine-blond tour guide instructed, "I'll show you the pressing machines."

"You mean they don't stomp the grapes with their feet?" Trent spouted, appalled.

"Please don't pay him any attention," Noelle interjected. "It's the sun." She nudged him in the rib with her elbow. "Behave," she whispered under her breath.

"Yes, Mommy."

She nudged him again, only harder. And they both giggled as they followed the small group.

Once back outdoors, Noelle playfully chastised Trent.

"Cole, why can't you behave yourself? You tortured that poor girl to death with your twenty questions."

"Aw, she loved it," he chuckled. "I'm sure we made her day."

Noelle shook her head. "You're probably right," she admitted.

He suddenly swept her up in his arms and spun her around until she squealed. Dizzy with laughter, they both collapsed on the grassy knoll.

"What do you want to do now?" Trent grinned as he nibbled on her lip.

"I'm starved. What about you?"

"Let's eat."

The pungent aroma of wine floated through the air. Trent spread a patchwork quilt on the grass, while Noelle unpacked the contents of their picnic basket.

"The inn thought of everything," Noelle commented, looking at the assortment of cheeses, dips, cold cuts, salad, fresh fruit and breads. "Maybe this is a feature that I could add to Liaisons," she mused out loud.

"You mean Liaisons doesn't prepare picnic baskets?" he asked, feigning horror. "Who would have thought such a thing!"

Noelle gave him a good shove. "Don't be obnoxious. It's just that I want to make sure that my guests have everything that they could want. I think picnic baskets would be a nice, homey touch."

"Believe me, baby, I'm pretty sure, none of your clients have ever sat their rear ends down on damp grass, fought off insects, or eaten food out of a basket." He took a hearty bite from his apple.

Noelle looked offended. "What is that supposed to mean?"

He sat up and looked at her. "You didn't create Liaisons for the non-wealthy, the underclass, and you know it. Liaisons is the hideaway for the rich, the elite. They don't come to Liaisons to be reminded of poverty. They want to be pampered, their every whim catered to with zest. They wouldn't know a picnic basket if it hit them in their Rolls Royces."

"That's a pretty narrow-minded conclusion," she tossed back. "Especially coming from someone whose had their share of the finer pleasures of life!"

He took the barb in stride. "I just think that when you dreamed of Liaisons, you wanted it to be as far away from all the poverty you've ever known. There's nothing wrong with that," he qualified. "But sometimes," he added thoughtfully, "we get so blinded by the beautiful life we forget where we've come from."

She turned away. He couldn't be any further from the truth at least where she was concerned. She wanted to laugh, but her anger and disappointment wouldn't let her. She'd expected that he would have thought more of her than that.

But she couldn't realistically expect him to be able to see beyond the obvious. Liaisons was a diversion. It was created for the very reasons that he mentioned, but the ultimate goal lay beyond the

naked eye. It was a part of her life that she'd
shared with no one. It was her one joy.

And she wasn't ready to part with that secret.
Not just yet.

She played along. "Perhaps you're right, Cole. I
probably have gotten too far away from my roots.
I guess I never thought of it that way before," she
said easily.

"I didn't mean anything by all that, Noelle. It's
just that I know you're such a caring person. I
wouldn't ever want to see you get jaded by everything that's around you."

"If I have nothing else, I have integrity. I could
never become *one of them*. But believe me, I know
what I'm doing."

Trent spotted the glint of challenge in her eye.
He believed her.

"I had a wonderful day," Noelle said to Trent
as they lay stretched out on the blanket, looking
up at the setting sun. "Thank you."

"I think," he replied, "it was something long
overdue for you. I would guess that you've spent
the past year doing nothing else but trying to get
Liaisons off the ground."

"That's true. I haven't had much of a social life
in so long, I'd almost forgotten how pleasant it
could be."

"The other day," he started tentatively, "you
asked me what were my plans for the future. But
what about you?"

She sighed. "I haven't given it much thought, actually."

"Have you ever considered taking over Jordan's business?"

"Jordan and I had very different views when it came to Maxwell Enterprises."

"Such as?"

She tried to think of a response that wouldn't sound too condescending.

"To put it simply, in business and in some aspects of his personal life, Jordan was a man strictly after personal gain. He had no concerns where it . . . came to the greater good."

Trent looked confused. "His business employed hundreds of people. That had to mean something."

Noelle pursed her lips, then took a sip of water before she spoke. "This may sound callous," she offered, "but in my opinion, Jordan took whatever he wanted at whatever the cost and generally gave nothing back. At least not on a humanitarian level," she qualified. "Jordan was propelled by money and power and what that could afford him. If someone else happened to benefit as a result, it was purely accidental."

Trent thought about it for a moment and had to admit that it was true.

"Did you ever discuss it with him?"

"Of course I did. But he wouldn't hear of doing anything differently. He said his business flourished with a strong hand and he didn't get into business for humanitarian reasons.

"Even though I resented his tactics and some of his ethics, I could never deny that he was incomparable when it came to business. You couldn't help but admire his ability to turn nothing into something. The barren lands of Sudan are a perfect example." *And so am I,* she thought. "No one imagined that it could be possible to establish a thriving enterprise in that region of the world," she continued. "Jordan had a vision and he made it a reality, whatever were his methods."

Trent leaned closer. "What would you do if given the chance?" he asked.

Noelle's eyes brightened. "If given the chance I would change the total direction of the company. Or at least expand its objectives." Her voice blossomed with excitement. "I would develop housing, schools, and hospitals in the areas where Maxwell Enterprises has its largest holdings. I would enlist the services of the community in building these facilities so that they would have a sense of ownership.

"Not only would they have jobs, but places to live and hospitals to attend to their health needs. Instead of constantly bringing in outside sources, use the internal resources," she concluded.

Trent was astounded by her insight and the validity of her vision.

"It's hard to believe that Jordan wouldn't have jumped at something like that."

"Believe it," she said simply.

"Have you ever discussed your ideas with—Trent Dixon?"

Her face hardened. "I have absolutely nothing to

say to that man. And certainly nothing that has to do with the business. He was a hired hand, paid to do Jordan's bidding. I'm quite sure that he wouldn't want to upset the status quo."

"Maybe if you . . ."

"Did you hear what I said?" she railed, her eyes flashing. "I have nothing to say to him. Nothing!"

She rolled her eyes in disgust and stared off into the distance. "My marriage may not have been made in heaven, but it was all I knew. All I had to rely on," she said in a choked voice. "Trent Dixon shattered my world. The only reason why Liaisons even exists is because of Jordan's death. It's a painful consolation. But it gives me the incentive to make it the best it can be. I'd like nothing better than to see Trent Dixon rot in jail for all eternity, and take Maxwell Enterprises with him. I have what I want," she added with finality.

Trent felt a chilling numbness slowly weave its way through his veins. Noelle's unyielding hatred for Trent left him without words.

It was painfully clear that Noelle would never forgive him, no matter what information he could come up with. And he could never tell her the truth.

The only way to convince her of his innocence would be to break his word to Jordan. That—he could never do.

He swallowed back the lump of acceptance. These next two days would be their last together. Of that he was certain.

Fourteen

Gina returned to her station at the front desk. The dinner hour was over and she'd made her rounds. In a matter of days Senator Thomas would arrive. Her pulse raced. How would she ever explain this mix-up to Noelle? Maybe, she thought, if she could find out who Cole Richards really was before Noelle returned, she could head off what she knew would be a disaster.

The spot just beneath her left eye twitched. The same sensation she'd had several weeks ago filled her. There had to be something she could do. But what?

The phone rang.

"Liaisons. Gina Nkiru speaking."

"Hello, this is Trent Dixon. May I speak with Mrs. Maxwell?"

Trent Dixon! "Uh, I'm sorry Mr. Dixon, Mrs. Maxwell is unavailable. May I help you with something?"

"We were to meet this week. But unfortunately something has come up and I won't be able to see her. Would you tell her that I'll call and reschedule?"

"Of course."

"Thank you."

The connection was broken.

Gina replaced the receiver. Noelle would be relieved, Gina thought, as she wrote down the message. She knew Trent Dixon wasn't someone Noelle was looking forward to meeting. At least that was one less thing to worry about. But Cole Richards, or whoever he was, was still an issue.

She hadn't spoken to Joseph since the night she walked out on him. Several times she'd attempted to call him but changed her mind halfway through dialing. This time she would swallow her pride. He was the only person she could think of that could find the answers. She prayed that he would help her.

The evening was warm. A soft breeze blew in from the partially opened window. The lights were turned down low and the murmurs of the television hummed in the background.

"Tell me more about your family, Cole," Noelle coaxed as they lay in each other's arms.

"Hmm, let's see. My older sister, Diane, she's the one with the twins, she works at a small law firm in Eaton."

"She's an attorney?"

"She thinks she is," Trent chuckled. "She's a paralegal, but you could never tell her she's not an attorney. Every chance she gets she's spouting the law, no matter what the topic."

They both laughed.

"But she's a doll. Unfortunately she can be a little hard around the edges," he admitted. "The firm she works for handles a lot of suits against large corporations and wealthy individuals who have, in some way, stepped on the toes of the little people. She considers herself a champion of the underclass. That compounded with a nasty divorce a year ago makes her a little difficult. But she's attending law school now. She should be finished in about another year. My other sister is Stephanie. Steph has nothing else on her mind except having a good time. She has more boyfriends than she can keep up with. She has the biggest heart of anyone so tiny. Everyone's issue is her personal heartache."

Noelle smiled, envisioning his night and day sisters. "And where do you fit in?"

"I'm the baby," he said humbly.

"And I'm sure you were spoiled rotten with two older sisters doting on you."

"I must admit, I had it made. But my parents didn't let me get away with much. They made sure that I knew how to do everything, including cooking to sewing. My mother always said I had to know how to take care of myself because she couldn't see how any woman in her right mind would put up with me."

"Were you a troublesome little boy?" she grinned, snuggling closer.

He laughed. "I was always in one scrape or the other when I was growing up. Usually it was because I had gotten involved in some outrageous scheme with my buddies from school. I spent an unusual amount of time in the principal's office."

"You certainly haven't outgrown your mischievous streak," she said, smiling as she recalled his behavior at the vineyards.

"Well some things never change," he said, rolling on top of her. "As a matter of fact," he kissed her lips, "I feel some mischief coming on right about now."

His mouth covered hers, while his searching fingers found their way beneath her short gown. Gently he caressed the tender flesh.

"I don't think you'll be needing this," he said in a raspy voice, skillfully slipping the gown over her head. He held her hands above her, dipping his head to suckle a taut nipple.

He felt her body tremble as his tongue circled the delectable orb.

"Cole," she moaned, "I want to touch you."

"No. Not this time. This is for you."

With each stroke of his tongue, with each tender touch he made her body come alive in ways she never knew possible.

Her mind ran in circles as she felt the flames of passion ignite within her.

Languidly his mouth sought out her moist center and lights exploded before her eyes. She cried out as her body involuntarily arched. Her shuddering moans crescendoed to ragged gasps filling the night air with erotic music.

He played along her willing body like a concert pianist propelling his instrument to greater heights. Her own spontaneous reactions incited him, filling him to near bursting.

She wanted to be with him always, she realized through the haze of her swirling emotions. She wanted to wake with him, sleep with him, share his dreams.

And as he gently buried himself deep within the satiny sheath, he said in a ragged breath just before his mouth covered hers, "I love you, Noelle."

The words so simple, yet so powerful, filled her with a warmth that was beyond reply. Let them be real, she prayed, as she clung desperately to him.

Joseph hung up the phone, still trying to absorb what Gina had said to him. This man that Noelle was with apparently wasn't who he claimed to be.

He rose from his seat by the window and crossed the small sitting room to the bar. He poured a glass of scotch over ice. If he were to discover who Cole Richards was, would Gina be willing to reconsider his marriage proposal?

She was scared. There was no question about that. Her job meant everything to her. More than he did, he realized, sadly. But maybe if he found a way to help her, she'd finally see just how important she was to him.

He took a sip from the glass. The information that Gina had provided was sketchy. And he couldn't rely on the profile that had been submitted to Liaisons.

He shook his head. This man was obviously after something. But what?

First thing in the morning, he'd make some calls. Hopefully, he thought, turning off the lights and walking into his bedroom, he could give Gina what she was looking for and she'd give him what he wanted most. *Her.*

Deep in thought, Nick lay in bed. He had some serious doubts about what he had done. He truly couldn't see how a phone call could actually help Trent out of this hole that he'd dug for himself. He said it would buy him some time. But time for what?

He clicked off the light. He could only hope that after the dust settled, Noelle would be able to forgive what Trent had done. Although he couldn't agree with Trent's methods, he could sympathize with his dilemma. Trent deserved some happiness. But for the life of him, he couldn't see how this could turn out happy for anyone.

Braxton looked over the documents with a sense of loss and relief. Carefully, he signed the last page and handed the papers to his partner, Scott.

"Signed and sealed," Braxton said, forcing a smile.

"You're sure you want to do this?" Scott asked.

Braxton nodded. "I've thought about it long and hard. It'll be the best thing for everyone."

Scott slipped the documents into a manila

folder. "I still think you should have discussed it with Tempest first. Secrets aren't what relationships thrive on."

"You know what she would have said. This way was best. Anyway, I'll still have my hand in things. My father built this architectural business from scratch. I don't intend to just turn my back on it completely. But my family needs me more than this firm does."

"You still have a ninety-day option, if you should change your mind."

Braxton heaved a sigh and nodded. "Listen, buddy, I have a plane to catch." He shook Scott's hand.

"Don't worry about anything," Scott offered.

"Why should I?" he joked, "I taught you everything you know."

Scott slapped him on the back, and grinned. "Yeah, right."

"I'll call you when I get to San Francisco."

Joseph was in his office earlier than usual. The staff had yet to arrive. He checked his fax machine. Waiting for him was the copy of the profile of Cole Richards that Gina had sent. He scanned the details.

Richards claimed to be a consultant for Jordan. That's odd, Joseph mused. He handled all of the contracts for every employee that Jordan hired. He'd never even heard of him.

He sat down at his desk and reviewed the other

details. Everything looked perfect. No wonder Gina didn't question anything.

He reached for the phone and dialed the number to the private investigator that he used from time to time.

"Good morning, Mike, Joseph Malone. Listen I need a quick favor. I want you to look into the background of a Cole Richards. He claims to be an aeronautical consultant, with a home base in New York."

"No problem. How soon do you need the info?"

"Yesterday."

"I'll get right on it."

"Thanks, Mike. There's a big one in this for you."

"Isn't it always?" he chuckled.

Joseph hung up the phone. "I really hope you appreciate this, Gina," he said out loud. But he had to admit, his own curiosity was getting the best of him. Why would someone want to pretend to be someone they're not in order to get close to Noelle? What did they have to hide?

Noelle and Trent spent the next day touring the countryside, stopping in at the little shops, picking up gifts and simply enjoying each other's company.

Noelle had a shopping bag full of souvenirs and Trent had a bag to match.

"I'm about shopped out," Trent breathed as they emerged from the last antique store on the road.

"What do you want to do now?" she asked.

"I hear they have a boat ride, well more of a yacht ride, just outside of the valley. How about if we take these back to the inn, change for dinner and spend our evening under the stars?"

"That sounds wonderful."

He leaned down and kissed the tip of her nose. "I was hoping you'd say that."

Hand in hand they returned to the car and headed for the inn.

On the return ride, Noelle leaned back and closed her eyes, letting the warm breeze whip across her face. She was in heaven. These past days with Cole had been more glorious than her wildest dreams. She felt like an entirely new person. A person who meant something. A person worth caring about for the *right* reasons.

She angled her head to the side to subtly study his profile. She smiled. Last night, he'd said he loved her. Did he really mean it? she worried again. She had been reluctant to bring it up in the fear that he may deny it. Or maybe he only said it because he felt he should. At least for the moment she could live with the glorious possibility that his feelings for her were real.

A part of her was still afraid to reveal her true feelings for him. She didn't want him to feel obligated to return the sentiments. He'd made it pretty clear that he wasn't making any promises.

She was a big girl. She'd just have to accept the fact that after this magical weekend Cole Richards might very well walk out of her life.

"What are you thinking about, baby?" Trent

asked, catching a glimpse of her out of the corner of his eye.

Noelle's smile was wistful. "Just that I wish that I had the power to freeze time."

He turned to look at her, brushing her chestnut hair away from her eyes. He eased the car onto the shoulder of the road. He turned toward her. "If we froze time," he said, loving her more with each passing minute, "then we'd never be able to reach our destiny."

"And where is that?" she asked hopefully.

He leaned across the stick shift and gently kissed her lips. His eyes caressed her face, so full of expectation he thought, his heart heavy with regret.

"Only time will tell," he answered finally.

She looked away, suddenly consumed by a sense of loss. She wanted him to want her as desperately as she wanted him. She wanted him to say more. To say that their destiny was one in the same. He wanted to go back in time and change everything—make it right.

"You're right," she said, forcing cheer into her voice. "And our immediate future is waiting for us at the pier."

They returned to the inn in silence, both trapped in their own tumultuous thoughts. Each wanting the same thing but unable to cross the barrier to claim it.

Beneath the star-encrusted sky, the *Alexis II* glided smoothly along the still waters.

Trent pulled Noelle closer, needing her nearness. He took a sip from his glass of champagne and looked toward the horizon.

"We'll be heading back to the pier soon," he said.

She didn't want to think about it. The closer they neared the pier, the sooner their night would end. And then tomorrow would come and they'd have to return to Liaisons.

She sighed. "As much as I love Liaisons," she looked up into his eyes, "I'll miss being here." She hesitated a moment. "I'll miss this time we've shared together."

He wished that he could offer her more than just the moment, but he couldn't. Instead he hugged her closer.

"Let's not think about tomorrow. Let's make the most of the time we have."

Noelle nodded, taking Trent's arm as they strolled along the deck.

"I've been thinking about your ideas for Maxwell Enterprises," Trent said, hesitantly. "I think you should do it. It would be just the thing to turn the company around. It's really suffering enormous losses because of the revolt. The people are revolting against the government because of all of the things that you mentioned."

"Is the company really in trouble?" she asked, hearing this news for the first time. The reports that she received on the company were generally glorious, with only hints of the real problems.

"From what I understand, things are getting pretty bad."

"Maybe that's why Trent wants to see me." She tossed the information around in her head. "If Jordan's company is in trouble, then Trent must want something from me that he can't handle himself. That would explain his sudden need to come to the States. But it still doesn't explain why he hasn't shown up yet, if the situation is urgent."

She looked to Trent for answers.

"Hopefully, when we return, we'll have some answers," he offered.

They disembarked from the yacht and walked toward the car.

"Think about it, Noelle," he continued. "Jordan groomed you for business and you've obviously proven that you have the capabilities to handle anything."

"You really think so?"

"I know so," he answered, helping her into her seat. He took his place behind the wheel.

"But Trent has complete control over the company. There's no way that he'd be willing to share in the power."

"Maybe you don't know him as well as you think you do."

She looked at him curiously. "You almost sound as if you do."

"No. Uh, of course not," he said quickly. "It's just that, well, maybe you should give him a chance. If Jordan trusted him, perhaps you can, too."

Hadn't Tempest said the same thing? Hadn't

Jordan said as much in his letter? Now Cole. She thought about it for a minute. She trusted Cole and she trusted his instincts. Maybe he was right.

"Before I make any decision one way or the other, I want to hear what your investigator friend has to say. If he can show me, without a doubt, that Trent Dixon has absolutely nothing to do with the crash—then—I'll think about it."

He stared straight ahead, keeping his eyes on the road. Ironically, his plan seemed to be working. He could only hope now that Nick did his part.

Fifteen

Tempest heard the sound of soft footsteps entering her bedroom. It must be Kai, she thought, pulling herself out of a light sleep. She glanced at the clock: 1:00 A.M. Kai couldn't possibly be hungry.

She sat up in bed just as the light came on.

"Braxton!" She came fully awake. "When . . . what?"

He crossed the room in long quick strides and sat down beside her.

"I've missed you like crazy," he said, covering her mouth with a warm kiss, stilling any further questions. He sat back and looked at her.

"I know it's early," he began, "but we need to talk."

Her heart raced. "All right."

"I know the past few months have been hell on you and Kai. I know I've been awful to live with, at least when I'm around," he added. "But things are going to change."

Tempest looked away, then back at him. "You've said that so many times, B.J., what makes now any different?

"I've sold the company."

Tempest paused before she spoke. "You did what?"

"I sold the company to Scott. He'll be running things from now on."

"You can't be serious. Why didn't you talk to me about it? That's a decision we should have made together Braxton. Didn't you trust me enough to discuss it with me?" She still couldn't believe that he'd made such a monumental decision without her. Maybe their marriage was in more trouble than she thought.

"I didn't tell you because I knew you'd say not to do it."

"But Braxton, that company means everything to you. It was your father's."

"I know. But it doesn't mean more than keeping you and our daughter happy. My months out of the country, and my hopping from one project to the next, have put a real strain on us. I haven't been there for you and Kai when I should have been. I'll do whatever it takes, T. I don't want to lose you, and I felt you drifting away. Or maybe it was me. I just couldn't stand it."

She was filled with mixed emotions. Everything she'd been thinking had been wrong. She'd been on the verge of accusing him of having an affair, and all the while he was . . . How could she have doubted him?

"So all those trips, all those hushed phone calls, they were about the company." Her tone was more of a statement than a question.

He nodded. "I had to make sure that everything

was in place. I had some developments underway and I couldn't step aside until I was sure that they were completed." He lowered his gaze. "I realize now that I should have been honest with you. It would have avoided so much hurt and confusion. I prejudged you, and I guess I was too stubborn to see past doing it my way. I know how persuasive you can be." He grinned slightly. "I didn't want you to talk me out of it."

"Are you sure this is what you want?"

"I'm positive."

"But what are you going to do?"

"I've leased some space in New York, near your office at the World Trade Center. I plan to set up operations there. But only for local jobs." He smiled. "No more jet-setting for me."

"I can't believe you did this," she said, fighting back tears.

"It's done. Now we can be a family. The family that you and Kai deserve. Nothing is more important to me than that. If I have the two of you, everything else will fall in place."

He lowered his head. "I think I got too caught up in the glamour of it all. Traveling around the world, making ridiculous sums of money. I'd forgotten why I'd gotten into architecture—to build houses for people. Not monuments to the wealthy who'll never really live in them."

"Oh, Braxton." She hugged him fiercely. "If this is what you want, then I want it for you. We already have enough money to last us a lifetime. I was just so afraid," she choked back a sob.

He eased her away and looked into her eyes. "Afraid? Of what?"

"I was afraid that you were planning on leaving me," she cried.

"Oh, God." He crushed her against him. "I'd never leave you. Never," he whispered against her hair. "You're my world. I couldn't make it without you."

"I've waited so long to hear you say that again."

He eased her down on the bed, hovering over her. "You'll never have to wait again," he promised. "I'm gonna keep reminding you every chance I get."

"No more secrets," she whispered softly against his mouth.

"No more," he promised.

Trent tossed his jacket on the chintz ottoman when he walked through the door of their room. His conscience had been gnawing at him relentlessly all evening.

He'd been so close to telling her the truth but had taken the coward's way out by trying to convince himself that the hurt to Noelle would be too devastating. The reality was, he was more afraid of what the truth would do to him.

At least he had been able to get her to rethink her stance on Maxwell Enterprises. Her vision was brilliant. It was exactly what the corporation needed.

"What are you thinking about?" Noelle asked, sidling up behind him.

He turned and pulled her into his arms. "This may sound very unromantic, but I was thinking about your plan to expand Maxwell." He looked at her speculatively.

"Oh." She backed away.

"I really believe that you should push for it Noelle," he urged.

Her eyebrows arched in question. "You seem overly concerned about Maxwell Enterprises. Any reason?" She folded her arms in front of her.

He swallowed and glanced away, not daring to meet her penetrating gaze.

"It's just that Jordan was a friend and I'd hate to see everything he worked for go down the tubes." He shrugged dismissively. "That's all. And anyway I'm sure that whatever happens would have some impact on you. Aren't you concerned about that?"

She moved his jacket aside and sat down, crossing her long legs at the knee. Her voice was decidedly flat.

"Liaisons has afforded me the ability to be independently wealthy. I've made some wise investments over the years. I'm sure I won't suffer one way or the other—no matter what happens to Jordan's business."

She stared at him hard, vaguely gaining a sense that there was more to his interest than he was letting on.

After Jordan's death, my goal has been to finally make a life for myself separate and apart from him and his name. I don't intend to spend the rest of my life living off of what he accomplished."

She thought of the enormous holdings that she had established in the reconstruction efforts of South Central L.A. After the riots, she had systematically sponsored many of the store owners and local contractors to rebuild. If she lived to be a hundred she'd never be able to spend all of the money that she would receive in dividends over the coming years.

So instead, she funneled the money to help the poor communities of California. She was adamant, however, about staying in the background and keeping her name out of the papers. But she gained her satisfaction from seeing the many victims of poverty gain a leg up on life.

"I never wanted to be a part of the big picture," she continued, keeping her thoughts to herself. "You don't have to hear applause to be appreciated."

"You never cease to amaze me," he said, kneeling down beside her. "Every moment that I'm with you, you reveal another layer of that Noelle Maxwell mystique." He smiled and held her hands in his. "What else do you have in store?"

She searched his eyes for some clue of what she was feeling. "Only time will tell," she answered quietly. For the first time since they'd met she had the fleeting sensation that she didn't know who he was.

Gina parked her Volvo in front of Joseph's ocean-front cottage. She'd taken a chance in coming without calling, but her nerves wouldn't let her rest. Noelle would be back tomorrow. She had to know what she was facing.

It was nearly 1:00 A.M. She'd left Carol in charge of things while she made the hour drive.

She was banking on Joseph's feelings for her to somehow help her out of this fiasco. He had no real reason to want to do anything for her, not after she'd walked out on him. But he'd at least listened to her when she'd phoned, although reluctantly. He said he would call her, but she hadn't heard a word from him since she sent the fax.

She couldn't wait any longer. Hesitantly, then with more determination, she walked up the four steps to the front door. The bell chimed.

Gina waited nervously, switching her purse from one hand to the other. She began to lose her resolve. What was she really doing standing on Joseph's doorstep in the middle of the night? She took a step back and started to turn away, when the door was pulled open.

"Gina?"

She spun around.

"Joseph. I, I'm sorry to just come by like this but . . ."

His voice was surprisingly gentle. "Do you want to come in?" He reached out and took her hand before she could respond.

"Can I get you anything," he offered, once they were inside. He poured himself a drink of scotch over ice.

"No. Thank you, I'm fine." She sat on the edge of the low sofa, her hands folded in front of her.

He leaned casually against the oak-finished bar, gazing at her appreciatively.

"So, to what do I owe this late-night pleasure?"

Gina studied her hands, then looked up. "I had to know if you found out anything," she said weakly.

"A simple phone call could have done the trick." He slowly walked toward her. "Are you sure that's the only reason you drove all the way out here in the middle of the night?" His finger stroked her cheek.

When he looked at her like that, as if she were the most important woman in the world, she couldn't think straight. He was right, and she knew it. She could have phoned. But deep in her heart she'd wanted to see him. Ever since their last night together, she hadn't been herself. Her temper was short, she hadn't slept well, and she'd made an inexcusable mistake. Mistakes were something totally out of character for her.

"You always could see right through me," she finally admitted, a glimmer of her true feelings dancing in her eyes.

Joseph took her hands and pulled her up. "I've missed you, Gina. I don't want to lose you." He sighed heavily and held her tightly against him. "I'll do whatever it takes to keep you in my life. No more pressure." He kissed the top of her head. "I promise."

She held him to her, pressing her cheek against his chest. She listened to the rapid pounding of his heart and realized that it matched her own. She knew how much it took for him to say what he did. Joseph Malone was a proud man and he'd put his ego aside for her. He'd willingly stayed in the background like the unmentionable lover in an illicit affair. He deserved better than what she'd given him.

She tilted her head back and looked into his warm eyes. "No more hiding, Joe," she said, feeling a sense of relief wash over her. "So long as you're with me, I'll deal with my father's outrage, Noelle's disappointment and anything else that gets tossed our way."

"Are you sure?" he asked, daring to hope.

"Absolutely," she smiled.

"You won't regret this, Gina." He kissed her lightly then with more urgency, his need for her mounting with every beat of his heart. "Stay with me tonight," he groaned against her mouth.

"I wish I could," she whispered, breathless with emotion. "But I can't. I left my assistant, Carol, in charge of things. I told her I'd be back in a couple of hours."

"Tomorrow then?" He caressed her hips, urging her closer against him.

"I'll be here as soon as I get off."

Reluctantly, she backed out of his embrace. "I'd better be going."

She picked up her purse and Joseph walked her out. When they reached the door, she stopped and turned. "I'd almost forgotten my other reason for coming," she said sheepishly. Have you heard anything?"

"Not yet. It'll probably take a couple of days."

Disappointment registered on her face.

"You said that this Cole Richards, or whoever he is, is with Noelle?"

"I'm pretty sure that they're together. Both of them left on the same day and haven't been back. She just seems so happy, Joe. I mean really happy for the first time in months. If I'm the cause of this imposter creating any trouble or hurting Noelle, I don't know what I'll do."

"Don't worry." He braced her shoulders firmly. "We'll get to the bottom of it. What troubles me," he continued, "is, what reason would someone have to conceal their identity from her? Why is it so important that she not know who he really is?"

"Maybe he's just some money-hungry con man out to see what he can get." But even as she said the words, she didn't really believe it herself.

"Perhaps," Joseph responded, half-heartedly. "I just have a nagging feeling that it goes deeper than that."

As Gina drove along the darkened highway en route to Liaisons, she had that same nagging feeling.

Sixteen

Trent and Noelle lay side by side, listening to the latest update on the revolt in Sudan. The United Nations was in the process of sending over an ambassador to see if he could initiate some sort of agreement between the rival forces.

The starving inhabitants were demanding a fair share in the running of their country. They wanted housing, jobs and doctors to care for the sick. Unfortunately, the newscaster continued, the government was unable to provide these things as the country was on the brink of financial collapse. Ambassador Kenyatta Nkiru was scheduled to arrive at the end of the week.

The wheels began to spin in Noelle's head. She sat up in bed.

"Cole, do you really believe that my plan could work?" she asked cautiously.

"Of course I do."

"But how could I ever hope to get it off the ground?"

He pulled himself into a sitting position. "I'm sure there's a way. You have plenty of contacts."

She thought about her options and then it dawned on her.

"Ambassador Nkiru is Gina's father."

Trent nodded. "Yes?"

"If I could meet with him before he left, maybe we could put together a proposal that everyone would be satisfied with."

"Are you sure you're in a position to pull something like that off?"

"I'd have to pull some money from the reconstruction in South Central," she blurted out, and wished she hadn't.

Trent's reaction was instantaneous. "You'd have to do what?"

She sighed in resignation, lying back on the down filled pillows. She stared up at the ceiling as she spoke.

"I've been contributing my dividends from Maxwell Enterprises and my investments into the rebuilding efforts of South Central. After the riots and I saw, first hand, the devastation, I had to do something. Even with government loans, it's not enough. Jordan never knew," she confessed. "He would have never understood."

Trent was momentarily speechless. To say that she was an enigma said little about Noelle. Before he'd met her, he believed her to be no more than a pampered princess. But day after day he witnessed the depth of her compassion, her intelligence, her acute business sense and her unbridled passion. Her own humility humbled him.

"Noelle, I don't know what to say."

"You don't have to say anything. And actually, I'd prefer that you didn't. I meant it when I said I didn't want to be in the limelight."

"But do you really believe that you can stay in the background if you present your case to Nkiru?"

"From the first time that I met him, I realized that he was a man of discretion. If I can be assured that my name won't be mentioned, I'll do whatever I can."

As casually as he could manage, he asked, "What about Trent Dixon?"

"I'll find a way to deal with him," she answered firmly. "If I have to buy him out, then I will. With any luck, he'll wind up in jail and he won't be my problem," she concluded with icy finality.

Trent felt the chill of her words as strongly as an arctic blast. He swallowed. "I know you're doing the right thing, Noelle."

"It's because of you," she said softly.

"Me?"

"Yes, you," she smiled, caressing his bearded cheek. "If you hadn't gotten me to really think about this, I don't believe it would have occurred to me to even try. You convinced me that it's possible."

"Noelle, you have talents that you haven't even touched yet. The future is yours for the taking."

"Is it?" she asked hopefully, searching his eyes with her own.

"Whatever you want."

"Anything?" She leaned toward him. Her heart pounded.

"Anything," he whispered as her lips met his.

Tentatively her tongue sought out his, inflaming her as they met. Her nimble fingers stroked his face, his bare chest. She began reacquainting herself with the rough and soft texture of his sienna skin.

He reached out to touch her and she held him back with a firm hand.

"This is for you," she said in a throaty whisper.

Her eager lips trailed down the length of his body, nibbling, kissing, awakening every fiber of his being.

She raised herself up, straddling him while holding his hand solidly in place above his head. Her eyes hung heavy with desire when she looked down at him, enclosing him within the heated walls.

She took him to heaven and beyond with each gyration, every rise and fall of her hips.

Her eyes slammed shut as he rose to meet her. She cried out as the sun, the moon and the stars all collided into a brilliant white heat within her.

She lost herself, consumed by her own driving need and his pulsing desire to sweep her above the mountaintops, across the valleys, soaring over the oceans to meet in a world that they had created.

He pulled himself away from her grasping hold, reaching up to cup her tender breasts, kneading the taut nipples until she called out his name in a mixture of agony and ecstasy.

They traveled together in a race older than time, searching for that supreme release that can only be found in the joining of two perfect lovers.

In one swift motion, he turned her onto her

back, hurtling them over the last soul-drenching mile of their sublime journey.

"I love you, too," she whispered in a ragged voice as the last shuddering spasm slammed deep within her.

And the pang of guilt twisted deeper into his heart.

Gina returned to the front desk, just as the phone rang. It was nearly 6:00 A.M. she realized.

"I'll take it," she quickly said to Carol.

"Liaisons, Gina Nkiru speaking."

"Gina, I'm glad I caught you. It's Noelle."

Gina held her breath. "Mrs. Maxwell, is everything all right? I didn't expect to hear from you."

"Everything is fine, Gina," she said wiggling away from Trent as he tried to nibble her ear. "I'm calling because I need to speak with your father. It's urgent. Do you think you can get in touch with him?"

It was 9:00 A.M. in New York, she quickly calculated. Her father was a notorious early riser. She was sure he had been up and around and in his office at the embassy for hours by now.

"Certainly. But I know he must be preparing for his trip. You did see the news?"

"That's exactly why I need to speak with him. *Before* he leaves," she emphasized. "Please try to reach him and you must impress upon him the importance of contacting me. Will you do that?"

"I'll—call—right away," she agreed, her exotic face creasing in wonder.

Noelle breathed a sigh of relief. "Thank you. I should be back no later than noon today. How is everything? Any important messages?"

Her heart skipped. "Everything is fine. There were a few messages," she added with hesitation. "But they can wait until you return."

"Good. Then I'll see you in a few hours. And Gina—"

She felt her stomach pitch. "Yes, Mrs. Maxwell?"

"Get some rest."

Gina smiled with relief as her stomach returned to its rightful place. "I was on my way."

"Good-bye."

Noelle hung up and Gina replaced the receiver with a shaky hand. Her conscience was troubling her so badly she'd begun to get paranoid, thinking that with every word Noelle already knew.

But she'd find out soon enough, she thought miserably.

She picked up the phone and dialed the embassy in New York.

Noelle and Trent sat side by side, each immersed in their own troubling thoughts. The short flight back to Cochran Airways was filled with unspoken questions.

She wanted to ask him; Where did they go from here? But she was afraid of the answer. She didn't think she could bear to actually know that their days together were coming to an end.

He wanted to ask her if she really meant what

she'd said last night, or was it only said in the throes of passion. He didn't dare hope that what she felt for him was real. It would only make their inevitable parting that much more painful.

"I hope Gina was able to reach her father," Noelle said lamely, attempting to break the heavy silence that hung between them.

"I'm sure she did. The only thing to concern yourself with now, is convincing him to present your plan."

"I just hope he'll have time to see me before he leaves."

They lapsed into another poignant silence as the Cessna hovered over the landing strip.

The plane gently touched down, and Trent automatically shut off all of the controls.

He turned to Noelle. "Well, here we are, safe and sound." His forced smile wasn't missed by Noelle.

Noelle looked away, but she was unable to hold back the thoughts that tripped through her head.

"Cole, before we go back, I have something I want to say to you."

He looked at her expectantly, with a mixture of false hope and much trepidation.

"Last night, I—I told you that I loved you— and . . ."

"You don't have to explain anything, Noelle." He reached for and held her hand.

"But I do. I know you said the same thing to me." She looked into his eyes and was rewarded with a nod of confirmation. "I don't want to hold you to that, and—I don't want you to feel obligated to—continue this relationship because of what I said.

"I mean, I realize that you, we, made no promises to each other." She looked down at their entwined hands, then eased hers away. "And I don't expect any now."

She sat back, straightened her shoulders and expelled a long-held breath.

She was offering him a way out, and like a fool he knew he was going to take it. Awkwardly, he cleared his throat.

"I—wish I knew what to say."

Her voice was thick with disappointment. "You don't have to say anything." She reached inside of her purse and retrieved her long-discarded, dark sunglasses. "Everything has been said," she added softly, slipping the glasses in place.

She forced a smile. "We should be getting back. I'm anxious to talk with Gina." She turned away, not trusting the dark glasses to hide the tears that welled in her eyes. She unhooked the latch of the door and with her back to him she said softly, "Thank you for an unforgettable weekend."

She stepped out of the plane into the blazing California sunshine.

As she sped along the freeway, she promised herself that she would not cry. If nothing else came out of this weekend with Cole, she had been made to realize that she had the power to change the destiny of thousands less fortunate. She'd discovered what real love truly felt like. She had uncovered her womanhood. And for those things she would always have a place in her heart for him.

Gina saw Noelle the moment she stepped through the revolving doors. Her pulse raced. She still hadn't heard from Joseph. And Cole Richards, or whoever he was, was no where to be seen.

Maybe she'd been wrong when she told Joseph that Noelle and Cole were together. Noelle had never mentioned anything, but Gina had a strong sense that something was going on. She could tell by the way Noelle's eyes sparkled whenever she saw him, and from the intimate way they spoke to each other whenever she caught a glimpse of them together.

Those things, compounded by the fact that both of them left Liaisons on the same day, had heightened her suspicions. Could she have been wrong?

"Gina," Noelle greeted. "How's everything? Did you speak with your father?" she asked anxiously.

"Everything is just fine. Here are your messages." She handed Noelle the rectangular slips of paper. She took them but didn't look at them. "I spoke to my father this morning."

"And?"

"He said he couldn't promise you, but he'd try to make a detour before he left. In any case, he said he would call you this evening."

Noelle bit her bottom lip as she pondered her

alternatives. "Would it be a problem if I contacted him myself?"

"I don't think so. I can give you the number." She quickly jotted down the number to the embassy on the memo pad affixed with the Liaisons letterhead.

"*Merci*. I'll let you know what happens." She turned without another word and headed to her suite, with her three-inch heels clicking purposefully against the marble floor.

When Noelle returned to her room she immediately went for the phone, her messages from Trent Dixon and Senator Thomas completely forgotten.

Trent sat in his car and watched Noelle's Mercedes until it disappeared along the stretch of highway. They had agreed that he would wait a reasonable amount of time before he returned. How long was reasonable? he asked himself. An hour? Two? Forever?

He wished that he could make things different. He wished that he could continue to be Cole Richards and never have to step into Trent Dixon's shoes again.

The irony was, for all of his deceit, everything was working out in spite of it. He hadn't given Noelle enough credit in the beginning. She was an intelligent, reasonable woman. He could have convinced her from the start that in order for Maxwell Enterprises to survive she would have to step in.

It was too late now. The damage had already been done. There was no going back.

He turned the key in the ignition and the Lexus engine roared to life.

Maybe the best thing to do would be to return to Sudan and try to put this behind him as quickly as possible—to forget Noelle.

He pulled off onto the highway and headed for Los Angeles. As the road unfolded before him, vivid images of Noelle sprung to life. Her smile. Her sparkling laughter. Her exquisite body wrapped in his arms.

At that moment, when he rounded the curve, he knew that he would never share a greater love, and what he was about to do would be the most difficult task of his life.

Seventeen

Noelle had been unsuccessful in trying to reach Ambassador Nkiru, but she'd left a message. Now there was nothing else she could do except to wait.

In the meantime, since Gina seemed to have everything under control, she began to unpack.

The first item that she touched brought back a pang of remembrance. She lifted the filmy nightie and held it against her face, closing her eyes as she brushed it against her cheek.

His scent still lingered on it. She held it closer as visions of their nights together filled her with an incredible warmth.

She'd given him an easy way out, and he took it, she thought, the hurt blooming anew. Was it that simple for him to walk away from what they'd shared? She couldn't believe that he didn't feel something for her. She knew, deep in her soul, that when he'd said he loved her, he meant it. How could he turn his back on her—on them?

Her gown floated from her fingers onto the bed. Floated away like the dreams that she'd had for herself and Cole.

Slowly she walked across the room to stare sightlessly across the expansive grounds that held Liaisons.

She had everything that anyone could ever want. Wealth. Power. The ability to make a difference. Even now she was on the brink of challenging the stone walls of a government.

But in truth, she had nothing. She was still the poor, orphaned girl serving food to the masses. The only difference was that the patrons dressed up for dinner, and the ambiance was the epitome of elegance.

Suzanne Donaldson was right when she said you could take the girl out of the swamp . . .

Who was she really fooling? All of her philanthropic work would never change who she really was. She'd believed that Jordan was her knight in shining armor. For a time he was. But even him, with all of his money, his gifts, his tutoring—he'd done it all for personal reasons, she realized sadly. Jordan's need to create something from nothing was manifested in her. She was his greatest creation. And her need to have her dreamlike life had allowed it.

But Cole, what were his reasons for wanting her, even briefly? She might never know, she concluded.

She sighed heavily. There was no point in berating herself for what had taken place between them. She had wanted it to happen and part of her would always be glad because of it.

She would treasure the memories and just tuck them away for safe keeping.

Noelle turned from the window, just as there was a knock on her door. Her heart leaped as she quickly crossed the room and entered the small foyer. *Cole.*

She pulled open the door, her face flush with expectation.

"I'm happy to see you, too," Tempest greeted, crossing the threshold and kissing Noelle solidly on the cheek.

Noelle struggled to hide her disappointment. "Miss me?" she asked, closing the door.

"Of course, this place isn't the same without you. Oh, Noelle," she clasped her hands to her chest, unable to subdue her happiness a moment longer. "He's back! Braxton's back." She looked up to the ceiling, a brilliant smile illuminating her face.

Noelle instantly pushed aside her own worries and took Tempest's hand. She led her over to the small couch and they sat down.

"Tell me. What happened?"

Tempest spun out everything from Braxton's surprise arrival to the sale of his architectural business.

"We're going to stay in New York," she concluded. "We're finally going to be a family. Kai is ecstatic. She and Braxton are spending the day together celebrating. *We* celebrated last night," she added coyly.

Noelle grinned knowingly. "I'm so happy for you. You see, everything did work out. I told you if you really love him, give him a chance."

"I cringe every time I think I almost accused him of having an affair." She shook her head. "I still can't believe that I could have thought such a thing. Harboring secrets and doubts can be devasating," she said softly. "If we had only talked with each other about how we really felt, so much pain could have been avoided."

She turned to look at Noelle and for the first time noticed the emptiness that was carefully hidden behind the practiced smile.

"What about you?" she probed gently. "I can tell something's wrong."

Noelle rose from her seat and turned away, crossing her arms protectively around her waist.

"Everything is fine."

"Look me in the eye and tell me that," Tempest insisted.

Noelle didn't move.

Tempest got up and came around in front of her.

Noelle angled her head to the side to avoid contact with Tempest's riveting gaze. She bit her lip to keep it from quivering.

Tempest held Noelle's arm. "What in the world happened? And don't tell me, nothing. I'm not leaving here until you tell me."

Noelle threw up her hands in defeat, then covered her mouth to stifle a sob. "Everything and nothing," she finally said in a weak voice.

"Very clever. Now what is that supposed to mean?"

Noelle sat back down, staring intently at the intricate pattern of the Oriental rug.

She started slowly, reliving each detail as she spoke, up to and including telling Cole that he didn't owe her anything.

When she finished, nearly a half hour later Tempest was shocked.

Here was a woman who she truly believed she knew better than anyone, only to find out that she'd been living in an unconsummated marriage for four, lonely years. What type of character must it have taken to stand it for so long and never whisper a word? Noelle's obvious loyalty to Jordan overwhelmed her. Tempest's admiration for Noelle amplified ten times over.

And now when she finally believed that she'd found that special someone, he, too, had abandoned her. Only this time it was much worse. Noelle was not in awe of Cole, as she had been of Jordan. She didn't feel obligated to stay with him. She was unquestionably in love with him.

"Less than a week ago," Tempest began, "you and I sat on opposite sides of the fence. It was *you* who gave me encouragement. It was *you* who told me to stick it out, because you knew how I felt."

She touched Noelle's chin, turning her face toward her. She looked deep into the sad brown eyes. "Prejudging nearly destroyed my marriage. Don't assume anything. If you love him, Noelle, don't let him go," she implored. "Everyone doesn't get a second chance."

"Did you make the call?" Trent asked Nick.

"Yeah. Just like you said."

Trent nodded and took a sip from his drink. He sat down on the couch and intently read the printouts that had arrived in his absence. Things were worse than he thought. He would have to return sooner than he'd planned.

"Is that all you have to say?" Nick probed, taking a seat opposite Trent. He'd been in the suite for over an hour and had yet to mention a word about his weekend other than Noelle's idea for development in Sudan.

Trent's jaw clenched. "I have to get away," he said, his voice devoid of emotion.

"You're just gonna walk away from her? No explanation? Nothing? I can't believe you'd do something like that."

"I don't have any other choice."

Nick shook his head in disappointment. "I would have thought you were a bigger man than that, Trent. Even for you this is low."

Trent jumped up, tossing the last of his drink down his throat. His eyes narrowed. "What would you suggest, O wise one?" he asked sarcastically.

"You know what I'd suggest. So don't ask."

"Oh, of course," he spat, his voice escalating in misdirected anger, "I should just walk right up to her and say, Noelle, I just wanted you to know that you've slept with your husband's murderer. See you later. Does that about sum it up for you, buddy?"

"Listen," Nick countered, his voice rising to match Trent's, "don't get pissed with me just because you let your hormones take the place of your brain! You knew what you were doing and you did it anyway. And the only person who's going to suffer is Noelle."

Trent turned on him. "Really? Do you honestly think she's the only one who's going to suffer?" His face hardened into a mask of pain. "Don't you think I'm feeling it, too?"

Nick crossed the room and stood in front of Trent. "I know you're feeling it," he said quietly. "That's why you've finally got to do what's right."

Trent turned away. "It sounds so simple," he said in a detached voice. "I only wish that it was." He hesitated. "But I know you're right," he admitted reluctantly. "You've been right from the beginning." He paused for a long moment. "I'll tell her," he said finally. "Once she presents this proposal to the Sudanese government, I'll tell her. I know that if I say anything now, she'll back out. And for all of the wrong reasons."

"I don't think you give this woman enough credit, Trent. From everything that you've told me about her she doesn't seem like the kind of woman who would put her personal opinion above the good of so many."

Trent shook his head. "I can't take that chance. This is too important. If I say anything now, I know she'll think I was just using her."

"Well, weren't you?"

"Maybe at first. But then," he looked across the room at Nick, "but then I fell in love with her, Nick, and everything changed." He hung his head. "Everything."

"And how does she feel?"

Trent swallowed. "She feels the same way." He spun away and pounded his fist against the wall, rattling the abstract portrait. "Damn it Nick, all I can think about is Noelle. I sleep, eat and dream her. I wanted her so badly, I just completely lost all sense of reality. And I still want her." His voice strengthened with determination. "I want her up until the very last minute I can have her."

He crossed the room in long, determined strides, snatching up his discarded jacket. "I'll call you," he said, as he slammed the door behind him.

The soft sound of music could just be heard over the surging rush of water. Noelle closed her eyes, letting the beat of the music and the pulse of the steamy water relax her.

She'd thought long and hard about what Tempest had said. She couldn't deny the fact that there were still too many things left unfinished between her and Cole. She owed it to herself to lay her cards on the table. She would go to him, she decided, and tell him exactly how she felt. She certainly had nothing to lose.

Noelle heard the insistent knocking on her door just as she stepped out of the shower. She slipped on a white silk robe and went to answer. Something must be wrong, she worried, crossing the room in bare feet. No one would come to her room, without calling first, unless it was an emergency.

She pulled the door open. Her heart lurched madly. And before she had a chance to react, Trent stepped through and pushed the door shut. Noelle took a cautious step back.

"Cole, I . . ."

He gathered her in his arms smothering her mouth and any questions in a soul-searching kiss.

Instinctively she responded, succumbing to the persuasiveness of his kisses. Her own spontaneous reaction to him rendered her powerless against the magnitude of his hunger.

Her head spun as the delightful shiver of wanting whipped through her. He'd come to her, she thought, wildly. Everything was going to work out.

Before she knew what was happening, Trent's nimble fingers had found their way between the folds of her robe, igniting the bare skin beneath. She let out a soft gasp.

Urgently he lowered her down to the thick carpeted floor. She clung to him, too overwhelmed to speak.

"I know I shouldn't have come here. But I can't stop thinking about you," he groaned in a ragged whisper, his breath hot against her exposed neck. Like a man starved for physical contact, he kissed her ears, her cheeks, caressed her narrow waist, suckled her breasts. "I couldn't imagine the night without you."

He rose up on his knees and tore the shirt from his body. The tiny buttons scattered across the floor. He quickly unbuckled his pants and kicked them away, holding her in place with the heated intensity of his gaze.

Then, as if in slow motion, he lowered himself above her. "I love you Noelle," he whispered, "more than I've ever loved any other woman. Don't ever doubt that."

It's true, her heart sang madly. She cradled his face in her hands, her eyes glistening with pure joy.

"I love you, too, Cole," she cried. "And nothing else matters." Her eyes slid shut as his lips met hers, her willing body welcoming their union.

Joseph stared in disbelief at the handwritten report in front of him. How could this be possible?

He turned over his options in his head. If he told Gina, she would be forced to confess her screw-up to Noelle and undoubtedly lose her job. If he went to Noelle, she would certainly think that he'd concocted the entire story.

He leaned back in his leather chair, steepling his long fingers against his chin. There had to be another way, and there had to be some crucial bit of information that he was missing.

He reached across his desk and buzzed for his secretary.

"Yes, Mr. Malone," Alice answered promptly.

"Alice get me the entire file on Jordan Maxwell. And check with all of the hotels in Los Angeles. I want to find out if Trent Dixon is registered in any of them."

"Right away, Mr. Malone."

There had to be something in the file that he'd missed. Something that would explain everything.

His private line rang.

"Yes?"

"Joseph, it's me Gina."

"Gina." He thought quickly. "I'm sorry but I still don't have anything yet. It's taking longer than I thought."

Gina swallowed. "Joseph, I just got a call from Senator Thomas. He pushed up his arrival. He'll be here late this evening."

Somehow Noelle and Trent found their way to her bedroom. A soft breeze blew in from the terrace window. The afternoon sun blazed through the sheer curtains. Noelle curled closer to Trent, listening to the pulse beat in his neck.

"I'm glad you came, Cole," she said softly. "There're so many things I want to say to you."

Trent took a deep, guilty breath. He knew he couldn't let her go on believing that there was any hope for a future with them. It was an impossibility.

He kissed the top of her head. "I'm leaving in the morning, Noelle," he blurted out before he had a chance to change his mind.

Her head pounded. She couldn't be hearing right. A suffocating sensation tightened her throat. *He didn't say that he was leaving.* "But you'll be coming back." She struggled for control.

"I don't think so," he answered softly.

A new anguish lashed at her heart.

"I got an offer to do a major consulting job in Washington. It could take—a long time," he added weakly.

Her voice trembled. "How long?"

"Months."

"I see." But she didn't see. She couldn't and she didn't want to.

She got up from the bed and slipped back into her robe, for the first time feeling naked before his eyes.

She wouldn't cry, she vowed. She'd walked into this relationship with her eyes wide open. No promises had been made. So nothing had been broken. Except her heart, which was shattering into tiny bits.

Her throat constricted. She spun toward him, her eyes burning with restrained agony. "Will you write?"

She sounded like a wounded child, begging for release from the pain, he thought mournfully.

He got up and went to her and was met with stony resistance. She kept her arms wrapped stiffly around her body.

He held her shoulders instead. "Noelle, I—I wish things could be different." He struggled for words. "I wish that our lives were different. But they're not. I can't offer you the things that you need. The things that you deserve."

You can, she thought wildly, feeling her world slipping from beneath her feet. *You are what I need. All that I need.*

She remained silent.

He turned away, unable to look at the despair that darkened her eyes.

"I'd better go," he said softly.

"I think that's best."

She stood motionless, facing the window, listening intently to every move of his departure.

The sound of his voice rocked her.

"I got the report from my investigator," he said to her stiff back.

Her voice was empty of emotion. "Just leave it on the table—on your way out."

The next sound she heard was the door closing softly behind him.

Slowly she turned around, her glistening eyes searching the space that they had so recently shared. *Empty.*

Drawn like a magnet, she walked over to the bed, absently touching the sheets. His scent still lingered in the air. She breathed deeply, and turned away.

All of the hurt, the loneliness, the insults, the inability to fit in, could never compare to the devastation that consumed her heart at this moment.

But as with all of the other hurts, she would store it away where it couldn't touch her. She would go on with her life as she'd always done. She would continue to conquer the obstacles and she would do it alone. As she'd always done.

Purposefully, she walked into the small sitting room and saw the thin brown envelope on the table.

She picked up the envelope and stared at it for several long minutes. Then she ripped it to shreds. Letting the pieces fall to the floor. The only emotion she had left now was her hatred for Trent. It would be what propelled her. It would make her forget Cole. She couldn't risk the chance that the words contained on those pages would vindicate him. Then she would have nothing to hold on to.

It was over, he thought, tossing the last of his possessions in his bag. He looked around the room for the last time.

I thought you were a better man than that. Nick's accusing words echoed in his head.

He picked up his suitcase and garment bag and walked out of the door.

Maybe he'd make a stop in Philadelphia and see his family before he returned to Sudan. He would need the fortification of his family to face the turmoil that would confront him in the coming weeks.

The company could survive only if Noelle's proposal was accepted.

He stepped onto the elevator. He'd have to find another job, of course, but that could wait. He pressed the button for the lobby. But he did want to tie up all of the loose ends.

Maybe one day, Noelle would somehow find out the truth about Jordan and find her way back to him. *Right.*

He cursed the day he'd made that pact. But if he hadn't, he might have never experienced the love he shared with Noelle. That would have to be his consolation.

He walked up to the registration counter.

"Mr. Richards," Gina said, *or whoever you are,* "what can I do for you?"

"I'm checking out." He placed his key on the countertop.

"Is something wrong? Are the accommodations a problem? I'd be happy to . . ."

"No." He waved his hand in dismissal. "Believe me everything here is wonderful." He smiled and the room lit up. Gina could instantly see Noelle's attraction. "I have some urgent business to attend to and I have to leave earlier than I expected."

"Well if you'll just wait a moment, I'll calculate your bill and draw up a check for a refund. Unless you'd prefer it in cash."

He reached down and picked up his luggage. "No refund is necessary."

"But Mr. Richards, our policy is . . ."

"Believe me, my stay here was well worth every cent."

"At least let me call Mrs. Maxwell. I'm sure she'll want to know you're leaving."

"She knows," he said. And Gina could have sworn she heard a tinge of sadness in his deep voice.

She followed him with her eyes as he crossed the marble lobby. Just before he reached the door, Noelle emerged from the elevator. For a brief, painful moment their eyes held. In that instant, Gina witnessed the undeniable electricity that sparked like fireworks between them, and the sadness that lingered in their gazes.

And then he was gone.

She saw Noelle raise her chin in determination as she turned and walked away.

* * *

Noelle sat in her office, perilously close to tears. She stared at the mail, the invoices, the reports without seeing them.

How long would the pain last? she wondered. A week? A month? Eternity?

One thing she was certain of, she realized, she couldn't allow what had happened between her and Cole to overshadow her entire life. If she'd learned one thing from Jordan, it was that you could never allow your personal feelings to compromise your business objectives.

She spun her chair around to face the window. In retrospect it was the same movement Jordan had exhibited when he was in deep thought, she realized suddenly. What would he have done, she wondered?

Then, a long-forgotten memory struggled to the surface and took shape in her head.

Jordan was sitting at his desk, much as she was now, pensively staring out of the window. Less than an hour earlier, they'd had a heated argument about his exporting of goods out of Sudan. She had been vehement in her disapproval and had questioned his ethics. She could immediately see that her emotional outburst affected him, even though his face remained impassive. But his dark eyes held the sting of her words.

When she'd walked into his office, much later, and found him there, his voice was calm, his eyes direct and full of purpose. He turned from the window to face her.

"I understand your objections to what I do, Noelle," he'd said. "But I can never let personal feelings, even yours, compromise my business objectives. Maxwell Enterprises is in the business of making money. What I do makes money. Unfortunately, it may not be in the manner you see fit." He stood up, his broad shoulders filling his Italian suit jacket. "One day you'll understand that."

Maybe now she finally understood.

She stood up. And her objectives were to make Liaisons the most successful enterprise of its kind. She would reshape Maxwell Enterprises. She would throw all of her energies and her resources to reaching her goals. And in time, Cole Richards would be no more than a vague memory.

She could do that, she thought, with renewed determination. She could wish him away. She could do anything. Hadn't she been told that a million times? She—was Noelle St. James-Maxwell. And the process would begin *now.*

Eighteen

Nick sat in open-mouthed disbelief. The magnitude of what Trent had revealed to him left him speechless.

Now everything made sense in a mad, almost insane kind of way. Jordan Maxwell had been a troubled man. A man consumed by his own power, and he had skillfully wielded that power around Trent.

"Who else knows about this?" Nick finally asked.

Trent heaved a sigh. "No one. The only person who could come close to putting the pieces together would be Joseph Malone, Jordan's attorney."

"You can't just leave it like this, Trent."

"I have no other choice. I swore I would never tell her."

"But what could it matter now? He's dead. And it wasn't your fault. She's got to find out eventually."

"Not from me. And now, in my stupidity, I've complicated matters so much that she'd probably believe that I'm making the whole thing up.

"You see, Jordan never wanted Noelle to run

the corporation out of loyalty. That was the one thing he was adamant about. He understood that the main reason why she stayed in the marriage was out of loyalty. He didn't want her to spend the rest of her life feeling like she owed him something. If she ever found out what was really going on, that would be her reason. That's just the type of woman she is."

Nick ran his hand across his smooth face. "I wish there was something I could do, besides say that I'm sorry."

Trent chuckled mirthlessly. *"You're* sorry. No one could be sorrier than I am."

"Did you give her the report?"

Trent nodded.

"Well, it clearly says that you had nothing to do with the crash. Wasn't that the proof that she needed?"

"I wish it were that simple. The report doesn't explain why I've been lying to her all of this time." He paused then looked directly at Nick. "And the report will never explain what really happened."

Nick frowned. "What do you mean?"

"There are things that have been removed."

Gina sat in her office and dialed Joseph's private line. He answered on the first ring.

"It's me Joseph. There've been some changes."

"What kind of changes?" he asked scanning the hotel information that Alice had just brought in.

"Cole Richards checked out about a half hour ago."

His head snapped up. "Did he say why or where he was going?"

"He just said he had some important business come up."

Joseph's jaw clenched. *He didn't go very far.*

"How soon can you get away?" he asked.

"I'm off at seven."

"Can you meet me at my house?"

"What is it Joseph? Have you found out anything?"

"Let's just say that the pieces are beginning to fall in place. I'll know more later. I have to make a few calls and go out for a while. I'll see you tonight."

He hung up, and quickly dialed the Los Angeles Hilton.

"Hilton Hotel," the clipped voice answered.

"Yes, I'm trying to reach Mr. Trent Dixon."

"I'll put you through to the switchboard."

The phone rang three times before it was answered.

"Hilton Hotel."

"Trent Dixon please."

"One moment."

The phone rang at least a dozen times. Joseph was just about to hang up.

"Hello?"

"Trent! Joseph Malone. I heard you were in town. I'm glad I caught you." He paused. "We need to talk. I'm on my way to your hotel. I can be there in fifteen minutes." Joseph hung up before Trent had a chance to respond.

"Ambassador Nkiru, I'm so happy you called."

"My daughter said it was urgent," he responded, the soft lilt of his homeland of Ghana evident in his voice. "What can I do for you?"

For the next half hour, Noelle laid out the details of her plan to Nkiru. "I have the resources to do this Mr.—Ambassador Nkiru. I'm sure that if you intervene with this proposal the government would be responsive." She held her breath.

Kenyatta Nkiru could hardly believe what he had just heard. How long had the government of Sudan waited for some relief from their poverty? The nations of the world had all but ignored them until it began to hit them in their pockets. Was this Noelle's objective also? He thought not.

"Mrs. Maxwell, your offer, though generous, may be too late. There has been such widespread destruction, it would take years to rebuild. What the people need now is food, immediate shelter and medicine. And who would train these people to do all of the things that you suggested?"

"Maxwell Enterprises would provide the initial training until the people were self-sufficient."

"You realize of course, that this idea of yours would be counterproductive to your own government?"

"What do you mean? How could the U.S. not want the people to be self-sufficient?"

"If all the people of the third world could fend for themselves there would be no need for *divine* intervention. The military budget is extremely high. And there are many who want to make sure that it stays that way. Now if there was no need to ship armaments and send in troops . . ." His voice trailed off.

A cold chill ran through her. "What can we do?"

"If you are as committed to this as you say you are, we'll find a way. Together. I'll be in touch with you as soon as I can."

"Thank you, Ambassador."

"No. Thank *you.*"

Noelle sat back, taking in the frightening words that had been hinted at but not spoken.

She was more determined than ever to make this a reality. And as much as she hated to admit it, she was going to need Trent Dixon's help. Whether she wanted it or not.

Nineteen

Noelle did a careful review of her financial assets. She would have to do some quick juggling.

She placed a call to her accountant, Sam Waters. Sam had been Noelle's personal accountant and financial advisor for the past five years. He knew her assets and liabilities like his own name. He was the type of man that she could call in the middle of the night and ask what her bank balances were, and he'd rattle them off without opening his eyes. Numbers were Sam Waters's life.

He'd given her sound financial advice over the years and he watched with pleasure as her fortune multiplied.

But Sam was annoyingly cautious, Noelle came to realize. He was never willing to take risks. He liked cold hard numbers, not big question marks.

That characteristic had them in their latest debate.

"I know what I'm doing Sam," Noelle said patiently for the third time. "I want my two largest personal accounts consolidated. I have to be able to show that I have the financial base to implement this plan successfully. I can't have my money spread all over."

"But Noelle," he cautioned, "do you realize the incredible amount of tax you'll have to pay on that money if you do that?" Automatically he punched numbers into his calculator.

"Of course I do. I worked out the figures. "$90,000.00."

She was right. As usual, he smiled. One thing he always admired about Noelle was her ability to manage numbers. She understood them and used them to her advantage. She would have made an excellent CPA, he always thought.

"All right. If you're sure," he finally agreed. "I'll get the ball rolling and contact the bank. They're going to have a fit when you pull out all of that money. It may effect your leverage with them if you ever want to borrow in the future."

Noelle thought about that for a moment. "You're right. Leave $100,000.00 in the account at Commerce and transfer the rest to First National. I'll send you my dividend check from Maxwell Enterprises, by messenger tomorrow. Deposit that with the $100,000.00. That should keep them happy."

Sam relaxed a little. "Wise decision. I'll call you tomorrow."

Next, she contacted her broker and advised her to liquidate $50,000.00 worth of her stock. Nina Armstrong was one of the top brokers in L.A. Her sixth sense when it came to picking the winners was almost eerie.

Fortunately, Nina took instruction extremely well and rarely did she question Noelle's judgment.

Noelle intended to use that cash to cover her monthly donation to the shop owner's fund in South Central. It would be a little short, this time, but she knew the anonymous donation would be well appreciated.

For the next two hours, Noelle sat in front of her computer, carefully detailing every phase of her proposal.

When she was done, the completed document was twenty pages long.

She leaned back in her seat and rotated her tight shoulders.

If only she could have the same control over her personal life, she thought miserably.

She pushed away from her desk and stood up. She'd promised herself that she would put Cole behind her and go on with her life. But it seemed as though whenever she took a breath she thought of him. *Maybe she should stop breathing*, she thought morosely.

She checked her gold, Cartier watch. The dinner hour was approaching. But she had enough time to change.

She switched off her computer and turned off the lights. Off in the distance she heard the low roar of a jet. Briefly she wondered if Cole was on that plane.

* * *

Joseph sat in the darkness of his den. The only light emanated from the last rays of sunshine.

His meeting with Trent had numbed him. He looked at the report that sat on his lap.

He had been so sure that he could nail Trent for somehow trying to manipulate Noelle. That theory went out of the window. Trent was as much a victim in this as Noelle.

He always knew that Jordan Maxwell was a force to be reckoned with. How many times had Jordan been able to convince wary stockholders that it was in their best interest to buy additional shares of stock, even when the stock market was falling? He was a great orator. He should have been in politics, Joseph mused. Jordan could make you believe that the moon rose at daybreak, if he chose. He was a shrewd businessman with the uncanny ability to zero in on a person's weakness and capitalize on it. What was more astounding was that it generally turned out to be in their best interest in the long run. Jordan ultimately achieved their lifelong loyalty as a result. Even from his grave, he was still the great manipulator. It was frightening.

After Joseph had departed from the suite, Trent and Nick sat quietly facing each other.

"What do you think Malone's going to do with what you told him?" Nick finally asked.

"I'm sure he'll go to Noelle with it. Why wouldn't he? I always knew he never gave her much credence. He'd probably get some kind of sadistic pleasure out of seeing the look on her face."

Nick hesitated a moment, reluctant to bring up the issue again, but knew that he must.

"Don't you think it would be better—a lot easier on Noelle—if it came from you? From what you're telling me about Malone, there's no telling what he might actually say."

Trent stared at his hands as if he hadn't heard anything Nick said.

Without a word he got up, shoving his hands in his pockets. His expression was impassive.

He gave Nick a sidelong glance. "You know I hate it when you're right. I'm going to take a shower and change. Then I'm going to drive out to see Noelle."

He started to move away, then stopped to toss a parting remark at the smug expression on Nick's face.

"I'm going, if for no other reason, just to shut you up. Finally."

"Whatever works," Nick grinned.

Noelle sat in front of her dressing-table mirror and applied a light stroke of coral lipstick to her mouth. With a thin black pencil, she lightly outlined the bottom rim of her eyes, making the chestnut brown orbs even more pronounced.

From her jewelry box, she selected a pair of diamond-and-gold teardrop earrings, the matching bracelet and choker.

She ran a wide-tooth comb through her chestnut hair, letting the satiny strands fall into place. Her hair had grown, she noticed, lifting the thick bang over her eyebrow. She decided not to cut it. *New life, new look,* she mused.

She had selected a sleeveless, calf-length Dior dress of off-white crepe. The two rows of buttons were fourteen-carat gold. The scoop neck showed off the choker to perfection. And the hip-high slits on either side gave ample walking room for her long legs.

She stood up and assessed herself in the full-length mirror. Now, if she only had someone to share her evening with, everything *would* be perfect.

She pushed aside the thought. She had guests who were expecting to see their sparkling hostess attending to their every need. She wouldn't disappoint them.

Trent slipped on his midnight blue Armani dinner jacket, over a pale-blue silk shirt.

He noticed a slight tremor in his fingers as he knotted the geometric, navy blue and pink silk tie. *Nerves.*

He stepped out into the sitting room, hearing the baleful strains of Nick's saxophone.

Nick stopped playing and looked up when Trent entered the room.

"Wish me luck," Trent said.

"You got it."

"See you later. Hopefully in one piece."

Trent tried to focus on the endless stretch of highway, but his thoughts kept drifting to his impending confrontation with Noelle.

How would he ever fully explain what he had done and why?

He stepped on the gas, screeching around the narrow turn, barely missing an oncoming sedan. *Damn, that was close.* His pulse raced as he tried to concentrate.

Images of Noelle loomed before him. He visualized her as he'd last seen her. The pain in her eyes was almost accusing. She didn't deserve that.

He wanted to erase that haunted look and replace it with the look of love that had filled and revived him. A look that he knew was reserved only for him.

His thoughts veered off to Joseph Malone. He stepped on the gas. He had to get to Noelle and explain before Joseph did. If he hadn't gotten to her already. If he didn't get to her first, he knew he wouldn't stand a chance in hell of salvaging anything.

His mind raced. His thoughts were colliding with one another. He didn't even see the other car coming.

Senator Thomas had yet to arrive before Gina left for the evening. If there was any justice in the world, maybe he would get called to make some national decision and not show up. Miracles like that never happen, she thought, pulling up in front of Joseph's white stucco house.

The house was dark. *Odd.* He did say to meet him when she got off.

Since he was expecting her, she used the spare key that he'd given her and let herself in.

She walked inside and switched on the hall light. That's when she saw his silhouette in the semidarkness.

"Joseph?"

She walked briskly down the corridor to the den. She switched on the light.

Slowly he turned his head in her direction. His smile was vacant.

"Joseph, are you all right?" She hurried across the room.

"Sit down."

She took a seat next to him and her heart raced with dread.

"What is it Joe? You're scaring me."

"I'm sorry. I didn't mean to. We need to talk—about what I found out."

"What is it?"

"I located Trent Dixon. I spoke with him."

Her eyes widened. "And?"

"I can't use what I found out, Gina. I won't. Noelle will have to find out some other way. It won't be from me."

"But Joseph, I don't understand. What could Trent have possibly said to you?"

* * *

Trent sat in his car, looking at the flashing lights of the police van up ahead. His head ached. He was lucky that the accident hadn't been worse. While no one was seriously hurt, the driver of the other car had insisted to the police that Trent must be drunk to have come flying around that curve and into the wrong lane.

Quick reflexes had allowed both drivers to barely escape a head-on collision.

Trent massaged his head. Joseph was probably bending Noelle's ear by now, he thought miserably. He couldn't begin to imagine what Joseph's version would do to her.

". . . Sir. Sir."

Trent snapped out of his thoughts and found a bright flashlight beaming in his face.

"Here's your license and registration. Do you want to go to the hospital?"

"No officer. I'm fine. Is it all right if I leave now?"

The officer looked toward the other vehicle. "You can go. But I suggest that you pay attention. These roads can be tricky if you're not familiar with them."

"Thank you, officer."

"Damn out-of-state drivers," he mumbled.

Slowly Trent eased the car out of the ditch and back onto the highway. *I'm probably too late*, he thought.

* * *

Noelle's first stop for the evening was the kitchen. It was bustling with activity.

Paul was busy giving out instructions and personally taste-testing the array of food and pastry that encompassed the entire state-of-the-art kitchen.

A cacophony of aromas assaulted her senses. She thought of her late-night dinners with Cole.

She moved on.

From there she went to the rooftop dining room. Tables were already occupied. She spotted Tempest and Braxton, their heads bent in intimate conversation. *At least someone was happy.*

She put her smile in place and stepped into the dining room.

There was a live jazz band playing some Miles Davis favorites in the background.

Noelle crossed the room and stopped at the table occupied by Gladys and Dionne, who after a little persuading agreed to do a duet at the end of the band's set.

After seeing to the seated guests, she went to the arch of the entranceway, to greet the incoming diners.

It seemed like an eternity since she stood in this very same spot and Cole walked through the door, she mused, smiling and shaking hands as the interesting assemblage of who's who entered the room.

Finally all but two tables were full. Satisfied, she turned away to make the rest of her rounds and walked smack into solid, hard muscle.

"This isn't the first time we've met like this,"

the voice that thrilled her said, bracing her shoulders to steady her.

Her eyes slowly trailed upward from the broad chest and locked onto the dark eyes that seemed to hold her in place.

Her voice sounded faint to her own ears. "Cole."

He felt her tremble through his fingertips.

"I had to come. I couldn't leave things the way they were between us."

She cleared her throat, and straightened her shoulders.

"I thought you'd made yourself pretty clear," she said stiffly. She eased out of his grasp, so he wouldn't feel the tremors that shook her body.

"Can we go somewhere and talk?"

"About what, Cole?" She wrapped her arms around her waist. Her eyes narrowed and her voice took on a steely edge. "Do you want to reaffirm your undying love for me and take me to bed—one more time, and then make your apologies?" she hissed. *She wouldn't cry.*

He lowered his gaze. "I deserved that." He looked up. "But it's not what it seems. It's much more complicated than that."

"Is it really?" she shot back.

"Please, Noelle."

For several interminable moments, they stood facing each other. A myriad of conflicting emotions assaulted her.

Her heart longed to be with him, to hear him out. Maybe there was some explanation that he could give her to take the emptiness away.

But her mind said—*no*. She couldn't subject herself to anymore hurt. It would be so much easier to just walk away. Yet she knew she would always have so many unanswered questions if she did.

"Please, Noelle," he repeated.

Her resolve weakened. She took a brief look over her shoulder. Everyone was absorbed in their conversation. The scene between her and Cole was going completely unnoticed.

"All right," she finally agreed. "Let's go out into the garden."

She brushed past him and walked out. Trent caught up with her as they reached the elevator.

Once inside they stood like two sentinels, stiff and silent. She wanted to ask him about the small gash over his eyebrow, but elected to feign indifference.

From the corner of his eye he watched her motionless form. She was so beautiful, and so hurt. His heart ached. It was his fault. She had every right to feel the way she did about him.

How could he make it all go away? He still struggled with the words he knew he would have to speak. What words could ever explain his role in this colossal game of deceit? She was right. All he really wanted to do was hold her—tell her how much he loved her and spend the rest of his life making her happy.

She couldn't look at him, because she knew if she did, she would run into his arms and tell him that nothing else mattered. Her heart pounded so forcefully it felt as if it would explode. Why had he come back? Why couldn't he just stay out of her life?

But deep inside of her soul, she knew that she would never stop wanting him even if he left this very minute and went to the end of the earth.

The doors slowly opened on the lobby level.

Noelle stepped out. Trent followed until they were side by side.

Trent saw him first, but it was too late.

Noelle kept her eyes straight ahead and didn't see Senator Thomas until she heard his voice.

"Noelle!" he called from across the wide corridor.

She stopped and turned, her eyes widening in surprise.

Trent tried to keep walking but Noelle stopped him with a touch.

Senator Thomas moved surprisingly quick for a man of his girth, Noelle thought absently.

The senator's smile was broad and encompassing, as he reached for Noelle and kissed her cheek. "Wonderful to see you."

Trent felt everything rapidly slipping away, when Thomas stuck out his hand.

"Trent Dixon. How long has it been?"

Trapped in a slow-motion nightmare, Noelle turned toward Trent and stared wordlessly at him as a wave of nausea threatened to overwhelm her.

Twenty

Her thoughts crashed against one another. Everything ceased to move. She couldn't think. She struggled to breathe.

This mustn't be true. But it was. Somewhere deep inside her soul, she knew.

The little slip-ups. His unusual knowledge about the business. The nightmare! It wasn't an air force accident. It was the crash with Jordan.

Lies! All lies!

She'd given herself to her husband's murderer. *Why was it so cold?* She began to tremble visibly.

"Noelle." The senator's voice drifted like a disembodied force to her brain. "Are you all right? You look ill."

Trent reached for her. "Noelle—please."

Her expression turned into a marble effigy of contempt. "Don't touch me," she whispered in a strangled voice.

Thomas scowled at Trent. "What's going on? Is he bothering you? I'll get . . ."

She held up her hand. "You're right, Richard," she said weakly. "I don't feel well." She didn't need a scene. Her smile was tremulous. "Working too hard. I just need some air."

She spun away, nearly running for the exit.

Trent started off after her, but Thomas grabbed his arm.

"I don't know what's going on here and maybe I don't need to know. But you and I have known each other for a while Trent, and your reputation with the ladies precedes you."

The senator remembered all too well their rivalry over the same woman. Trent had won, and the senator's pride was still bruised, years later. That score was never settled. But Noelle wasn't that kind of woman. He'd realized that, years ago, the moment Jordan had introduced his new wife.

"I'd hate to find out that you're the cause of her distress." His stony eyes locked with Trent's. "You do understand me?"

Trent snatched his arm away. "You're right, Richard, this doesn't concern you." He turned without another word and ran for the exit.

By the time he reached the garden, Noelle was in her car tearing out of the driveway.

Burning tears nearly blinded her as she sped down the open roadway. Her head was pounding. She had to get away, as far away from Trent Dixon as possible.

How could she have been so blind, so gullible? She'd been used, masterfully, by the one man she'd sworn to despise.

"Oh, Jordan, I'm so sorry," she cried out loud. "You wanted me to trust him and unknowingly I did. I trusted him with my heart, my body."

Every scene of their lovemaking burst before her eyes. An agonized scream tore from her throat.

The high beam of headlights reflected in her rear-view mirror. Another car was barreling down on her. *Cole—Trent*. She stepped on the accelerator.

The speeding Lexus raced to close the distance between them.

Noelle took a sharp turn onto the back road that she knew so well. Within moments, she was swallowed up in the darkness.

Trent lost sight of her as the taillights disappeared into tiny specks.

Twenty-one

Noelle continued to drive with no destination in mind. She kept driving aimlessly down the road until she reached the highway entrance. Somehow she found her way onto the exit to Los Angeles. All she knew was that she had to put as much distance as possible between her and Cole—Trent Dixon.

When she finally slowed down she was in the heart of Los Angeles. She looked around and saw the marquee of the Los Angeles Hilton Hotel. *This was where she'd seen him that day.*

What made her pull into the garage and walk to the reception desk, she didn't know. She seemed to be drawn by an invisible magnet, but hoping to find what?

"I'm looking for Cole, I mean, Trent Dixon's room," she said to the hotel clerk. How long would it take her to get the name Cole Richards out of her mind? she wondered absently.

"I'll ring the room," the clerk advised.

"I'd, uh, prefer if you didn't," Noelle said, putting on her best smile. "I want to surprise him."

"It's really against hotel policy," the clerk protested. "Mr. Dixon didn't advise us to allow . . ."

"Is there a problem?"

Noelle turned in the direction of the voice. A rather tall, unquestionably handsome man, dressed in faded jeans and a T-shirt approached. By his outfit, he couldn't be hotel staff, Noelle quickly surmised, unless he was security. She'd leave quietly, she thought.

Nick stood next to Noelle and immediately knew who she was. Everything that Trent had said about her was magnified a hundred times over.

"You must be Noelle," he said, his soothing voice putting her at ease. He looked across the desk at the clerk. "It's all right, miss," he smiled.

He took Noelle's arm and angled his chin in the direction of the lounge. "Let's go in here."

Obediently, Noelle allowed herself to be escorted into the dimly lit room.

He helped her into her chair and took a seat opposite her at the round table.

"Would you like something to drink? You look a bit shaken."

"No. No thank you." She fidgeted with the paper napkin and wondered, again, why she had come here.

Nick tried to figure out how to break the ice. She was obviously so distressed that she would walk away with a complete stranger.

"I guess you're wondering who I am," he said looking at her from beneath long, curling lashes.

She twisted her napkin between her fingers and didn't respond.

"I'm Nick Hunter, Trent's friend."

For the first time since they sat down, she actually looked at him.

Her eyes registered on his face. "You're a friend of Cole's?" She swallowed. "Trent's?"

Nick nodded. "He came to see you, didn't he?" he asked gently.

Her bottom lip quivered. "Yes."

"Then you know everything."

She stared directly at him, each word that she uttered a condemnation, cold and exacting.

"All I know, Nick Hunter, is that your friend lied to me for some sick reason. He used me for his own, personal satisfaction. And I fell for it—every sweet word." Her voice broke. "Every sweet touch."

She turned her head to hide the tears and abruptly rose from her seat. "I don't even know why I came here."

Nick got up and put a restraining hand on her arm. "Wait. Please. What did he tell you?"

"He didn't tell me anything. We ran into an old friend of his."

"Joseph Malone?"

"What?"

"Did Joseph Malone come to see you?"

She frowned in confusion. "Why would he?"

"He paid Trent a visit today."

"What? Why?"

"Please sit back down," he urged. He released her arm when she did.

"Listen, Trent got in this thing way over his head." Nick took a breath. "The bottom line is, he made a promise, more of a pact with your husband. A pact that he swore to Jordan he'd never reveal to you."

"What kind of pact?" Noelle asked bewildered. "What are you talking about? And what does Joseph have to do with it?"

"Trent wouldn't tell me everything. And I left the room when Malone showed up. All I know is that it had to do with the accident. Trent didn't cause it. Jordan manipulated him, and ultimately you as well."

"You're lying for him. I don't believe you!" she said through clenched teeth, her eyes sparking with rage. "Trent did it. What other reason could he have for trying to pass himself off as someone else? He knew how I felt about him and about what he'd done. It was the only way he could—get to me. To score some points."

"You don't have to believe me, Noelle. But believe this. I've known Trent Dixon for more years than I care to count. And what I know about him is that he's a man of his word." His voice softened. "He'd risk losing you rather than break that promise he made to Jordan. That should say something about the kind of man he is."

He halted, waiting for his words to sink in. "Another thing I know—he loves you. And I don't think you'd be this upset if you didn't feel the same way."

He reached across the table and covered her hand with his. "You fell in love with the man, not the name. Doesn't that tell you something?"

Noelle looked at Nick, seeing the sincerity in his

eyes. And suddenly she knew that what he'd said was true.

"So what do I do now? I've got to know. If Trent won't tell me, then I know who will." She abruptly rose to leave.

"Where are you going?"

"To see Joseph Malone."

Nick got up. "I'm going with you."

They walked toward the exit.

"Where's Trent?" Nick asked.

"I don't know. He tried to follow me, but I lost him on the back roads out of the villa."

"He'll eventually come back here. Do you want to wait it out?"

"No. I need to talk with Joseph, now. The next time I see Trent I want the slate to be clear between us. He'll never have to tell me anything he swore he wouldn't."

Maybe it was better this way, Trent thought as the lights from the airstrip winked, up ahead. Maybe he deserved this for using Thomas' name. Maybe it was fate.

Fate had taken it out of his hands.

He switched on the windshield wipers as a slow drizzle began to fall.

Everything was coming apart. In ten days the banks would demand their money and when they didn't get it, Noelle would lose Liaisons. And if she doesn't step in as CEO, as required by the agreement, Maxwell Enterprises will collapse. But

Jordan, Trent mused, I believe Noelle may just outwit you this time. *The student teaching the teacher.* Noelle was resourceful. She had a brilliant mind and more business acumen that even Jordan had given her credit for. Knowing Noelle as he did, Noelle would find a way to run Maxwell and keep the villa. He felt certain that she would be able to put her plan in motion. Would it be in time?

He parked the car in front of the hangar and got out.

Bill Cochran trotted out to meet him.

"Mr. Dixon. What are you doing out here?"

"I need a plane," he stated in a flat voice.

"I'll juice one up for you. Going far?"

His laugh was hollow. "As far as I can."

Moments later he was in the air, soaring above the clouds, high up in the environment that he loved.

He let his mind wander, forgetting about the rain, his fears. He forced his body to relax as the comforting sensation of flight seeped through his veins.

Thunder rolled around him, but he ignored it. He should have followed Nick's advice a long time ago, he mused, as the tiny plane was buffeted around the heavens.

Visibility was getting poor, and the winds were picking up. He checked the dials. He was losing altitude.

He tried to pull the nose up but it wouldn't budge.

He tried again.

Nothing.

Bill Cochran cupped his hand over his eyes and looked up. He could have sworn that plane was at a funny angle. He shrugged. Dixon knew what he was doing. He turned to get in out of the rain when he caught a glimpse of thick, black smoke trailing through the air.

He trotted forward to get a better look, when flames leaped from the engine. He tore off toward the hangar to call for help, when the explosion threw him to the ground.

Twenty-two

By the time Noelle and Nick pulled up in front of Joseph's house, it was raining heavily.

"Maybe we should have called first," Nick said, quickly coming around to open the door for Noelle.

She stepped out. "No. That would have just given him time to think of a way out of it."

They darted toward the door together and stood under the shelter of the canopy. Noelle rang the bell.

"Are you expecting anyone?" Gina asked, slipping into a robe.

Joseph frowned. "No. I'll get rid of whoever it is." He opened the door. His face reddened.

"Noelle?" He tightened the belt on his robe and looked nervously at Noelle and Nick. "What are you doing here? Is something wrong?"

"Something is very wrong, Joe. And I think you know about it."

"If it's something to do with the will, I'd be happy to . . ."

"It's a lot deeper than that," she said, cutting

him off. "May we come in? Or would you rather have this conversation on your porch?"

He quickly glanced over his shoulder, thinking of Gina.

"Come in," he said finally. He led them into the den.

"I understand you've already met Nick Hunter," she said following him down the hallway.

"Yes," he answered halfheartedly. "We've met."

After they were seated, Noelle wasted no time in getting to the point.

"I know that Cole Richards is really Trent Dixon. I want you to tell me the rest."

"How did you find out?" Joseph asked slowly.

"Senator Richard Thomas arrived at Liaisons this evening. He recognized Trent. It seems they're old friends."

Joe pursed his lips. "Then I don't see why you're here."

Noelle leaned forward. "I need your help Joseph. I know we haven't had the best of relationships over the years, but I hope that you will put your feelings for me aside and tell me what was in Jordan's codicil. Whatever it is, it's the reason why Trent felt compelled to masquerade as Cole Richards." She paused. "Trent won't tell me, because he made some sort of pact with Jordan. You were Jordan's attorney. You had to be a part of it."

Joe leaned back and rested his head against the cushion. He inhaled deeply, weighing his options. He could stick by lawyer-client privilege. But at this point, he knew that premise was absurd.

He looked across at Noelle for a short moment and in that instant he plainly saw the love she had for Trent. He'd seen the same look in Gina's eyes. It was undeniable. And for the first time in his life he understood it.

His conscience tore at him. From the day that he'd written the document, he knew it was a cruel epitaph. But who was he to argue? Jordan was one of his biggest clients.

"Tell her, Joseph."

All eyes turned toward the doorway where Gina stood.

Noelle's mouth opened, but no words came out.

Gina walked to Joseph's side and took his hand. "Believe me, Joseph didn't know that Trent Dixon was masquerading as Cole Richards." She sat down on the arm of the chair. She looked at him, then back to Noelle who was still trying to digest what was unfolding in front of her.

"He only found out yesterday that Cole Richards never existed."

Noelle finally found her voice. "Did you know what was going on Gina?"

"No, Mrs. Maxwell. Believe me, I had no idea. I only found out he wasn't who he said, when the senator called."

Gina lowered her eyes. "I let it slip that his reference, Cole Richards was staying with us. The senator had never heard of him. I guess I panicked. I called Joseph. When you called, I was too afraid to tell you. I was hoping that Joe could help in some way. And he did."

Gina turned to Joe. She took his hands in hers, giving him the strength and comfort that he needed.

"Tell her the rest," she urged him gently.

Slowly he nodded. "It'll probably be easier if I just let you read the codicil."

He pushed himself up from his seat and left the room. In his small office he spun the dial on the wall safe.

"How long have—you been seeing each other?" Noelle asked Gina hesitantly.

"Almost two years. He's really a wonderful person, Mrs. Maxwell," she emphasized. "I know that may be hard for you, or anyone to believe, but he is."

Noelle looked at Gina and saw the strength of her love and conviction reflected in her eyes. "Gina, if you feel that strongly about him, then I know it must be true." She smiled gently. "I always told you I had the greatest confidence in the world in you. As long as you're happy, that's what's important."

Joseph stood in the doorway, catching the last strains of the conversation. He and Gina had greatly underestimated Noelle Maxwell. He'd been wrong about her from the beginning. He had been so blinded by the dollar signs and protecting Jordan's interests, when he really should have been protecting Noelle's.

Maybe now he could begin to make that up to her. This was the first step.

He walked into the room. Without a word, he handed her the copy of Jordan's codicil.

Twenty-three

The rescue squad combed the wooded area. Wreckage was everywhere. But no body had been found.

The news crew from KABC in Los Angeles were the first reporters on the scene.

"This is the kinda stuff that makes the eleven o'clock," Bill overheard one of the cameramen say.

He stayed as far away from them as possible. He didn't want to be interviewed.

The fire department worked feverishly to extinguish the many small blazes that had erupted from the sparks.

Bill nervously paced back and forth in front of the hangar. He knew there'd be an investigation. His father would be furious. It was his responsibility to make sure each aircraft was in perfect running condition.

But over the past few months, revenue had been low. Bills were piling up. So he'd used shortcuts to curtail some of the costs. Instead of bringing in the technicians to service the planes, he'd done much of the maintenance himself. He'd been lucky. Until now.

* * *

"Over here!" Bill heard one of the workers yell.

There was a flurry of activity as a half-dozen men from the rescue squad, followed by two cameramen and the anchor woman from KABC, ran toward the beckoning voice.

Moments later, the screeching wail of the ambulance's siren pierced the night air.

Bill watched in dread as the red and white vehicle raced down the roadway.

A short, rather heavyset man approached and identified himself as Detective Dumont.

"You run this operation?" he asked, gruffly.

Bill nodded, nervously. "Yeah, me and my pop."

Dumont pulled out his notebook and began to ask a series of questions.

"What was the time of departure? Did the victim seem sober at the time? Where was he going? Was his pilot's license checked?"

Dumont scribbled down all of the answers, then snapped his book shut.

"Oh, one more question, Mr. Cochran. Is there anyone that you know of that should be contacted?"

"He was here the other day with a lady," Bill offered.

"You have a name?"

"Noelle Maxwell."

Dumont's eyes widened. "*The* Noelle Maxwell that just opened that ritzy joint in the valley?"

"Yes sir."

He flipped his pad back open and made a note. "Thank you. I'll be sure she's notified."

He had always wanted to get a peek at Liaisons. Now he had a damned good reason.

Noelle was visibly shaken when she completed reading the contents of the will.

"I—just can't believe Jordan would do such a thing," she said in a strained monotone. She looked up at Joseph as if searching for some explanation.

"He was determined that you would take over the running of the company. At any cost," Joe said. "Trent was to see to it that you were capable of managing it. Jordan knew that you would never do it voluntarily because you'd always been very clear in your views of the corporation and its methods of operation. So Jordan made sure you had no alternative. He used Liaisons as collateral for the bank loans. And he knew you'd do whatever it took to save Liaisons. You would have to step in as CEO with all of your resources. Jordan viewed Liaisons as a lark, so to speak. If you found a way to keep it . . ." Joseph shrugged his shoulders.

"Trent was caught in the middle," Nick added. "Even though he had promised Jordan that he would carry out his wishes, he wanted to ensure that you didn't lose Liaisons in the process."

"That would explain his insistence on my pursuing the expansion of Maxwell Enterprises," Noelle said almost to herself. "But something else is missing," she continued. "Jordan was not the kind of man to just blindly pursue anything. I realize that his company meant everything to him. Something motivated him to go to such lengths, beside the fact that he wanted me to run it."

"The only person who would know that is Trent," Joseph said.

Noelle rose. "I can't thank you enough, Joseph," she said sincerely. "I know this was difficult for you to do."

Joseph heaved a sigh. "It's something I should have done a long time ago."

Noelle and Nick returned to the car.

"I've got to find him, Nick," she said, quickly turning on the ignition. "He's off somewhere believing the worst, thinking that I hate him for what he's done. I've got to find him before he leaves."

Twenty-four

It was well after 2:00 A.M. by the time Detective Dumont arrived at Liaisons.

As soon as he stepped through the door the atmosphere made him hold in his stomach, stand up straight, and wish that he had shined his shoes.

Self-consciously, he smoothed his wrinkled suit as he approached the reception desk. He tried not to act like a tourist as he took in the decor from the corner of his eye.

Carol was completely absorbed in her latest romance novel. She had just reached the part where the two lovers were on the brink of making love.

Dumont cleared his throat so loudly, she dropped her book with a thud.

"I'm so sorry," she apologized, her face crimson with embarrassment. "May I help you?"

He flashed his badge, and she nearly choked.

"I'm looking for Noelle Maxwell," he said sternly, enjoying the look of fear in her eyes. That was the one pleasure in being a cop, he'd always thought, you had the power to intimidate. And he enjoyed it to the fullest every chance he got.

Carol swallowed back the knot in her throat.

"Mrs. Maxwell is not in the building." She tried to remember what she was supposed to say next, but the big burly cop who looked like he wanted to grind her to pieces, made her forget everything.

He wanted to laugh, but instead he hardened his look even more. He leaned across the counter.

"Do you know how she can be reached?"

"I can call her on her car phone," she offered up as sacrifice.

"You do that."

With shaky fingers Carol punched the numbers into the mobile phone. It rang ten times before she hung up.

"No answer."

"Okay." His demeanor softened. He'd had enough fun for the evening. "When she returns, or as soon as you hear from her, tell her that a friend of hers, Trent Dixon, is in Memorial Hospital. She should try to get there as soon as possible."

Carol quickly jotted down the information. She looked up and smiled weakly. "I'll be sure to give her the message."

"Good girl." He started to leave, then stopped. "How much does it cost to spend a night in a place like this?"

"$2,500.00," she said, "all amenities included," she added gaining immense pleasure from the look of astonishment on his face.

He left without another word.

Carol looked down at the neatly written message and wondered who Trent Dixon was.

* * *

Noelle hadn't said a word all the way back to the Hilton.

Once they returned to the suite, and discovered that Trent had not come back, Noelle insisted, against Nick's protestations that she had to get back. The combination of the emotional shocks that she had endured—together with pure exhaustion—were taking their toll. She wanted to be alone. She needed to think.

"Are you sure you can make the drive back alone?" Nick worried.

"I'll be fine. I've done it dozens of times. And anyway I want to be there in case Trent decides to come back."

She reached through the open car window and clasped his hand. "Thank you for everything, Nick. Trent is really lucky to have a friend like you."

He gave her a half smile. "I tell him that all the time."

"Call me when he arrives. I'm beginning to worry."

He hadn't wanted to say anything, but he was starting to worry also.

Dr. Kevin Holloway was the Chief of Surgery at Memorial Hospital. He was on duty when Trent was rushed into the trauma room. He'd practiced internal medicine for nearly twenty years. Most people would be hardened by the pain and suffering they witnessed daily. But for Kevin Holloway, each case was special and each patient's life was just as precious as the next.

"Vitals are weak, doc," the EMS worker said. "We had to resuscitate on the way over."

Holloway quickly peered into Trent's dilated pupils with his pen light. His trained eyes did a rapid visual assessment of the external injuries, while his fingers gently probed the inert body.

He looked over at his nurse. "Get Carson in here, stat. I'm going to need him in the O.R. If he's not in the building, have him paged. And order a CAT scan."

"Yes, doctor." The nurse rushed from the room.

Moments later, the squalling sound of the intercom blared throughout the hospital.

"Dr. Matthew Carson. Dr. Carson, trauma room one, stat."

Within moments, Matthew Carson appeared at Trent's side. To look at him, one would never imagine that this painfully thin, rather meek-looking man, was one of the leading neurosurgeons in the state. Most people thought that he was no more than twenty-five years old. He was much closer to forty.

"What've we got?" Carson asked.

"Plane crash. He's pretty messed up inside," Holloway explained. "We're trying to stabilize him before going into the O.R. No known relatives. The police are trying to track them down."

Carson took a look into Trent's eyes. "Hmm, not good. Has a CAT scan been ordered?"

"Done."

"Has he been conscious at all?"

"Not a peep. That's why I want you in the O.R. to observe. Just in case."

"Let's go. I'll look at the pictures then."

Each step was a task. Every fiber of her being ached. Her eyes felt like they had been loaded with sand. Her brain seemed to have turned to sludge, from her having tried to absorb everything that had taken place over the past few hours.

She still found it hard to believe the things that she'd been told. She thought she knew her husband. In reality, she didn't know him at all.

Jordan had been driven by his own obsession for control.

From the moment that he'd walked through the doors of her aunt's cafe, he'd controlled her life. She had been so desperate for escape from the life she lived, that she had willingly succumbed.

Even now, when she had finally found her place in the world and a man to share it with, he was still in control.

Noelle pushed through the doorway of Liaisons. She wouldn't allow him to control her any longer. If she'd learned nothing else from Jordan, she learned what power can do. And she intended to use hers to the fullest.

She was so caught up in her own thoughts, she

didn't stop by reception, but went straight to the elevator. She'd take a quick shower and then call Nick. Hopefully, Trent had returned by now.

She pressed the UP button, just as Carol ran up behind her.

"Mrs. Maxwell."

Noelle spun around, a smile of greeting on her face.

"Mrs. Maxwell," she began breathlessly, "the police were here."

The smile faded in degrees. "What?"

She nodded vigorously. "He left this message for you." She stuck out the slip of paper.

Noelle read the words and her hand began to tremble.

"How—long ago was he here?"

"About an hour." Carol looked at Noelle's stricken face. "Are you all right, Mrs. Maxwell?"

Noelle nodded, but knew she was far from all right.

She felt frozen. For several moments she just stared at the piece of paper. She couldn't think straight. She didn't know what to do first.

The elevator door opened and Noelle snapped to attention. She had to go to him.

"If anyone is looking for me, I'll be at Memorial Hospital."

She brushed past Carol, ran across the corridor and out the door.

Twenty-five

Memorial Hospital was more than a half hour away. Only critical cases were taken to Memorial. Her heart pounded. *Trent was critical.*

She floored the gas. She'd be there in fifteen minutes.

Nick couldn't sleep. The soundless television watched him. He glanced at the bedside clock. It was almost 4:00 A.M. Trent hadn't returned and he hadn't called.

Maybe he'd gone back to Liaisons. He reached for the phone. But something on the screen caught his attention. He pressed the volume button on the remote control.

". . . we're here at Cochran Airstrip where a little more than an hour ago, a small aircraft registered to Trent Dixon, an employee of Maxwell Enterprises, has gone down . . ."

Nick sat straight up in the bed.

". . . the victim has been rushed to Memorial Hospital in critical condition. We'll have . . ."

He didn't hear any more. He grabbed the phone and dialed Liaisons.

Mrs. Maxwell isn't available," Carol informed the caller. "She left about five minutes ago."

"Did she say where she was going? Nick pressed.

"Oh, yes. She's on her way to Memorial Hospital. She did say to . . ." The dial tone hummed in her ear.

Carol shook her head dismissively as she replaced the receiver. *This has been some night.*

Nurses and doctors alike turned and stared when Noelle ran down the hospital corridor to the information desk.

She looked like someone straight out of a Hollywood movie, from her obviously expensive clothing to the stylish hairdo, right to those brilliant brown eyes.

Breathless, Noelle stopped at information.

"There was a man brought in about an hour ago. Trent Dixon. Where is he?"

The overworked receptionist checked the computer.

"He's in surgery, ma'am."

She felt faint.

"Are you a relative?"

"Yes. No." Noelle wrung her hands. "I'm a close friend."

"You can go up to the third floor. Dr. Holloway is in charge of the case."

"*Merci.*"

When Noelle arrived on the third floor, she was escorted to a small lounge area by a nurse.

"It may be a while," the nurse advised. "There's a coffee machine against the wall."

"Will someone let me know what's happening?" She knew she sounded like a frightened child but she couldn't help it.

The nurse patted Noelle's shoulder. "As soon as they come out of surgery, I'll let Dr. Holloway know you're here," she said soothingly, seeing the anguish in her eyes.

Noelle swallowed and struggled not to cry. "Thank you."

The nurse turned away and left Noelle alone in the room.

"I can't lose you. Not now," she cried in a strangled whisper.

"How are his vitals?" Holloway called out over his mask.

"Weak. His pressure is dropping. Fast."

The surgical nurse wiped Holloway's brow.

"I can't stop this bleeding."

"We're losing him, doc."

Suddenly, the ominous sound of the heart monitor blared in a piercing, steady drone.

"Paddles!" Holloway barked. *Don't let me lose this one,* he prayed.

Nick rushed through the lounge door, and found Noelle huddled in the corner of the tweed sofa.

She looked up and the agony he saw in her tear-filled eyes tore through his gut as sharp as a samurai sword.

He hurried to her side and put his arm around her trembling shoulders. The last of her strength crumbled. Hot tears ran down her cheeks as deep sobs racked her insides. He held her in silence until the tears slowly ebbed. His eyes asked the unspoken question.

"He's in surgery," Noelle was able to say.

Nick briefly shut his eyes in relief. "Have you heard anything?"

She shook her head. "How did you know?" She sniffed back the tears and wiped her eyes with the paper napkin that she'd balled in her fist.

"It was on the news."

"A car accident?" she asked, bewildered.

"That's what you think happened? Didn't anyone tell you?"

"No. Tell me what? Nick, what happened?"

He took a breath. "Trent was flying. He went back to Cochran and rented a plane. I don't know all of the details, but the plane went down. He was apparently thrown clear—before it exploded."

She felt as if she'd been slammed against a brick

wall. She wanted to scream, but no sound would come from her mouth.

The nightmare came hurtling back. Only now she was fully awake. *Jordan. Trent.* It was happening all over again and she felt herself slipping into that dark abyss of unspeakable pain.

"There's nothing else we can do," Holloway said heavily. He left the operating room.

Exhausted, mentally and physically, he stripped off his hospital garb.

Carson joined him at the sink. "You think they found any family members?"

"Hopefully."

"You want to tell them, or should I?"

"I guess I should. I'm the doctor of record."

Carson patted him solidly on the back. "If it's any consolation buddy, you did a helluva job. No one else could have done more."

Holloway barely nodded his thanks.

Twenty-six

Noelle and Nick both jumped up when a grim-faced man in a white hospital jacket came to the door. He stepped inside and approached Noelle.

"Mrs. Maxwell?"

She nodded.

"I'm Dr. Holloway.

She shook his extended hand.

Noelle held her breath and prayed.

"Please tell me, Doctor."

He looked at Nick.

"It's all right," she assured, the panic rising. "He's a close friend."

When they were both seated, Dr. Holloway explained what had transpired.

"Mr. Dixon sustained internal as well as head injuries. He was in shock and unconscious when he was brought in. We repaired what we could, and set his leg. During the operation his heart stopped."

Noelle's breath caught and she covered her mouth to stifle a cry. Nick held her hand.

"Go on, Doctor," he said.

"We were able to revive him," he paused, "but he's in a coma."

Noelle's eyes squeezed shut.

"Now, I'm not promising anything. I want you both to understand that. However, the next seventy-two hours are critical. He lost a great deal of blood and we don't know the extent of the damage to the brain. He's going to receive the best medical care possible. But it's up to him. He has to want to pull through."

Dr. Holloway stood up. "If there's any way you can contact his family, I would suggest that you do."

"When can I see him?" Noelle asked in a tight voice.

"He'll be in recovery until tomorrow afternoon. Then we'll move him to intensive care. I would say tomorrow evening."

They both nodded.

"You both might as well go home and get some rest. There's nothing else to do right now." His voice softened. "Your friend looks like he's in good physical condition. That's a plus in his favor."

They both nodded, the first glimmer of hope shining faintly.

"Get some rest," Holloway said again. "And please leave a number where you can be reached. Just stop off at the nurses' station on your way out."

When they were alone, Noelle collapsed in Nick's arms. The tears that she had fought to hide while the doctor was with them, were released in low, tortured sobs.

"He'll be all right," he soothed, gently rubbing

her back. "You heard the doctor. Trent is strong. He'll pull out of this."

"All I can think of," she choked, "is that I'm going to lose him. It's like Jordan all over again. And I don't think I can live through it. I want to have the chance to tell him that everything is going to work out. I want to tell him how much I love him," she cried.

"You will," Nick assured softly. "You will. Now, let's go home and get some rest."

When they'd reached her car, Nick put his arm around Noelle's shoulders. "Drive carefully," he advised.

"Why don't you stay at Liaisons," she suggested. "We have vacant rooms reserved for the staff in case of emergencies. No one is scheduled to spend the night," she said, easily recalling the staff log.

"Sounds great. It'll give me a chance to see what Trent has been raving about. He thinks the world of you," he said softly, a warm smile playing at the corners of his lips.

She looked up at him, her eyes softening, "I feel the same way about him."

By the time they arrived at the villa, the sun was high in the sky. Several of the early risers were already on the tennis court, and there was a lone rider taking a turn around the track.

To Nick it seemed that he'd stepped into his wildest fantasy. He was dumbfounded. He began o look at Noelle with a newfound respect. Trent was right, he mused. She is remarkable.

There was no doubt that Liaisons was her creation. Every sculpture, window dressing, piece of artwork all had her distinctive signature.

"It's a bit small, don't you think?" he teased.

Noelle laughed for the first time in what seemed like weeks and it felt good. She took his arm. "You haven't seen anything yet, Monsieur Hunter."

Once Noelle stopped by reception to let Carol know she had returned, she personally escorted Nick to his room.

Noelle looked hesitant as she opened the door a crack.

"I do want to apologize that there were no full suites available. I hope that you'll be comfortable here." She opened the door the rest of the way.

Nick stood in the doorway with his mouth open. "This is the staff quarters? How can I get hired?"

Noelle breathed a sigh of relief. She wanted him to be comfortable.

He stepped in and sunk into the two-inch thick, oriental carpet. The room was done in muted shades of grey and mauve.

The cozy living room was fully equipped with a high-tech stereo system, a fully loaded bar, and an efficiency kitchen.

The bedroom repeated the same shades with the addition of a soft green that ran throughout the printed draperies and matching bed ensemble.

"I'm sorry that there's no Jacuzzi, but you're welcome to use the one in the gym."

"I'll keep that in mind," he grinned.

"Well—I'll let you get settled. There are a million things I need to take care of."

Nick walked over to her and braced her shoulders. He looked into her questioning eyes. "Please try and get some rest. I'm sure your staff is capable of handling everything."

She looked away. The hard and painful realities came rushing back.

"I'll try. I'm going to call the hospital and see if there's been any change."

"You'll let me know if you hear anything?"

"Of course."

She turned to leave, then stopped at the door. She looked at Nick over her shoulder. "Thank you for everything, Nick. And most of all thank you for helping me to see beyond the surface."

"No thanks needed. Everything is going to be fine. Count on it."

She pressed her lips together and nodded.

Noelle returned to her room. Alone, again the tumultuous thoughts enveloped her.

Heavily she sat down on the couch.

Was it just yesterday that she and Trent had made love not two feet from where she sat?

Slowly she got up and walked to her bedroom door. For several long moments she stood there recalling awakening in Trent's arms.

Her eyes misted over when she remembered, all too painfully, the moment she heard the door close behind him.

She would give anything to have even those last moments together again. To be held in his arms—to be loved by him again.

Her throat tightened. She turned away from the telltale bed, knowing she would not be able to sleep.

Crossing the room, she went to the phone and dialed the hospital.

There'd been no change, she was informed, and he hadn't been moved out of recovery. His condition was still critical, but stable.

She thanked the nurse and hung up. Looking down at the telephone table, she caught a glimpse of the edge of a piece of paper sticking out from beneath her address book.

She picked up the slips of paper that had the telephone messages.

Senator Thomas will be arriving tomorrow.

Trent Dixon will not be meeting with you as planned.

Her heart skittered, when she saw the note with Trent's name on it. Even though Nick had confessed that he'd placed the call at Trent's request, hoping to buy more time, it was still disturbing to be plainly reminded of the reasons behind it.

She studied the neatly written notes in Gina's familiar handwriting. The last few hours of her life had almost been prophesied on two tiny pieces of paper.

Would anything have been different if she'd seen them sooner? Could this tragedy have been avoided if she'd mentioned to Trent that Senator Thomas was arriving?

There was no point in trying to go back, she realized with a pang. There was nothing she could change about the past. All she could do now was pray that Trent would be a part of her future.

She shuddered to think that the last time she saw him could be the final time.

Twenty-seven

After a quick, refreshing shower and a change of clothes, Noelle went to the lower level to check on things before going to the hospital.

Gina was at the desk when she arrived. The look of sympathy in Gina's eyes told her that she already knew.

"I'm sorry, Mrs. Maxwell. I saw the news report. How is he?"

"He's critical. And he's in a coma." She swallowed. "They, the doctors, don't know when he'll come out of it."

"I don't know what to say."

"I'll be staying at the hospital. I want to be there when he wakes up."

"Of course. Do you want me to stay over?"

"If you don't mind. I'd feel much better knowing that you're here. Oh—one more thing. I put together a proposal that your father needs to review before he leaves. It's in my office. Would you be sure that he gets it in the overnight mail."

"I'll take care of it and call my father to let him know to expect a package."

"*Merci.*" She hesitated, while Gina watched expectantly. "Gina," she began slowly, "I just want to say that no matter what difficulties Joseph and I have had in the past, I'm truly happy for you both. I know you were reluctant to let me know about your relationship and I understand your reasons. But I hope we can put that all behind us."

Thoughts of Trent surrounded her as she spoke. "Life is too short," she said with quiet conviction, "to let past wrongs stand in the way of the future."

"Thank you, Mrs. Maxwell. You don't know what that means to me."

"I think I do," she smiled. "And I also think it's time that you started calling me Noelle."

As Gina watched Noelle depart, she once again had to marvel at the extraordinary woman that she was. Even in the midst of everything that she was enduring, she still had time for others.

She could only hope that, one day soon, Noelle would finally have the happiness that she deserved.

Before leaving for the hospital, she went to her office and called her accountant, Sam and her broker, Nina. Both of them confirmed that the transactions had taken place.

Noelle paid Tempest and Braxton an unannounced visit. For the next hour, she told them everything that had happened—at least all that she knew.

Tempest held her, letting her cry softly, while Braxton tried to reassure her that Trent would pull through.

By the time she left them, she felt physically spent yet emotionally lifted. True friends was something that she desperately needed, right then, and they had proven themselves once again. They had not judged, or condemned, but had been loving and supportive.

"Don't forget the words of wisdom you gave me," Tempest said, standing with Noelle at the door. "If you love each other, be patient." Tempest smiled and Noelle hugged her.

"I'm going to miss you terribly," Noelle whispered softly, hugging her tighter.

"I wish we didn't have to leave, but we have to get back to New York tomorrow. But you know I'm always just a phone call away," Tempest said softly. "I'll be here until tomorrow night if you need me."

"Thank you for everything. I'll call you. And give Kai a kiss for me."

"I will."

After Noelle left, Tempest stood for several moments facing her husband.

"She's been through so much, B.J., my heart aches for her."

He gathered his wife in his arms and kissed the top of her head.

"She's found her happiness, baby. I just hope that she'll stay as happy as we are."

* * *

Nick quietly hung up the phone. He covered his tired eyes with his hands. That had to be one of the most difficult calls he'd ever had to make.

The doorbell chimed. He pulled himself off the side of the bed and went to answer it.

"Noelle, come in." He could immediately tell that she'd been crying. Her eyes were slightly red and puffy. He began to think the worst.

"Has something happened? Did the hospital call?" They walked into the small living room and sat down.

"No. No." she quickly answered. "I called, but there've been no changes."

"I was able to reach his sister, Stephanie, in Philadelphia." He shook his head. "She was almost hysterical. But she calmed down long enough to say that she would inform the family."

Noelle took his hand. "I know that must have been difficult for you."

He heaved a sigh and nodded. "She said she'd call back once they made flight arrangements. So I need to stay here and wait for the call."

"Of course."

"Anyway," he tried to smile, "Trent doesn't need to see my ugly mug when he opens his eyes." He saw her lip tremble. "He will open his eyes," he repeated with certainty.

"And I want to be there when he does." She got up and walked to the door. "I'll call you as soon as there's any news. If you need anything at all, let Gina know. She'll take care of it. I'll also make arrangements for Trent's family to stay here at the villa. It'll be too much for them to try to arrange for a hotel on such short notice."

Nick shook his head in amazement. "I know they'll appreciate that."

"It's the least I can do." Her voice threatened to break. "I just feel that somehow this is all my fault."

"That's absurd. You couldn't have known."

She looked directly into his eyes. "If it hadn't been for me and my obsession with trying to prove that Trent was guilty of . . ." she looked away, "he wouldn't have felt forced into this twisted scheme." She spun away, suddenly ashamed.

Nick grabbed her shoulder, turning her around. His eyes zeroed in on her. "Don't do this to yourself. You're as much a victim in all this as Trent. What matters now is not who's wrong, but what you're going to do to make things right."

She bit down on her bottom lip. "I know you're right but I can't help how I feel. I've spent the past year fueling my hatred for a man I'd never met, blaming him for something he didn't do." She looked up at him, her eyes laden with guilt. She shook her head in despair. "I'll never forgive myself if I don't get the chance to make it up to him."

She wrapped her arms around her waist. "I can't imagine what he's been going through for the past year. I even went so far as to destroy the report he'd gotten because I didn't want to find out that I may have been wrong."

"That's all behind you now. Think positive."

"I'll try."

* * *

Noelle tossed a small overnight bag, filled with toiletries onto the passenger seat of her car, along with a light blanket and a pillow. She was determined that she was not moving until he awakened. If they threw her out into the hall, at least she would be prepared.

She'd dressed in a designer jogging suit of purple and white with matching Nike sneakers. The waiting may take some time, she'd reasoned, at the very least she wanted to be comfortable.

She'd taken care of all of the tiny details at the villa and was confident that Gina could handle any problems that might arise.

All she had to do now, was focus all of her energies on Trent.

Twenty-eight

Noelle took a steadying breath as she stood outside of Trent's hospital room. She drew on the final reserves of her strength to help her face whatever lay on the other side.

Doctor Holloway had warned her that it could be an unnerving sight. He'd offered to accompany her, but she had adamantly declined.

She pushed open the heavy blue and white door. The stark white walls rushed toward her, while the mournful bleeps from the monitors seeped through her veins, becoming one with her own heartbeat.

She felt like she was suffocating. She took deep, gulping breaths. For a split second she shut her eyes, as she stepped across the doorway. She knew that just beyond the jutting wall was Trent.

Steeling herself, she slowly walked around the curve.

Her heart slammed against her chest. She covered her mouth to smother the gasp that rose from the pit of her stomach.

Her throat constricted as she cautiously stepped forward. He was so still, unmoving beneath the sterile white sheets. The only sign that he was even breathing was the steady beep of the monitor.

Carefully she drew closer until she was inches from his side. A hot tear rolled down her cheek when she looked down at the bruised face. There was a thick bandage over his right eye and another on his cheek. She swallowed back the knot of anguish that lodged in her throat.

Her fingers trembled as she reached out to touch him, needing desperately to confirm, for herself, what the machines already knew.

The instant that her fingertips touched his warm flesh, a sudden wave of euphoric relief swept through her.

Her eyes filled and ran over.

"Trent, you're going to be fine, *cher*," she cried softly. Gently she stroked his arm. "I'm here. We have so much to talk about. So many things I need to say to you."

She lowered her head and lightly rested it on his chest. The steady beat of his heart filled her.

"I love you, Trent," she cooed. "Nothing else matters except how we feel about each other."

Blindly she sat down on one of the two, white plastic chairs. For the next few hours, she sat unmoved, talking softly to him, believing, without a doubt, that he heard every word she said.

Nick found her quietly talking to him, smiling intermittently as she revisited their brief, but passionate time together. He felt like the third wheel, rolling in on a very intimate moment. He turned to leave.

"Nick." The strangely ragged voice reached across the sterile room.

"Hi," he whispered almost as if the sound of his voice might awaken the sleeping patient.

Noelle motioned him over.

"Any change?" he asked, pulling up the matching white chair.

She shook her head. "He hasn't moved." She continued to stroke his arm. "But I know he hears me," she firmly stated, as if challenging Nick to disagree.

He chose to ignore the statement, rather than upset her. He'd never believed all that stuff about talking to people in comas. It might work on television, but this was real life.

Instead, he stated, "I heard from Trent's sister, Stephanie. They can't get a flight out until tomorrow. They'll arrive early in the morning. She said the family really appreciates your offer."

"So they'll be staying?"

"Yes."

"Good. I'll let Gina know to make arrangements." She turned her attention back to Trent.

"Have you seen the doctor?" Nick asked.

"He was here when I arrived. He said Trent is stable and we'll just have to wait."

"Why don't you go for a walk. Take a break and stretch. I'll stay here with him."

She shook her head emphatically. "He may wake up, and I wouldn't be here. I can't leave," she insisted.

"Okay. Have you eaten?"

The mention of food suddenly reminded her of how hungry she was. She hadn't eaten since early the day before.

"Food has been the last thing on my mind," she said with a fragile smile. "But I am hungry."

"I'll see what I can find in the hospital cafeteria."

"Something light for me," she said. "Fruit or a yogurt. I don't want to send my stomach into shock."

"No problem. I'll be back shortly."

She turned back to Trent's still body. Lovingly she caressed his cheek.

"I think I understand why you had to do what you did," she said softly. "I thought I knew my husband, but I didn't. What he did to you I can never forget. But we can't let that stand between us." She remembered Tempest's words, *harboring secrets and doubts can destroy a relationship.* "Trent," she pleaded, "come back to me so that I can make it all up to you."

A nurse entered soundlessly, did a brief check of the monitors and changed the I.V. just as Nick returned.

He placed the small tray on the bedside stand. It went unnoticed by Noelle who kept her eyes locked on Trent.

Without a word, Nick gently patted her shoulder. This was their time, he thought. He wasn't needed there. Quietly he closed the door behind him.

* * *

The sun was slowly setting over the mountain-tops. Noelle switched on the small nightlight. Slowly, achingly, she rose from the chair.

Her body was painfully stiff from having sat in one place for so many hours. She arched her back and rotated her head.

On shaky legs she walked toward the window. She looked through the partially open blinds. She saw the weaving roads, the flow of human traffic, the flickering lights. Life moved on, she realized, even as one life hung by a precarious thread.

She twirled the wand on the venetian blinds, letting the last rays of sunlight filter through.

Suddenly, she spun around when a soft groan mixed with the tin-tin sound of the blinds.

With renewed agility, she ran across the room.

"Trent," she whispered. "Trent, it's me, Noelle." Her voice began to tremble. "I'm here, sweetheart."

She held his hand tighter, willing him up from the darkness that had captured him. "Come back to me. You can do it," she urged.

Ever so slowly his fingers wrapped around her hand. A ragged groan rose from deep within his throat. His eyes flickered open, then slid closed.

"I love you, *mon cher,*" she cried. "Please!"

Somewhere far off he heard that familiar voice, that he so loved, drift to him like a lazy tide. Every nerve-ending in his body screamed in pain.

But the voice soothed him, almost lulling him back into that peaceful sleep where there was no pain, no agony of loss.

He had nothing to come back to. There was no reason to fight against the darkness. The only thing he had ever really wanted was not to be had by him.

It was better this way, his mind said. It's easier to just let go and get swept away to eternal peace.

But that voice kept calling out to him, whispering, reaching out, not letting him escape. He couldn't fight the voice. It was more powerful than the desire to sleep.

"Noelle." The raw whisper was the sweetest symphony to her ears.

She held his hand to her face. "I'm here, I'm here." Her throat ached as she fought to control the scream of joy that struggled for release.

The agonizing effort to open his eyes, was almost more than he could stand. But he had to reach the voice.

Gradually his eyes opened.

She stroked his head and leaned over the guard-rail, directly in his line of vision.

"You're back," she cried in a strangled voice. "You're back."

Hot, salty tears flowed unchecked down her cheeks and onto his.

She rested her head on his chest. "Everything is all right now," she said.

Weakly he squeezed her hand and somewhere deep inside his soul, he knew it was.

Twenty-nine

"Well," Dr. Holloway said, giving Trent a brief exam, "you're a very lucky man. You have a difficult recovery ahead of you and you'll probably experience severe headaches for a few days. Maybe weeks. But," he turned to include Noelle in his smile, "I predict a full recovery. Don't stay too long," he added. "Our patient is going to need a lot of rest."

"When can I leave?" Trent croaked.

"That depends. I'll have Dr. Carson run another series of head x-rays. So long as there's no infection from the operation and the pictures are good, I'd say in about a week. Maybe less."

"Thank you, Doctor," Noelle grinned.

"You'll definitely need peace and quiet during your recovery. You won't be able to get around much on that leg for a while either."

"Don't worry, Dr. Holloway." She looked at Trent with adoring eyes. "I intend to take very good care of him."

Holloway winked at Trent. "You're luckier than I thought." He walked to the door. "I'll check on you in the morning."

Nick approached the bed with a big grin on his face. He said in a stage whisper, "If they're worried about head injuries, they can forget it. With that hard head of yours it would take an atom bomb to do any damage."

"Very funny," Trent tossed back in a hoarse voice. "Anyway, step aside, you're blocking my view."

"Hey," Nick held up his hands. "No problem. Consider me gone." He gave Noelle a kiss on the cheek. "I'll see you later." He turned back to Trent. "Your whole family will be descending on you tomorrow. Don't let her wear you out!" he teased.

"Beat it," Trent warned with a crooked smile.

Nick waved good-bye and left.

Noelle took a deep breath and stepped closer. "How are you feeling?"

"Sort of like I've been in a plane crash." He tried to laugh but a sharp pain shot through his head.

Noelle clutched his hand. He closed his eyes and spoke through the pain. "Did you mean it—when you said you'd take care of me?"

She leaned down and kissed his forehead. "Of course I did."

"Good." He began to drift off to sleep. His voice was thick. "I—like the sound of that. We have—so—much to talk about. So much I need to tell you."

Noelle stroked his arm. "We have plenty of time for that," she whispered, but he was already sound asleep.

* * *

After speaking briefly with the doctor, he assured her that Trent would sleep through the night. Noelle took the opportunity to return to Liaisons. She wanted to personally see to the accommodations for Trent's family.

Suddenly, the thought of meeting them made her nervous, as she strutted through the two adjoining suites that were set aside for their use.

She spewed out rapid-fire instructions. "Please be sure to stock the refrigerator with soft drinks, juices, condiments and light snacks from the kitchen," she instructed Joann, her head of housekeeping. "We don't have information on their dietary requests. So we'll just have everything available."

Noelle's trained eyes rapidly assessed the rooms. "We just received a new shipment of floral bedding. Have these bedrooms changed. I want the rooms to have a cheery atmosphere. They'll need it."

"Yes, Mrs. Maxwell."

"Be sure that there are fresh flowers and baskets of fruit in both suites."

"Yes, Mrs. Maxwell."

Noelle looked around anxiously. She wanted everything to be perfect, and realized that she was transferring her anxiety to Joann. She turned and looked at Joann who stared back with something resembling awe.

"I'm sorry if I sound too demanding," Noelle apologized. "It's just that these visitors are very important to me."

"No apology necessary. I understand." She felt thrilled just to be in the same room with Noelle.

"Merci." She smiled warmly at Joann and hurried from the room. She'd already arranged to have a car pick them up from the airport and bring them to Liaisons, then to the hospital.

She mentally ticked off the things yet to be done as she entered the elevator. *Call hospital, change clothes.* Her stomach growled. *Get something to eat!*

The elevator doors opened and she went directly to her room. She looked around as if seeing through new eyes. The last time she was in these very same rooms, she was filled with apprehension and cold fear. Now, she felt like she could finally smile again.

Trent was going to be well. They were going to work things out between them. True, there were still a lot of unanswered questions. But they would all be answered in time. Liaisons was flourishing and she had very positive vibrations about her proposal to Nkiru.

Everything was right with her world. She had someone to love and he loved her. She felt alive and vibrant again.

Nothing could change that.

Noelle prepared for her evening tour of the villa. Now that Trent was stable, and she had the assurance from Dr. Holloway that Trent would sleep through the night, she didn't feel guilty about meeting her routine obligations.

She selected a coral cocktail dress of satin with a chiffon overskirt in a pale orange. The combination gave the dress an iridescent shimmer.

The wide waistband gave unquestionable definition to her narrow waist. The bodice was framed by stand-away off-shoulder sleeves, giving the observer an ample view of the satiny copper skin.

She felt radiant and she looked it as heads turned when she entered the dining room.

Almost immediately, Senator Thomas saw her enter and motioned her to his table. He'd hoped to see her tonight. He'd desired Noelle from the moment Jordan had introduced them years ago. Seeing her again served to reinforce that desire. He'd never dared to cross that line while Jordan was alive, knowing that Jordan would have ruined him without batting an eye. Plus Noelle never seemed to be the kind of woman who would cheat on her husband.

But now. Now was a different story. Jordan was definitely out of the picture and her would-be suitor was incapacitated.

"Please join me for a few moments," he requested when she'd reached his table.

"Just a few." She sat down as he helped her into her seat. He stood behind her for several moments longer than necessary, deeply inhaling her intoxicating perfume.

"Noelle, you're looking—extraordinary," he breathed heavily. His eyes raked over her. "I hope you're feeling better. I was worried." His light brown eyes reflected concern.

She smiled confidently. "I am. Thank you, Richard."

At first glance, Richard Thomas gave the impression of being a rather average-looking man, Noelle always thought. But upon close observation he was decidedly handsome in a practiced sort of way.

His smooth ebony skin was flawless, his dress impeccable and the full head of salt-and-pepper hair capped off the look of distinction. Richard Thomas was a big man in stature and gave all who met him a sense of trust and security. He inspired confidence—an attribute that had made him adored by his constituency.

"I heard about Dixon. Sad." He shook his head slowly, the picture of concern. "Have you gotten any word on his condition?" He looked at her from beneath long lashes.

"As a matter of fact, I was at the hospital when he came out of the coma."

Her face visibly brightened, Richard noticed, annoyed. *Dixon wouldn't get this one.* Not if he had anything to do with it.

"The doctors say he'll be fine," Noelle added.

"I'm sure he will be. Trent and I go back quite a way. Actually I met him for the first time when Jordan purchased this villa. Dixon has a very unscrupulous reputation." He chuckled lightly. "I hope you weren't taken in by any of his, uh, schemes." He took a sip from his glass of wine.

Noelle frowned. "I'm sure that whatever Trent may or may not have done in the past has no bearing on who he is now."

Richard pursed his lips, covering them with his finger.

"Oh, Noelle," he said in a patronizing tone, "no wonder Jordan was so madly in love with you. You're still so innocent."

Noelle stiffened. "You don't know anything about me," she snapped.

"Please I didn't mean to offend you." He placed his hand on her bare arm and his fingers began to tingle. "It's just that," he looked around as though making sure they couldn't be overheard," I wouldn't want to see you hurt." He paused for effect.

"Trent Dixon has a long track record for romancing rich women and taking them for all they're worth. He has a very expensive lifestyle. Even Jordan couldn't afford his habits," he chuckled again.

A hundred troubling thoughts ran through her head at once. *The lies.* His interest in what she did with the business. *The lies.* If he married her, he'd be set for life. The community property laws in California were very liberal. Had she been blinded again?

"I don't see how all of this has anything to do with me," she said, cautiously.

"Of course it doesn't have anything to do with you. But you can never be too careful. I just feel it's my duty—as a friend of Jordan's to—warn you."

He smiled, watching her expression change from confidence to doubt as his words slowly penetrated.

"Please excuse me." She pushed away from the table.

He stood up. "I was hoping you would stay for dinner."

"I'm sorry, Richard." She felt confused and suddenly afraid. "I still have rounds to make."

"Maybe tomorrow then?"

"Maybe." She hurried from the room.

What Richard said couldn't be true. Trent wasn't after her for her money. He couldn't be. It was Jordan. Jordan convinced him to trick her into running Maxwell Enterprises.

Her mind spun. But what kind of man was Trent? She had no idea he lied before since the lies flowed so easily. Had he always lied—even to Jordan?

The pulse in her temple began to pound. She rushed for the elevator and ran into Tempest as she was coming out.

"Noelle, where are you . . ." She saw the stricken look on her face. "What's wrong? Has something more happened to Trent?"

Noelle shook her head. "I-I'm just tired. I was going to my room."

Tempest looked at her skeptically. "I know you, and I always know when something is wrong."

How could she tell her that she'd been a fool—that she'd been used?

"I'll be in my room, Noelle if you want to talk."

"I'll be fine," she said weakly. She stepped into the elevator, leaving Tempest with an unsettling feeling.

* * *

Alone in her room, she went over every detail from the moment she'd met Trent.

Every move that he'd made had been choreographed to seduce her. He clouded her head with words of love. He praised her business sense. He sympathized with her marital problems.

She had been so starved for love and affection, she played right into his hands.

Within hours his family would be arriving and she'd have to pretend to be cordial. She'd have to pretend that nothing was wrong.

A chill ran through her. She couldn't face him. She wouldn't look into his eyes and feel weak. She wouldn't listen to anymore lies.

Anguish gripped her. She fell onto her knees, huddling into a tight ball and cried. She cried for all of her losses—her parents, her youth, Jordan and Cole. Cole because that's who she fell in love with. But he was gone forever.

Thirty

At 10:00 A.M. the white, stretch limousine carrying Trent's family pulled in front of Liaisons.

Stephanie hopped out first. Her large brown eyes widened in astonishment. "Damn!"

"Watch your mouth!" her mother, Janice, warned as she stepped out of the car. But even she had to stop in wonder as the enormous villa spread out before her.

"Don't get all excited," her older sister Diane stated. "You know how these rich people are. She'll probably write this off as some tax deduction." She turned up her broad nose in distaste.

"Your antiestablishment rhetoric is rearing its ugly head again," her mother said.

"Diane," Steph cut in, "lighten up."

"I just want to get to the hospital," Janice said, "and get my son home."

Gina buzzed Noelle on her office intercom.

"Yes, Gina."

"The Dixons are here."

"Thank you."

Noelle had hardly more than an hour sleep all night. She kept seeing Trent lying so helpless in the hospital. Then she'd heard Richard's scathing denunciation.

Maybe Richard was wrong about Trent, she'd told herself at least a hundred times. But then reality would hit and all of the events that had led to this moment confirmed her fears.

Her head ached. She felt hollow, devoid of emotion.

Somehow she'd make her excuses. She wasn't going back to the hospital.

Her private line rang.

"Yes? Noelle Maxwell."

"Noelle. This is Ambassador Nkiru. I presented your proposal at an open session of the U.N. this morning."

This morning? she thought she was confused, then remembered that it was one o'clock in the afternoon in New York.

"I have good news. It was decided that I would present the offer to the Sudanese government."

He sounded so enthusiastic, she thought absently. Her voice was empty. "That's wonderful."

"However," he rushed on, "the cabinet members want to meet with you."

"That's fine," she continued in the same monotone.

"They want you here by tomorrow. Can you arrange for a flight?"

Her excuse dropped in her lap. She didn't have to pretend to have a headache, or sudden illness. Maybe when she arrived in New York, she'd just stay for a while.

"I'll be there."

"Excellent. I'll book a room for you at the Plaza. And Noelle, you're doing a wonderful thing."

She broke the connection without commenting further. Now to face the family.

"I hope you liked your rooms," Noelle was saying as she escorted them back to the limo.

"Everything is exquisite," Janice said enthusiastically.

Diane looked at Noelle from the corner of her eye and was painfully reminded of Roxanne, the woman who had lured her husband away from her and his family. She swallowed back the knot of remembrance. So what if the champagne gold pantsuit that Noelle wore so gracefully was a Halston original, or that the studs in her ears were real diamonds, she thought jealously. So what if she was gracious and thoughtful, she mused angrily, unable to find the flaws that she sought. She knew her type. And the quicker her brother was out of this fake world the better off he'd be.

Didn't the dark glasses clearly state that she was a product of her environment? What did she have to hide? Diane went on silently.

"Give my best to Trent," Noelle forced herself to say.

"Aren't you coming?" Janice asked.

Stephanie looked at Noelle quizzically and could have sworn she saw shadows of pain lurking in her brown eyes just before she slipped on her dark sunglasses.

"No. I can't. I have to go out of town—on business. I'm sure Trent will understand." She smiled. "Now that his family is here he doesn't need me hovering around."

Stephanie watched Noelle closely and listened to the very subtle tremor in her voice. She'd always been good at seeing beyond the surface and this woman was definitely hurting. She wondered why.

Noelle waved until the car was out of sight. Without looking back, she went directly to her office to make her flight arrangements to New York.

"You can't all go in at once," Dr. Holloway advised patiently. "Two visitors at a time and only for five minutes each."

There was a loud groan from the family and verbal protestations from Steph.

"We flew all night, have been terrified about my brother, and we only get five minutes! That's totally unfair."

Dr. Holloway gave her that doctorly look that he gave to all difficult family members. "We have to think about what's best for the patient. If he gets too tired, it will take longer for him to recover. You don't want that, do you?" His steady gaze included everyone.

"Hospitals have rules, Steph," Diane admonished in that know-it-all tone that Stephanie hated. "Just like there are laws that have to be followed.

If not, there'd be total chaos." She gave her sister a self-satisfied look.

Stephanie cut Diane a sidelong glance and rolled her eyes. She was about two seconds from telling her ever-righteous sister just where to go. But refrained since they were in front of a stranger.

"I only want what's best for my brother," Stephanie assured the doctor.

"Very well. Two visitors. Five minutes."

They all nodded in agreement. Dr. Holloway continued down the hall.

"Steph you go first," Diane said. "I'll go with Mom." They both knew from experience that Diane was the only one who could control their mother's hysterics, especially when it came to Trent. The last thing that Trent needed now, was his mother falling apart.

"Come on Ma," Diane directed, taking her mother by the arm and moving her away from Trent's door. "Now you be strong," she cautioned in a no nonsense voice. "You don't want to upset Trent." She looked over her shoulder at her sister with an *I have everything under control look.*

Less than a minute after Stephanie had entered the room, Trent's struggling laughter could be heard. Steph always had that effect on him, Diane realized grudgingly.

"So that's *the* Mrs. Maxwell. Nice to have *friends* like that. She's pretty wonderful," Steph added with a conspiratorial wink. "A person could get used to living like that. She have any brothers?"

Trent winced when he chuckled. "Sorry Sis."

Stephanie pouted, then stepped closer. "You just get well, baby bro'. I'll find me a man on my own," she teased. She smiled down at Trent and her heart swelled. She loved her brother dearly and couldn't have loved him more if they had been joined by blood. It was like that with all three of them, even though Diane did get on her last nerve. Their adoptive parents had raised them to love each other unquestionably.

"Get some rest," she said kissing his cheek. "You're gonna need it," she added. "Ma and the wicked witch are next."

Trent tried not to laugh because it hurt too much.

"I'll be back tomorrow," Stephanie said. "I can't wait to get the full tour of Liaisons." Her face beamed. "No one back home is gonna believe me."

She bent down and kissed his cheek again. Her eyes softened. "I love you," she said in a near whisper.

"Same here."

"See you tomorrow."

Moments later Diane and his mother walked in. He could immediately see that his mother was struggling for control and that Diane had her under strict orders.

Janice hurried over to his bedside and gently embraced him. "Oh, my poor baby," she wailed. "What have you gone and done to yourself now?"

"I'll be okay, Ma," he said, trying to sound stronger than he felt.

Diane stepped closer. "I hope that you're planning on pursuing an investigation. I'm sure you can sue the company."

"I just want to get out of here, Di."

"Well you'll be coming home with us to recuperate."

"No. I'm staying at Liaisons."

"You need to be home with your family. This whole glitzy life out here is not you. And your friend Noelle is just like all the other rich and famous."

"You don't know her," Trent snapped back, feeling his temper rise. Diane could raise his blood pressure in a wink. "She's not like Roxanne." He mentioned her ex-husband's mistress.

Diane felt the implication of his words as if she'd been slapped with a cold towel. "Believe me, I know her type," she sniffed.

Trent didn't have the strength to argue.

"I want you to come home, too, sweetheart," his mother pleaded. "I'll be there to take care of you."

"Ma, I appreciate that, but Noelle has already made the same offer. It'll be easier on me if I don't have to travel for a while."

"She must be planning on getting you a nurse," Diane said, "because she's not going to be there."

Trent frowned. "What are you talking about?"

"When we were leaving today, she said to send her regards and that she was going out of town on business."

Trent felt a sinking sensation in the pit of his stomach. She wouldn't do that without calling. What could have happened?

"We'll see you tomorrow, Son." His mother kissed his forehead. Diane did the same.

Trent gave them a faltering smile as they left.

For several moments, Trent lay staring up at the ceiling. Diane must be wrong, he concluded. He knew how she felt about wealthy people. She was always barely able to hide her contempt for the work he did with Maxwell Enterprises.

Noelle wouldn't just leave without saying anything, he reaffirmed. Any minute now, she would walk through that door.

By late afternoon, she hadn't arrived. Nor had she called. The sinking sensation intensified.

He couldn't stand it any longer. Painfully, he inched his way toward the bedside phone. The normally simple task took agonizing minutes to accomplish. He was bathed in sweat.

Panting he dialed Liaisons.

Minutes later he was hanging up. Disbelief clouded his thinking. *Mrs. Maxwell is out of town for an indeterminate length of time,* he was informed. He'd tried to reach Gina, but she was unavailable.

She'd just left, without a word. He couldn't understand that.

He looked up and Nick walked through the door.

"Where's Noelle?" Trent demanded.

Nick stood next to the bed. He avoided looking into his eyes. Trent felt ice spread through his belly.

"She said to tell you that she's leaving on business." He halted. His gaze wavered.

"And?"

"And she hoped you'd be long gone when she returned."

Thirty-one

Noelle arrived in New York and checked into her hotel room at the Plaza.

She didn't notice the exquisite decor or the breathtaking New York skyline that was visible from her bedroom window. All she could think about was Richard's very candid characterization of Trent and what a fool she had been.

She sank down on the bed. Even after everything that had happened between her and Trent, she had allowed herself to be persuaded to believe that he had been sincere in his feelings for her. She had given him a second chance, despite her reservations. That was all part of the act, Richard had said.

She'd never admit to him that she too had been taken in by Trent's charm. It was too humiliating and too painful.

Mindlessly, she undressed and crawled beneath the covers, wishing that she could stay there, hidden away from the world forever.

Even in her dreams she found no refuge in sleep. With every toss, every turn, Trent was there, smiling, caressing, loving her, making her feel complete. Unwillingly she felt her body ignite with an undeniable longing.

And then the adoring eyes would change to jeering ones, taunting her, laughing at her. She struggled to get away, running down a dark road, but everywhere she turned, once-friendly faces changed to mocking ones—pointing laughing fingers at her.

At the end of the long road, Trent stood with open arms beckoning her to him. Weightlessly, she ran to him, with joy bubbling in her throat. He'd come to rescue her. Just as she reached him, the light of love in his eyes was extinguished, replaced with contempt.

Long fingers reached out for her. She screamed and came fully awake.

She sat up in bed, shivering, burning tears running down her cheeks. She hugged her knees to her chest, and let the pain-filled sobs envelop her.

Trent awakened the following morning with that same sinking feeling. Maybe it was all a dream, he thought, but he knew that it wasn't. He still could not imagine why Noelle would leave him.

Maybe her being at the hospital, sitting at his bedside had been an act. How many times had he heard how important it was for the coma victim to feel that there were people around who cared. It was crucial to their recovery.

He closed his eyes. Noelle was just that type of person. He could very well imagine that she would totally set aside her own feelings for someone else.

He'd been surprised even to find her at the hospital. The last time they'd seen each other he felt the power of her hatred.

Last night, before Nick left to return to New York, he'd said that he and Noelle had talked. He said he was sure she understood that he wasn't to blame. She seemed convinced. Even Nick couldn't understand the sudden change.

Maybe he'd just do like his folks had suggested and return with them to Philadelphia. It was becoming obvious, with each passing hour, that Noelle had closed the chapter on their lives. He would tell the doctor he wanted to leave immediately. The sooner he put some distance between himself and Noelle the better.

Miraculously, Noelle had been able to sound coherent as she stood before the cabinet of the United Nations.

Her confidence grew from her firm belief that she could make a difference. In clear, nonpolitical language, she reviewed the details of her reconstruction efforts in Sudan.

"You were magnificent," Ambassador Nkiru stated to Noelle over lunch. They were dining in one of the rooms reserved for cabinet members.

"I just wanted to emphasize how important this is." She took a forkful of her seafood platter.

"You're sure they'll be able to keep my name out of it?"

"All that will be mentioned is that this is an endeavor by Maxwell Enterprises."

She looked down at her plate. Trent would get the credit and that was fine. Let him have it. She'd firmly outlined the reorganization process to the note holders and had guaranteed repayment of the loans. She was no longer in jeopardy of losing Liaisons. She no longer had the desire to care.

"How long will you be staying in New York?" Nkiru asked.

She smiled wanly. "I haven't been to New York in years. I think I'll just take my time and see the sights."

"I'm sure you'll find plenty to do." He pushed away from the table, wiping his mouth with the paper napkin. "I've got to be going. My plane leaves in an hour. Will you be able to get back to the hotel? I can get a car."

She held up her hand. "Please don't bother. I'll be fine. And I could use the exercise." She stood up and firmly shook his hand. "Have a safe trip."

"And you have a pleasant stay."

It was still early afternoon when Noelle stepped out of the United Nations. The warm spring air was filled with the sounds of birds, laughter and promise.

With no specific destination in mind, she strolled

casually along the busy Manhattan streets—a sharp contrast to the lull of San Francisco.

She peeked into the elaborate store windows and pangs of melancholy rushed through her. She and Trent had done the very same thing in the Napa Valley. It seemed like a lifetime ago.

Everywhere that she looked, couples were holding hands, touching, hugging one another, whispering words of love. Spring was the time for love, she thought miserably.

She moved on and kept walking until she found herself at Twenty-eighth Street and Fourth Avenue.

The bold gold letters splashed across the crystal clear windowpane caught her attention. *Rhythms.* Curious, she came closer to read the posting in the window. It was a supper club with live jazz entertainment. It may be a bit early for dinner, she realized, but she could hear the soft beat of the music beckoning to her.

Her spirits lifted. When was the last time she was out alone, doing something spontaneous? She couldn't remember. She thought about it for a minute and decided to go in. The combination of aching feet and a budding appetite were the final motivators.

Once her eyes adjusted to the dimly lit interior she could see that the club was actually a converted brownstone.

The front of the club had a small dining room and bar as well as a working fireplace. The hard parquet floors were covered with bright African print area rugs. Large plants stood in the corners.

Since no one seemed to be rushing to seat her, she took a quick tour.

Upstairs were three large rooms, one for dancing and two for dining. Each of them had a small bandstand for entertainment. Several tables were occupied and the sound of Nancy Wilson's voice filtered through the hidden speakers.

Just as she was about to descend the stairs, she caught the sound of a very familiar voice in the midst of a conversation.

Nick turned almost at the same moment that she did.

Her brown eyes widened in shock. What was he doing here? The next to the last person she needed to see was a friend of Trent's—especially this friend.

She turned away and began to go downstairs, but not before Nick grabbed her arm.

"Wait a minute," he commanded.

She spun around, her eyes glaring in anger and humiliation.

"What are you doing here?" he demanded to know.

"I could ask you the same question," she snapped back through clenched teeth.

He walked down two steps and stood directly above her.

"This is my place," he said simply. "And quite frankly I don't know if I want you in here. Anyone who could do what you did to Trent isn't welcome here." His eyes hardened into narrow slits.

Noelle swallowed back her astonishment.

"Are you crazy?" Her voice rose and customers

began to stare. "What *I've* done?" she asked incredulously. "He—he used me!" she cried. "He was going to do to me what he'd done to all the others. It all fits, and you were a part of it. You helped him with his lies."

"To all the others?" Nick's glare lost some of its steam. His utter disbelief momentarily derailed her anger. "Now you're talking crazy."

"Oh really." She tugged her arm away. "I had a chat with Senator Thomas. He told me everything."

Nick rolled his eyes up toward the ceiling. "Come on," he ordered. "I'm gonna talk and you're gonna listen." His unwavering tone didn't leave room for argument. He ushered her down the staircase.

He found an unoccupied table in the far corner on the ground floor. They had complete privacy.

Nick folded his large hands on the table. He lifted his eyes to look at Noelle.

"Let me get right to the point. Richard Thomas is a pig."

"Sure, tell me anything to cover for Trent." She turned her head away and folded her arms, stubbornly in front of her.

"I'm doing the talking, remember?" Nick said stonily.

She snapped her head around, her eyes challenging, but she did not speak.

Then in gentler tones, he continued. "A nasty rivalry has been going on between Trent and Richard for years. Richard was really head over heels in love with this woman in Texas when we were stationed there. But she only had eyes for Trent. Richard also wanted Jordan to put out large amounts of money to finance his reelection bid. Trent convinced Jordan that it wasn't a wise move because of Richard's negative third-world views. Jordan agreed. And . . ." Nick added, looking at Noelle hard, "rumor had it that Richard had his eyes on you, but was too afraid that Jordan would cut him off at the knees if he ever tried anything."

Noelle leaned forward in her seat and covered her face with her hand. "He told me all of that to get back at Trent," she said in a hollow voice.

Nick nodded. "Richard has a very long memory, but a very short attention span. His relationships never last."

"I just walked out on him," she said looking across the table at Nick. "I never gave Trent a chance. I was so anxious to believe the worst. How can I keep doing this to him?"

"You can't."

She caught his pointed look.

"I've got to get back and settle things once and for all." She stood up. "I wouldn't blame him if he wanted nothing to do with me."

"He's not that kind of guy." The warmth in his smile echoed in his voice. "If you give him half a chance, I bet he could prove it to you."

Noelle's eyes filled with gratitude. "How many times am I going to have to thank you?"

"As often as necessary," he grinned.

* * *

When they reached the exit, he pulled out a business card from the pocket of his jacket and handed it to her.

"The next time you're in New York, look me up. My home number is on the back."

She reached up on tiptoe and kissed his cheek. "I certainly will."

Noelle took a cab back to the Plaza. In no time at all, she'd packed her bags and had contacted the airport. There was one more flight out to LAX Airport. She would have to be on standby, but she didn't care.

She arrived in Los Angeles at 7:00 P.M and took a cab straight to Memorial Hospital, only to be informed that Trent had signed himself out less than eight hours earlier. She couldn't speak with Dr. Holloway, he was in surgery.

All she could do now was return to Liaisons and hope that he'd gone there.

An hour later she walked through the doorway of her villa. Gina was at the front desk.

"Mrs.—I mean, Noelle, we didn't expect you back so soon."

Noelle's heart raced. "Are the Dixons still here?" she asked in a rush.

"No. They checked out early this afternoon."

She dreaded the answer to her next question. "Did Trent go with them?"

"His mother said they were picking him up from the hospital on their way to the airport."

Noelle felt all of her hope slowly seep out of her like a leaky tire.

"Thank you, Gina." She turned away. There was nothing else she could do. At least for now. What she needed was some rest. The rapid change in time zones was catching up to her with a vengeance.

She blinked her eyes hard to clear them. Her legs began to feel like they were weighted down with cement. The short walk to the elevator was like traveling a desert mile.

She pressed the Up button, and then took a peek in the lounge. While she waited, Richard came out.

Rage bloomed with frightening potency within her. The strength of it gave her renewed vitality.

Richard caught sight of her and came in her direction, his smile broad and inviting.

Noelle stood motionless, her ability to camouflage her innermost feelings swung into full gear. She smiled sweetly.

"Noelle, I've been looking for you. I'd hoped that I could persuade you to join me for a—late dinner."

"Richard," she said calmly, the smile never leaving her face, "the sight of you turns my stomach." He blinked back his shock. "If you want a meal, or anything else for that matter, I suggest, strongly, that you get it somewhere else. The last place I ever want to set eyes on you again," she continued in that same sweet voice, "is in my villa! Save your maligning verbiage for the Senate floor."

His mouth dropped open and he took a faltering step back as though struck.

She turned triumphantly on her heels and stepped into the elevator feeling utterly wonderful.

When she reached her room she knew it was too late to call Nick in New York.

She dug in her purse and pulled out his business card and placed it on her nightstand. She'd call him first thing in the morning.

Diane had decided to take a week off and help her mother care for Trent. She couldn't be happier to have her brother home again. She just wished he would stop brooding. She knew it was about Noelle, but he was better off without her. He just didn't know it yet. She had the perfect woman for him, a friend of hers who worked at the law firm. As soon as he was better, she'd set something up.

Trent lay in his old room, listening to the familiar sounds of his childhood home.

He thought of Noelle. He had hoped that they would finally have a life together. But it was painfully obvious that she hadn't forgiven him.

He had no one to blame but himself. He'd lied to her, over and again. He deserved the sentence that had been meted out to him. But that would never stop him from loving her. With every breath he took, he thought of her. The pain was more powerful than the physical injuries he'd sustained. Those injuries would heal, but the loss of Noelle would always leave a dull ache in his spirit.

He looked toward the phone and thought of calling her. Maybe if he had the chance to explain, he could somehow make her understand that he never set out to hurt her.

He turned his head away. There was no point, he decided. She'd made her decision. He'd have to respect that.

He forced his eyes to close and instantly visions of Noelle blossomed with life.

Noelle awakened with the sun. It was nearly 9:00 A.M. in New York. She reached for the card on the table and dialed Nick's home number. A sleepy female voice answered, then gave the phone to Nick.

"I'm sorry to call so early, Nick, but Trent signed himself out of the hospital. I'm sure he's in Philadelphia."

Nick grunted. "Hold on."

Several moments later he was back on the line. "This is the number to his mother's house."

She quickly copied down the number. "Thanks again."

"You're batting a thousand," he teased. "Good luck," he added seriously.

She depressed the button and quickly dialed the

number. Her pulse pounded in her ears. She felt warm. Please be there, she silently prayed.

The phone rang four times on the other end before it was answered.

"Hello?"

"Mrs. Dixon?"

"Yes."

"Good morning. This is Noelle Maxwell. I'm trying to reach Trent."

Janice Dixon flinched. She remembered all of the things that Diane had said to her about this woman. Maybe Diane was right. She'd already seen how hurt Trent was now. She wanted the best for her son. She cleared her throat.

"I'm sorry, Mrs. Maxwell he—doesn't want to speak with you. And I think it would be best if you didn't call back. But thank you again for your hospitality." She quickly hung up, and for an instant she wondered if she'd done the right thing.

Noelle swore that her heart stopped beating.

Thirty-two

For the next three weeks, Noelle functioned as if she were in a dream. She couldn't remember ever feeling so empty inside.

Even the news that her proposal had been accepted didn't revive her crushed spirits. She simply called Mr. Takaka in Hong Kong and explained that Trent was temporarily unable to run the operations and he would have to begin the reorganization of Maxwell Enterprises. She seemed to have lost interest in everything.

She continued to meet and greet the continual flow of guests. She attended all of the necessary meetings, and took a trip to Washington to meet with the Secretary of State to finalize the plans and keep a watchful eye on her business. But her heart was not in it.

Sitting alone in her room one evening, her phone rang. She had long since stopped hoping that the caller would be Trent.

She answered the call in the same monotone that had become a part of her.

"Hello?"

"Mrs. Maxwell?"

"Yes. Who is this?"

"Mrs. Maxwell, this is Stephanie Dixon, Trent's sister.

Her stomach lurched and she sat straight up.

"Yes, Stephanie, is something wrong? Has something happened to Trent?"

"Something's wrong all right, and that something is my big-mouth sister, and gullible mother."

Stephanie went on to explain that her mother had blurted out to her the conversation that she had with Noelle and how she wasn't sure that she'd done the right thing by not letting her speak with Trent. Stephanie was livid.

"Trent never knew that you called. And he's too stubborn to contact you. I don't know what went on between the two of you," she continued, "but I can't stand for my brother to be hurting like this. I know he loves you. He has that same look in his eyes that you did. And the only time he seems to brighten at all is when I mention your name."

Noelle choked back a sob of joy.

"He still can't get around very well. But he's using crutches. So do you think you can come out here?"

Ecstasy bubbled in her voice. "I can be there tomorrow," Noelle gushed.

"If you can tell me what time your flight is arriving, I'll meet you at the airport."

"That would be wonderful."

"Take my work number and call me as soon as you can."

"I will. Thank you, Stephanie. Thank you so much."

"Anything for my brother," she said. "You're just the medicine he needs."

Noelle could barely sleep. Her thoughts scrambled around in circles. Would her prayers finally be answered? It was almost more than she could stand.

She was so anxious to see him, she arrived at the airport more than an hour early. The added wait only heightened her anxiety.

Suppose Stephanie was wrong, she worried on the five-hour flight. Suppose Trent didn't want to see her after all this time. What would she do?

By the time the plane landed she was a nervous wreck. Luckily, as soon as she walked through the arrival gates, she spotted Stephanie waving at her.

"I didn't tell him you were coming," Stephanie said as she drove the red Acura Legend skillfully through the Philadelphia traffic. "The surprise will do him good."

"What if he refuses to see me?"

Stephanie turned briefly and looked at Noelle's troubled expression. "He wants to see you," she said with assurance. "Believe me. He's just too proud to admit it." She patted Noelle's hand. "Everything is going to be fine."

Soon they pulled up in front of a small frame

house. The front lawn was neatly manicured and the house itself gave off a feeling of serenity.

So this is where Trent grew up, she thought, imagining him as a boy running through the yard.

"Here we are," Stephanie announced. She hopped out and opened the door for Noelle, who suddenly seemed frozen to her seat.

"Don't look so panicked," she said. "He won't bite your head off. Come on," she coaxed with a smile.

Noelle stood nervously at the front door, while Stephanie dug in her bag for her keys. "My mother is out," she informed Noelle. "And thank heavens, Diane is back at work. So you two will have the house to yourselves."

She opened the door and they stepped inside.

Noelle was pleasantly surprised at the size of the house. It was much larger than she'd envisioned.

The entry foyer led to the living room where Stephanie instructed her to wait.

"He's probably in the backyard," she said. "Wait here. I'll be right back."

Noelle paced like a caged tigress, barely taking in her surroundings. What did catch her eye was the row of photographs that graced the mantel.

There were several pictures of Steph and Diane at various stages in their lives. But the ones she really looked at were the pictures of Trent.

There was one of him in his Little-League uniform—photos of his graduation from high school and college—and a picture of him in his air-force uniform, his chest full of medals.

She turned, suddenly, her heart thundering when she heard voices approaching.

"I told you I didn't want to see anyone, Steph," Trent growled.

"Well at least try to be nice."

"Who is it anyway?"

Stephanie didn't have to answer as she left him at the door and quietly slipped away.

His large, muscular body framed the doorway, and Noelle's heart stood still. He was more gorgeous than ever she realized with a pang. And the slight scar over his right eyebrow gave him an even more devastating look.

When he saw Noelle standing there in a sunshine yellow dress, he was certain that he was imagining things. His head pounded. He wanted to move toward the apparition but his feet seemed to be glued to the ground.

"Noelle?"

The sound of her name coming from his lips filled her with an exquisite joy.

She took one cautious step forward, another and then another, until she was only inches away.

His crutches clattered to the floor as he reached out and crushed her against his body. She was real!

"Noelle," he said over and again. His lips swept down on hers, burning against her, filling her with unimaginable sweetness.

She moaned helplessly against his mouth, touching him, stroking him, relishing in the feel of him against her.

His honey sweet tongue dove into her mouth,

searching wildly for all that he'd thought he lost. His fingers raked through her hair, kneaded her spine, pulled her ever closer to his hardened body.

She arched her neck as his mouth trailed hungrily down the open collar of her dress. She cried out his name when his scalding lips touched the half moons of her breasts.

Languidly he raised his head and stared deeply into her tear-filled eyes. "I never thought I'd see you again," he said in a ragged whisper. He stroked her cheek as if still not believing that she was real.

"So many things have gone wrong between us, Trent," she said in a shaky voice. "I want to make it right."

"I've missed you so much Noelle," he said, taking a reluctant step back. "I thought I'd go out of my mind because I believed you'd walked out on me."

"I was a fool to let anything or anyone come between how I feel about you."

"And how *do* you feel about me?" he asked, a soft smile teasing the corners of his mouth.

"I love you madly."

He exhaled deeply. "Let's go outside and talk," he said. "There's so much I have to tell you. And if we stay in here," he added his eyes raking over her, "there's no telling what may happen. I'd hate for Mom to walk in on us in a compromising position." He grinned mischievously.

She tossed her head back and laughed out loud, a deep and soul-stirring laugh that lifted her spirits to the heavens.

* * *

Under the warm afternoon sunshine, Trent, in measured tones, explained to Noelle what had happened on the day that changed their lives.

"Jordan was very ill, Noelle," he began slowly. He turned his head and looked at her. "He was dying of cancer."

Noelle's eyes registered shock but she didn't speak.

"He didn't want you to know. He knew that if he told you, you would stick by him out of loyalty. He couldn't bear having you watch him deteriorate. He said it wasn't fair to you after everything that you'd been through with him.

"I never understood what he meant by that until you told me about your marriage." He took a deep breath. "He convinced me that the only way out was to orchestrate his death." He paused. "I did rig the plane."

Her heart jumped.

"But that's not what caused the crash. We were hit by lightning just like the reports said. That's what actually caused the malfunction."

Noelle covered her mouth with her hands.

"In his own way, Jordan was doing what he thought was best for you, Noelle. He never wanted me to run Maxwell Enterprises forever. It was for you. He wanted to show you and the world that you were capable of handling it. You'd never have to feel inferior to anyone again. He wanted you to have Maxwell Enterprises. But he knew you'd never take it willingly, so he fixed that too."

"The bank loans, using Liaisons as collateral," she said in a faraway voice.

Trent nodded.

"I was to give you one year to get the villa off the ground and out of your system. When everything fell apart you'd have no other choice but to take the reins if you wanted to save the villa. He knew that would be your motivation. The only thing he didn't bargain for was that Liaisons would be so successful in such a short period of time."

"You knew how important the villa was to me," she said softly. "You wanted to make sure that I didn't lose it."

He nodded.

"And you believed that if I knew who you were from the beginning I would have found another way out of Jordan's plans for me."

"That's part of it," he admitted. "But from the first time that I saw you, I wanted you." His eyes held hers. "I knew how much you hated me. If you realized who I was, I wouldn't have gotten within a mile of you.

"I made a promise to Jordan, and I'm a man of my word, Noelle. I idolized Jordan." His eyes drifted off toward the horizon as distant memories rushed past. "He was more than just my employer, he was my friend. He was like a father to me, and I think he knew that's what I needed. And like a dutiful son I pledged my allegiance to him.

"Even though I stood the risk of losing you, I

couldn't tell you." He hung his head, then looked up. "And then I fell in love with you and I couldn't back out. I wanted you more than life itself and the thought that you would turn away from me because of who I was—it terrified me."

She reached out and touched his face. Tears of happiness and regret slid freely down her cheeks.

"You'll never have to worry about losing me. I almost let my misplaced hatred destroy me, destroy us. Nothing can ever come between us again." Thoughts of Tempest and Braxton swirled before her. They too had come perilously close to losing each other because of doubts and pride. But their love had bound them irrevocably together as Trent's love and hers would do.

He brushed the tears from her face. "Jordan truly loved you in his own way, Noelle."

"I see that now," she said sadly. "Maybe by some strange twist of fate, this was all meant to be." She smiled wistfully. "If I know Jordan, he probably had this whole thing planned." She could easily imagine that Jordan would have dropped Trent in her lap, somehow, mystically knowing the outcome.

She looked off toward the drifting clouds and remembered Jordan's words in his letter. *Put your trust in Trent.* And she knew that she would.

Epilogue

The wedding of Noelle St. James-Maxwell to Trenton Mark Dixon hit every reputable newspaper and tabloid in California.

Her gown was hand-sewn and imported from Paris and copied in every bridal shop across the state. All of the major networks carried coverage of the elaborate wedding held on the great lawn of Liaisons.

Tempest walked regally as her matron of honor and Nick stood proud as Trent's best man. Even Ambassador Nkiru attended and gave his blessing to Gina and Joseph.

All of Trent's family attended and even Diane had to admit that her brother was really happy.

Noelle's aunt Chantal sat in a place of honor and cried bittersweet tears at the extraordinary beauty of her niece.

Every celebrity from sports to the big screen was in attendance. It was truly a fairy-tale wedding come true.

Hundreds of miles away, Noelle and Trent spent their honeymoon night under a blanket of stars on a secluded strip of the Riviera. The warm breeze blowing off the ocean gently caressed their beach-clad bodies.

Noelle snuggled closer to her husband. "Can it always be this way?" she asked softly, stroking the warm skin of his bare chest.

Trent kissed the top of her head. "For as long as we make it," he answered.

Gently, he rolled on top of her. His dark eyes swept lovingly over her face. "I've searched for you all of my life, Noelle. And with every breath I take I promise to spend the rest of my days making your every wish come true."

His mouth slowly descended onto hers, sending spirals of desire shooting through her. She held onto her husband, wrapping him in the warmth of her love.

They had traveled a long and painful road to find each other, but their triumph was well worth the struggle that they had endured. They no longer had to be satisfied with stolen moments of happiness. They had forever.

As Trent gently eased her suit from her body and joined her, forever, with him, she knew, unquestionably, that she had found the love that she had been seeking. The ghosts of her past were finally at rest. And silently she thanked Jordan for sending real love to her—at last.